CAUGHT BETWEEN

PHILIP M. BUTERA

JaCol Publishing Inc.
Copyright 2020 © by JaCol Publishing Inc.
Illustrations Copyright © 2020 by JaCol Publishing Inc.
FIRST PRINTING
July 2020
All rights reserved
JaCol Publishing Inc.
195 Murica Aisle
Irvine, CA 92614
818-510-2898
Editor-in-Chief: Randall Andrews
www.jacolpublishing.com

ISBN: 978-1-946675-56-9

No part of this publication may be reproduced in whole or part, or stored in a retrieval system, or transmitted in any form, or by other means, electronic, mechanical, photocopying, recording, or otherwise without written permission of the publisher, except in the case of brief quotations embodied in critical articles and reviews. The classroom teacher may reproduce the materials in this book for use in a single classroom only.

Black/white shield cover by James T. Catalano

Parker H. Catalano (parkercatalano@gmail.com)

Gray scale Cover by Maria Cristina Delayo

CONTENTS

Testimonials vii
Introduction ix
Foreward xi

Prologue 1
Chapter 1 3
Chapter 2 30
Chapter 3 52
Chapter 4 80
Chapter 5 93
Chapter 6 121
Chapter 7 126
Chapter 8 156
Chapter 9 167
Chapter 10 203
Chapter 11 228
Chapter 12 243
Chapter 13 246

About the Author 249

I want to thank The New York Public Library and the New York City Police Department. I want to also thank for their tireless support through the years: Joyce Metzger, Susan Roberts, Joanne Schmidt, Caron Cersosimo, James Cellini, Barnabas Britt, Michael Anderson, Philip T. Butera, Rose Butera, and Elizabeth Luxon.

*Dedicated to the beautiful and wonderful
Joyce Metzger*

Testimonials

"An actual account of a New York City cop. Is he a good guy, bad guy, or caught between? Every turned page of this novel is time spent in the lives of real cops—a gripping and captivating police story with a provocative ending."

    Patrick Pesce, Lieutenant, NYPD, retired, author of "Blue Memories – Life in Law Enforcement."

"The subject of this frightening true story had a sixth sense when it came to police work and always seemed to be in the right place at the right time, except for once. His story is one of the most interesting, intriguing, and exciting I've ever read. If you like books about real cops involved in real life or death situations, read this one."

    Stuart Milisci, Sgt. NYPD, retired, author of "Confessions, Lies, and Secrets."

INTRODUCTION

"Caught Between" is based on an actual incident, though names and places are changed. Over the years, I interviewed and researched this story. I spoke with key players and spent numerous hours in the New York Public Library.

This is a case where everyone and every organization involved just wanted it to disappear. The police didn't want to investigate the shooting; the truth was inconsequential. The Mafia issued a contract on the shooter's life, but they hated the heat. The Feds wanted complete control and promised they would make it all go away. The case became a gnarled knot that kept getting tighter yet looser at the same time. Most stories have twists and turns; this story is all twists and turns.

The chief investigator would find extensive evidence to both exonerate and condemn the officer who did the shooting. He also discovers a ruthless and corrupt "system." Like unpeeling an onion, in the end, questions remain – what is relevant, what is not, and does truth matter?

I have written this story in the first person so the reader can interpret the information as the investigating detective received it. Jump into his shoes, and discern for yourself, was the shooting, excellent police work, or premeditated murder?

Philip Butera

FOREWARD

Based on a true story

On April 1, 1973, high ranking Mafioso trigger man, "Crazy" Mario Zicaro was enjoying an early dinner with his family at Lombardo's Seafood restaurant in Manhattan's Little Italy. Reno Piantini, another Mafia henchman from a different crime family, walked into the restaurant, went directly to Zicaro's table, and opened fire, cowboy style, with two .38-cal. revolvers. Ten shots were fired directly at Zicaro. His death and the brazen way he was murdered raised eyebrows among the New York crime families. But what annoyed the bosses most was Reno Piantini's boss, Stefano Gambacorda, now cemented his position as the undisputed head of organized crime across the country.

PROLOGUE

MONDAY, JUNE 30, 1975
3:50 P.M.

NYC POLICE RADIO
    CENTRAL: 1013 - Assist police officer, corner of Vermont and Ivy
    CENTRAL: Signal 1013 - Shots fired Vermont and Ivy
    CENTRAL: 1013 - In 5th Precinct. A police officer needs assistance.
    CENTRAL: 1013 -1013 - Shots fired.
    5 IDA: At scene. Unfounded.
    CENTRAL: 1013 - Confirmed. Two men in a shootout at the corner of Vermont and Ivy.
    7 DAVID: At scene - witness states one man had a police shield around his neck, jumped in a Yellow cab in pursuit of late model white car.
    5 IDA: At the scene, witnesses state two cars sped off down Vermont.
    CENTRAL: Cab traveling on Vermont
    5 IDA: In pursuit.
    CENTRAL: Shooter is now at St. Vincent's Hospital.

CHAPTER 1

TUESDAY, JULY 1, 1975
7:30 A.M.

"MURDER!" The word reverberates in my head like a cathedral bell.

"Yeah, murder. Do you understand, D'laska?" Chief Roberts repeats the bitter words, "Cold-blooded murder."

Roberts pauses, self-assured, and strides the short distance toward the narrow, smoke-stained office windows. He's a short, thin man with a small pot belly and a drooping lower lip. His cheap summer suit is draped over his narrow shoulders.

Roberts twists his face into a grimace, and the deep lines around his beady eyes turn him into an ugly rodent.

"Listen D'laska," his voice booms with authority from across the room, "this guinea cop, Louis Calabrese, shot and killed the only son of Reno Piantini." He sighs. "Even you know who Reno Piantini is, right? The madman that gunned down 'Crazy' Mario Zicaro."

Roberts lights a cigarette. "Reno made sure that kid was feared and respected by all those low life dagos. Nickie never screwed up. No arrest records. Calabrese gets out of work early, rushes into Manhattan from Brooklyn, spots Nickie supposedly about to shoot two spics. He interferes, there's gunplay, a car chase. Nickie Piantini is dead, and this Calabrese is telling police sergeants, captains, and inspectors to go to hell because he used to be assigned to Street Crime. Then get this—the guinea demands his P.B.A. attorney."

"Do you have a motive?"

"The New York Police Department has you to find that out."

I feel the perspiration gathering on my forehead. "How was Calabrese handled? Like a cop or a criminal?"

The blue vein in Roberts' temple pulsates. "Stefano Gambacorda is God to criminals. Reno Piantini is one of his top lieutenants. Piantini's kid is shot down in broad daylight under baffling circumstances. Does that answer your question, D'laska?"

"Why me? I don't investigate Organized Crime or Internal Affairs cases."

"I'd like to know that myself. With all the capable detectives in this city, why was a schmuck like you chosen?"

The air bristles with tension.

The hatred in Roberts' eyes drills into me. "Your guardian angel, the fine Chief McConnell, has faith in you, and he's taking full responsibility for his decision."

I run my hands through my hair.

Investigating a cop isn't a job most cops enjoy. There's a sadistic pleasure attached to scrutinizing a fellow officer.

Smoke billows from Roberts' crooked mouth. "It's about time you did some real police work."

I stand and stare at him. "Can I go?"

"No! Sit down till I dismiss you."

My jaw clenches as I comply.

He moves like a sloth to his cluttered desk, crushes his cigarette among a pile of other discarded butts, picks up a ruler and slaps it against his palm. "I don't care for your psychological methods, D'laska. I thought you were lucky in solving the Lafayette Hotel stabbings, and I didn't think you deserved to be promoted to detective sergeant though you passed the exam. But I have my orders. Your assignment is to find out how much of Calabrese's story is true. I already know he's a murderer. You'll be working directly under

McConnell, but I'll be watching you. When you screw up, and you will, I'm gonna come down on you like a big brick on a little pile of shit."

"Now, can I leave?"

"Take these reports with you. One more thing, the clock is ticking, college boy."

TUESDAY
8:00 A.M.

Outside, dusty-brown clouds and smog filter out any brightness. Everything is a gritty gray that darkens daily.

I stare from the station house steps. The stench of decaying garbage permeates the dead air. The Department of Sanitation has been on strike for over a month, along with the firemen. Walls of stinking garbage move closer to the center sidewalk. They tumble into the street; drivers scatter the debris, adding pockets of nauseous odors into the foul air.

The city is on the brink of fiscal collapse, supposedly. Two thousand cops lost their jobs this morning why couldn't one of them have been Roberts? His ambitions have never been a secret. He's left claw marks behind on his trail to the chief of detectives. I tug at my tie and unbutton the top of my shirt. The humidity is oppressive. There's no breeze, and the temperature must be eighty, and it's still morning.

I thought I had put to bed the whispers behind my back, the snickers of ignorant men who wanted their kids to go to college but despised an educated man. McConnell fixed me this time. He's going to tell me he's done me a favor. Meanwhile, Roberts will dig my grave. It's hard for any cop to survive the smell of Internal Affairs.

I remove a folded sheet of paper from my top pocket, my schedule. An appointment with Connors, one of the two high-ranking officers at the crime scene. At eleven, I meet Officer Louis Calabrese at the morgue.

TUESDAY
8:30 A.M.

THE FIFTH PRECINCT is on Canal Street, another brick building with frosted glass block windows bordering Chinatown and Little Italy. This neighborhood is a siege of movement.

The station is crammed with people shouting at each other. I squeeze through the thicket to the duty sergeant's desk and ask where I can find Connors. He points down a narrow corridor.

After a second hard knock, a coarse voice within the office shouts, "Wait." A few seconds later, I'm ordered to come in.

The craggy man watches me approach. Captain Connors sits behind a large old wooden desk in the center of a dingy office. The room is saturated with stale air. Neither of the two frosted windows is open. I'm sure they're nailed shut.

I introduce myself.

"Whatta ya want, Alaska?" Connors says. "I'm busy." He puts his hands below the desk. We're not going to shake hands.

"It's D'laska. I'm looking into the Piantini shooting. You were in charge at the hospital?"

I take a seat across from him.

Connors brings up his leathery hand and rubs it under a wrinkled nose. "You with Internal Affairs?"

"Chief McConnell's office."

He snorts. "Why?"

"Didn't Chief Roberts call you?"

"Jim McConnell called me about this. And I told him what I thought."

"I need some questions answered."

"So, do I. You attached to Patrol?"

"No, Homicide."

Connors twists his mouth. "Alaska, Jim McConnell runs Patrol. What's the connection?"

"Special assignment."

His laughter echoes through the stagnant room. "Two thousand cops were laid off this morning, and they got Homicide detectives playing hop-scotch for wops."

Connors' skin is loose, drooping from heavy lines under his sunken eye sockets. He runs his tongue along his liver-colored lips. "In the old days, shit like this would have been taken care of immediately. Without special assignment guys." He laughs again—the kind of bitter cackle that's more of a contemptuous attack.

Connors could have helped write the "old school" manual. Twenty-five years of change hasn't been agreeable to him. He detests modern times, modern methods, and modern cops. For him, iron-ruled police authority has become watered-down law enforcement, and he despises the loss of power.

I scan the room—old plaques, old headlines, old faces in old frames. A tired-looking St. Patrick stares down at us from behind his desk.

He picks dry skin from his nose and examines it. "What do you want to know that I didn't tell McConnell?"

I come forward in my chair, cupping my hands. "What happened yesterday?"

He pounds his bony fist on his desk projecting a pencil to the floor. "What happened? That wop Calabrese shot one of his own fuckin' kind, for a favor to some other wop. That piece a shit refused, refused to obey my orders. He ignored me like I was a nothing. I fuckin' axed him straight questions. He was deaf for ten minutes. When I demanded answers, he played with his prick. This jerk told me he left work at four. It was four when he told me that."

He pounds his hand a second time. "I axed him a civil question, where he was assigned, and he becomes annoyed and tells me, 'Street Crime.' Over twenty years I've been on the force, and I've seen a million lying pricks, and that includes Calabrese. Street Crime, I told him, Street Crime has been dismantled for now. He looks at me with this stupid guinea smirk and says, 'Street Crime' again." Connors leans over his desk. "So, I say. What're you doing in Manhattan? He just looks at me like I'm nuts and he knows St Peter. I shouted in his ugly face, 'Where you from?' Then he says he's from Brooklyn. I ask, 'What precinct in Brooklyn?' He doesn't answer. I ask him again what's he doing in Manhattan. He ignores me, acting like he's too busy to answer my questions; he just stands there bobbing his spaghetti head. I say, 'You here fuckin' some broad?' You know how guineas are—they'll jump on anything. I demanded answers. He says to me, a captain, 'What fuckin' business is it of yours?' In the old days, I would have put that little wop in hell with all the other worthless guineas."

Connors' lips are moist and caked with spit. He lights an unfiltered cigarette and bellows out thick smoke from the sides of his mouth. He stares at me for a long moment as if he were examining dirt under a magnifying glass. His words come out fast. "How do you spell your name?"

I go along. "D apostrophe L-A-S-K-A."

"What kinda name is that?"

I mask my disgust. "Captain, I'd like to bring back something constructive to Chief McConnell."

"If you ain't proud to say it, you ain't Irish. That's for sure."

"Please continue, Captain."

"How did a good Irish name like Michael get connected with such an awful last name?" He inflates his chest and hangs one arm at his side. "What more don't you know?"

I take a small notebook from my inside pocket and dart past the first pages until I come to the name I'm looking for.

"What happened when Captain Rocca from the Sixth Precinct arrived at the hospital where Piantini died?"

"The Italians drove back to the scene of the shooting. Leaving me, of course, to restore order."

I flip back a few pages. "Calabrese shot Nickie Piantini on the corner of Vermont and Ivy in Little Italy. Wounded, Piantini drove two dozen blocks into the Village to St. Vincent's Hospital. Piantini staggered out of his car in front of the hospital. Calabrese arrived seconds later and confronted Piantini, but Nickie collapsed in the street. Hospital personnel rushed Nickie into the emergency room."

Connors shakes a finger at me. "Immediately after Calabrese first spotted Piantini, but before he approached and shot him, Calabrese demanded a gas station attendant to call nine-one-one and report a ten-thirteen. That cop in trouble call produced a lot of action, patrol cars rushin' to be heroes, sirens blastin', lights flashin', mass confusion. You had ambulances, fire engines gettin' involved. All this commotion alerted every asshole in a twenty-mile radius.

"There must have been a hundred civilians gathered outside the hospital creating even more confusion. I had squad cars arriving every second and everybody wantin' to know what happened. I have no answers cause Captain Rocca took Calabrese back to the scene to find witnesses. I told Rocca there wouldn't be any, but he went anyway."

I study Connors for a moment before I stand. "You're implying the killing was premeditated. Then you assume he was in Manhattan to meet a woman. Isn't that contradictory?"

He takes a long last drag on the cigarette, crushes it on the side of the wastebasket, leans forward, and pushes aside papers atop his desk, his face is freckled granite. "Italians have three major faults: they lie, they cheat, and they kill their own. Calabrese is a real Italian. He came over the bridge into Manhattan to kill Piantini. That was set up from at least Friday when he requested an early out for Monday. Then, sooner or later, he was gonna meet some broad either to prove how tough he was or to collect payoff money. Maybe both."

"You, Captain Rocca, and an inspector questioned Calabrese till almost midnight. Did he stick to the same story?"

"The son-of-a-bitch never gave one straight answer except maybe to his guinea lawyer. If I'd been left alone with the bastard, I would have got the truth." Connors points a crooked finger at me. "Calabrese is guilty. I'll stake my reputation on it. I just want to know how much other shit he's gotten away with."

Connors stands. He once had a build, now his shoulders are rounded, and his chest has slipped toward his waistline. He adjusts himself before offering his limp hand. "Give Chief McConnell my best and tell him if he needs anything else not to send any messenger boys, just call me direct."

I shake his hand and say, "According to his report, Calabrese contends there was a second person in Piantini's car."

Connors sighs with unsuppressed annoyance. "Alaska, no one saw any fuckin' body in Nickie Piantini's car. Not the gas station guy. Not the cabby Calabrese flagged down and had follow Piantini's car. Calabrese jumped from the cab to a squad car two blocks from the hospital. The two officers in that car didn't see the second guy. Finally, when Piantini slammed on his brakes in front of the hospital, nobody saw another person get outta that car."

"Why would Calabrese lie about a second person being in the car?"

Connors stops halfway to the door and looks hard at me. "The prick is guilty."

"Was any blood other than Piantini's found in the car?"

"Don't try and make an asshole of me, Alaska. No."

"It's D'laska."

"Who cares?"

"Calabrese stated he fired five shots. Two bullets hit Piantini; one just after Piantini shot at and missed Calabrese, the other as Piantini was struggling to get back into his own car. Calabrese quickly fired the other three shots at a second man who was hiding under the dashboard of Piantini's car. That means there are either bullets or blood there."

Connors spits some tobacco from his lips.

I continue, "Calabrese's report states the only reason Piantini got away was that after emptying his gun, Calabrese had to retreat. So, if no blood was found, what about bullets?"

He ignores my question, waving me toward the door.

I fake a smile. "Where's the car now?"

"Impound center. Who gives a shit! "

"The forensic report didn't mention fingerprints."

"That's Forensics' problem." Connors opens his office door, gloating over his own imagined importance.

I step out and turn back to him. "Who's the most informed detective to talk with about Nickie Piantini?"

"Go upstairs and ask for Olearczyk. That Polack's been here for fifteen years."

As I approach the stairwell, I hear Connors' voice echoing in the hall. "Hey, what the hell kinda name is Alaska, anyway?"

TUESDAY
9:15 A.M.

THE DETECTIVES' central area housing is filled with outdated furniture. The closed windows are painted gray. One long row of dim fluorescent lights stains the ceiling with a grayish-green shadow. The scattered men ignore me as I walk through the hinged gate into the pen. I approach a hunched forward detective. He has a disarming, heart-shaped face and pecks away at a typewriter.

"I'm looking for Detective Olearczyk?"

He shakes my hand. "I'm Flip Olearczyk. What's up?"

He's near forty with thinning straight brown hair and a lanky build.

"D'laska. Homicide. Captain Connors said you'd be the one to talk with about Nickie Piantini."

"Captain's a prince, ain't he?"

The lines at the corner of his eyes ebb and grow as he squints at the black machine. "I hate typing."

We slip into a small interrogation room. Olearczyk grabs a metal chair slouches and folds his hands on his head. "What d'ya need?"

I push a chair close to the table. "Tell me about Nick Piantini."

Olearczyk shakes his head. "He was no charm school graduate. I want to congratulate the cop who shot him. I mean that. I practically watched that punk grow up. Typical mobster's son. He was known to his father's friends, and he used that to his advantage. When Reno Piantini killed Mario Zicaro and went into hiding, the kid knew he was being protected by the big boys. No one was going to screw with him. So, he pushed his weight around pretty good." Olearczyk runs a long finger under his nose and grins. "I'm sure you've read his file. What do you really want?"

"Any ideas on why Nickie Piantini would be at Vermont and Ivy at three forty-five on Monday with a gun in someone's face?"

Olearczyk runs a St. Christopher's medal up and down a silver chain around his neck. "Any reason! Nickie was heavily involved in numbers, card games, bookmaking, dope, carjacking, shakedowns, robbery, and any other shit he could get away with."

"Tell me about his personality."

"He was a mean, tough, sadistic mobster who would muscle anybody he could—but smart enough not to step on any serious toes. He hustled guys his own age. Weaker guys, from the neighborhood. Nickie was built like a bull, over two hundred pounds, and in good physical shape. He used his strength and his father's reputation to intimidate everybody he came in contact with. Including cops. He even tried with me."

I grimace and Olearczyk notices.

Olearczyk gives me a long, steady look, staring as if I'm familiar from somewhere. After a moment, he excuses himself and walks out the door.

The room smells of confined air and old confessions. When Olearczyk returns, he has two Styrofoam coffee cups. He drops small packets on the table. "Powdered milk."

He sits, sipping his coffee.

"Michael D'laska. I remember your name, a Master's Degree in Psychopath Psychology or something like that. They did a feature article about you in one of the police magazines a while back. You collared that schizoid who was raping and stabbing women at the Lafayette Hotel?"

"That was a few years ago."

Olearczyk waits a long minute. "Why is Homicide, Psycho Homicide, asking questions about Organized Crime? That's Larry Ring's area. Are you working on his unit?"

"I'm doing some preliminary legwork for Chief McConnell."

"McConnell!" Olearczyk shakes his head. "Why is Patrol involved?"

I shrug.

Olearczyk stirs his coffee with his finger. "What are you investigating exactly?"

"They want a complete picture of Piantini and the cop who shot him."

"You're making it sound like something is wrong with the shooting."

"McConnell wants a report." I sound lifeless—noiseless, like crumpled cellophane hitting the floor and reforming.

He grins. "From what I remember of that article, Chief McConnell sort of sponsored your education didn't he?"

"Does that mean you're not going to tell me about Nickie Piantini?"

Olearczyk gulps his coffee and grins. "Nickie enjoyed power. Liked to drink and gamble. He loved being important and spending money to impress whoever noticed him."

"How ambitious was he?"

"He wanted to be bigger than his father."

"Would he have?"

Olearczyk's careful. "He had a way to go."

"Many enemies?"

"Half the neighborhood, but that's only a drop in the bucket compared to his father."

"Where did Nickie Piantini hang out?"

Olearczyk puts St. Christopher between his lips while adjusting himself in his chair. "There are three main spots. Three Deuces is a daytime sports bar, run by the wife of a small potatoes hood who's doing time for burglary. They run a moderate book from there. Marlowe's on Mulberry is the other popular joint owned by a clean Polack who thinks he's an Italian. That's the nighttime hot spot. The high-class place is Pieri's, of course. Everybody knows it's run by the mob. You could try Fat Sam's Italian Gardens."

I don't like to drink anything I can't see through, but I take my first sip of coffee. It's horrible. I dig for my notebook. "Reno Piantini has been in hiding since the Zicaro murder. Will he surface now?"

Olearczyk tosses his cup into the wastebasket. He wags his head.

"Reno Piantini wasn't the perfect father. It's hard to tell. It's no secret the feds have been trying to set up a deal with him for a while. This might be the right time."

"Is it possible another Mafia family set up this shooting to force Reno Piantini out of hiding?"

Olearczyk freezes, glaring at me: "You think Nickie was killed by a dirty cop?"

"I'm just making inquiries."

"The morning papers say the cop risked his life."

"I'm not denying that I'm just making inquiries."

Olearczyk reflects for a moment. "You're working both sides of the street, aren't you, D'laska?"

I sigh. "No cop wants to wonder if his partner is on two payrolls."

Olearczyk rolls his eyes. "I guess those psychology classes at college taught you how to phrase things, so you don't answer a question."

"Who will benefit the most by Piantini's death?"

"Check out a clever young climber named Claudio Cellini. He will seamlessly control what Nickie lost."

Olearczyk brings his wrist up to check his watch. "Anything else?"

"You didn't answer my question. Do you think this shooting could have been set up to force Reno into the open?"

Olearczyk scratches the back of his head. "You're asking me two questions in a very tricky way. If I say yes, then I'm setting up a fellow cop. If I say no, I'm lying. Better if you talk with Larry Ring over at Organized Crime." Olearczyk gives me a sideways stare. "Or Internal Affairs."

I stand.

He opens the door with a small smile. "One last thing."

"Sure."

"Shake Officer Calabrese's hand for me. He killed a real bastard."

TUESDAY
11:12 A.M.

. . .

WHAT AM I MISSING? A cop killed a criminal. This isn't a rarity in New York. If they think the cop is dirty, assign this case over to I.A. If they believe the mob is flexing its muscle, let Ring and Organized Crime takeover.

They questioned Calabrese for hours yesterday. What do they expect me to find that they didn't? Last night, they couldn't make a reliable connection between Nickie's death and Calabrese's statements. This morning, by some miracle, they think it's all going to fall into place. Roberts and Connors want to hang him, but someone is preventing them from making that move. It can't be McConnell alone.

My thoughts run in an endless circle. Why choose me? I enjoy the challenge of analyzing what a psychopath's next move will be and outmaneuvering him—what I despise is asking questions about other cops. The more you probe, the uglier you become.

I squeeze into a parking space a block away from the morgue at Bellevue. It's standard procedure for an autopsy to be performed on a victim killed by a cop, so McConnell arranged for Calabrese to meet me at the main entrance.

A new blue Chrysler is double-parked in front of the morgue. Two Hispanics lean on the fender. They look me up and down as I pass. The radio volume could crack the old Greek face of the building.

The heavy morgue doors close out the sticky humidity, exposing me to the marble silence. Moments later, a medium height and build well-dressed man enters. His determined face and nose are round. His hair is thin, sandy brown, short, and combed forward. He lifts his shoulders and rolls his head from side to side before talking with the receptionist.

"Hello, I'm Louis Calabrese." He unbuttons his Italian silk suit jacket to present his badge. "I'm here to identify the body of Nicholas Piantini."

I approach him. "Calabrese, I'm D'laska." We shake hands while evaluating each other.

Calabrese has a meticulous order about him, the opposite of mine at the moment.

We walk down the corridor, aware of our footsteps on the tiled floor. We get in the elevator.

"Where you from?" Calabrese asks.

"Homicide."

He squares his shoulders before speaking again, "Homicide! Detective-sergeant? I guess you're good at taking tests? I don't see many of you guys out on the field."

I shrug. "I like the streets."

"Yeah, me too. I've been working Street Crime for five years, ya know? At least till a couple of weeks ago. Dumb ass politicians. Why dismantle the most productive unit on the force?"

I continue the conversation as we walk down the hall. "You were one of the original two hundred officers chosen for Street Crime. That's impressive."

"I gotta knack for the streets. Know what I mean? Some guys are good at homicide or arson or vice. My partner, Gino Guzzetta, and I were the best on the streets. We could spot a job goin' down ninety-nine percent of the time."

WE SHOW A GUARD OUR BADGES. He folds the *Daily News* and without comment leads us into a small, cold, antiseptic room where the only sound is a dull hum of fluorescent lights. There are three metal tables, each draped with a white sheet over a dead body.

The guard glances at a three-by-five card. "Number 1609W, Piantini? The stiff on the end cart."

Calabrese's jaw tightens, hardening his face when his eyes are fixed on the man he killed. Purple scalpel slashes cut the length of Piantini's torso radiating from two dark holes, one in the upper chest and the other in the belly. Calabrese is unemotional, but I catch a slight grin at the corner of his mouth before the guard drapes the body.

Calabrese signs the appropriate forms, and we ride the elevator in silence. He holds the door open for me, and as I pass, he asks, "Homicide, you said. Not Internal Affairs?"

"Homicide."

We walk up the corridor, past the receptionist to the exit. Loud salsa rhythms from the blue Chrysler greet us as we walk down the long funnel-shaped steps. There's a string of double-parked cars now, but the Chrysler is the only one idling with two Hispanics sitting on the hood.

Calabrese looks over at me and shakes his head. "Believe these assholes?"

We walk parallel to the street away from the music toward a small coffee shop on the corner of the next block. Calabrese walks with a confident head-turning, chin-thrusting, shoulder-swaying motion.

While we walk, the distant Spanish music squeezes through the overflowing mounds of garbage lining the storefronts.

Calabrese has two prominent personality characteristics: he's self-controlled and calculating. Both contradict the frantic descriptions given of him after the shooting.

We enter the busy coffee shop. Calabrese says, "How long have you been a detective sergeant?"

"Little over three years."

"How long on the force?"

"Since December sixty-six, mostly Manhattan. A lot of nights. The department put me through graduate school."

He lifts his head to rub his chin. "Yeah, I never had much time for school. I figure the streets are school enough for cops. You a lawyer or something?"

I slide into a booth. "Criminal psychologist."

Calabrese gives me a condescending smirk. "Psychologist, ah?"

We begin piling the egg-stained breakfast plates and the cigarette-filled coffee cups away from us. We glance at menus. Calabrese leans back to keep his suit from brushing against the table. It's a contrived, awkward situation.

He tucks his menu between the crusted sugar shaker and empty napkin holder and returns his hands to his lap. "So. Tell me why we're here."

"I need you to tie up a few loose ends."

"A psychologist from Homicide is gonna tie up some loose ends?"

"We're just having a conversation."

"Homicide means something stinks."

"Why don't you explain to me what happened. Cop to cop."

Calabrese is a closed man, not very permeable. "We both know I went through this from four o'clock yesterday afternoon till midnight. My story hasn't changed. Nobody listened last night." He wags his index finger back and forth between us. "So, why should you listen now?"

"I've read the reports. I've just come from Captain Connors' office. He doesn't seem to be a very opened-minded guy. I need your side of the story."

Calabrese smirks. "That Irish bastard doesn't believe I shot Nickie Piantini in self-defense. He tried hard to fuck me last night, and I didn't appreciate that."

A plump waitress takes our order while trying to remove a brown stain on her uniform. We both turn our heads to the window. The blue Chrysler is still double-parked in front of the morgue.

Calabrese grew up in Coney Island and ten years of being a cop in crime-ridden places like Harlem and Brooklyn have left deep cynical scars on him. He holds down his starched white collar as he lifts his chin and stretches his neck. "I'll explain, and then you can tell me why Homicide, and not Internal Affairs or Organized Crime?"

I nod. "Fair enough."

Calabrese draws in a large breath and tries to hide his annoyance. "I was filling my car at the gas station on the corner of Vermont and Ivy when I heard a yell. I looked around. Diagonally across the street from the station along Ivy, I saw this big guy in a white suit leaning into this idling green Pontiac. I knew this guy came from the white Cadillac directly in front of the Pontiac because the engine was running and the door was wide open. I notice this guy in the white suit pointing a gun into the driver's face. I figure the guy in the white suit is an undercover cop making an arrest. Who else walks around with a gun in his hand in broad daylight except for a cop? I told the gas station attendant, 'Call nine-one-one and report a ten-thirteen is going down.' I remember repeating, 'Make sure you say, a ten-thirteen cop in trouble."

The waitress brings two cups of coffee. I push the coffee I didn't order to the side.

I place my elbows on the table. "What did you hear the guy in the white suit yelling?"

"At first, I couldn't make out the exact words. I just heard yelling. When I got closer, I heard Piantini yelling, 'You motherfucker, give me my money.'"

"You heard him say, 'You motherfucker, give me my money.' You saw him holding a gun inside the car at the driver's face, and you thought Piantini was an undercover cop?"

Calabrese's answer is stiletto quick and challenging. "No, when I heard that, I knew he wasn't a cop. I was closer to him then. Let me go on."

I raise my eyebrows.

He says, "You got a problem with that?"

"Go on."

"I ran across Vermont dodging traffic. While I was running, I pulled out my shield. Once on the sidewalk, I headed the short distance toward Ivy. I had my gun out. As I approached, I heard Nickie Piantini say clearly, 'You motherfucker, give me my money.' He was leaning into the Pontiac. He had the driver by the shirt with a gun to his head. Then I knew this wasn't a bust, and he wasn't a cop. I identified myself. He turned around and fired at me."

"Did you get a good look at the men in the Pontiac?"

"No, just a flash. I'm pretty sure they were spics." Calabrese sips his coffee and makes a face.

"How far away was Piantini when he fired at you?"

"Twelve, thirteen feet. I was stepping off the curb. He was against the door of the second car."

"How many bullets did he fire?"

"A quick two. One when he was turning away from the driver to face me. A second when he actually saw me."

"He fired in your direction. First, without seeing you, he aimed to where he thought your voice originated. Then a second time a moment later while facing you. What did you do then?"

That smirk comes back to the corner of his mouth. "I fired back, hitting the son of a bitch. He spun around and began to stagger toward the Caddie. I shot him a second time as he was getting into the car. He shut the door, and I ran to him. When I got to the window, I was surprised. A Hispanic guy is cowering underneath the dashboard on the passenger's side. I realized instantly the odds of me being killed just doubled. My aim changed from Piantini to the other guy, and I fired three shots, emptying my gun."

Our waitress hands me my spinach omelet and places a turkey club in front of Calabrese.

When I press my fork into the omelet, a small stream of milky-green liquid runs to the outer circle of the plate. Calabrese lifts a wedge of his sandwich, and a thick gold bracelet falls to his shirt sleeve. He's wearing a gold wedding ring and a diamond adorned with rubies on his right pinky.

I encourage him to continue. "You emptied your gun into the car. What happened then?"

"I backed away quickly from the Caddie, ducking behind a parked car. Almost immediately the Caddie skidded off, making a left onto Vermont. I flagged down a cabby with my badge. The cab weaved through traffic on Vermont."

Calabrese takes an absent bite of a potato chip. "The Caddie headed up Vermont, then made a right on Sixth. At Greenwich and Christopher, I spotted a patrol car, so I ran to it. The two officers listened, but they didn't give a fuck 'cause at midnight they were being laid off. They gave me some bullets, and we followed the Caddie. Piantini made rights on Seventh and on Eleventh, stopping at the entrance to St. Vincent's Hospital. We were about five car lengths behind him. I left the patrol car, and as I approached the Caddie, Piantini appeared, his white suit was soaked with blood. He walked from the driver's seat to the back of his car. I yelled for him to stop. He staggered and collapsed in the street. I ran to the Caddie and threw open the passenger door. The car was empty. Somewhere between Ivy and the hospital, the Hispanic guy had got away. Meanwhile, people flew out of St Vincent's—doctors, nurses, security guards, nuns, some black broad with a clipboard wanting information."

Our waitress refills his coffee cup.

"That's it!" he says. "Except that bullshit with Connors and some big shot Inspector afterward."

"Tell me what happened after they took Piantini into the hospital."

"Just so there's no misunderstanding, I killed someone who tried to kill me. You want to hear about the departmental fucking I took last night? I'll tell you because that's why you're here, ain't it, D'laska? 'Cause I pissed off that Irish prick enough for him to cry to his Irish City Hall connections. Those bastards want to screw every Italian 'cause they know we're better than them." Calabrese pushes his coffee away harder than he intended, brown liquid erupts from the sides of the cup and spills into the saucer.

"How did you feel when you found out you killed a Mafia leader's son?"

Calabrese has a cocky smile. "It didn't bother me."

"Reno Piantini is a powerful man. You aren't the least bit nervous?"

"When I became a cop, I realized the worst that could happen to me is I could die, and we all die sometime."

"Isn't that easier said than done?"

He waves his hands to dismiss that question. "Why Homicide?"

"Special Assignment."

"I killed some wise guy last night in self-defense, and those Irish bastards got a college guy to squeeze my balls. Why?"

I push my hair from my forehead and fall back in the booth.

"Why a psychologist? They think I'm nuts because I killed a wise guy's son?"

"The ten-thirteen must have produced several patrol cars. A lot of commotion."

Calabrese rolls his neck from side to side. "Now, there are a lot of cop cars, bystanders were shouting and media people sticking microphones in anybody's face they thought was important. Then this fuckin' Connors appears and tries to corner me. I could tell immediately he was a typical Irish prick who hates Italians. He started accusing me the instant he saw me. Like I'm the criminal who just shot a cop, not the reverse. Then this Italian, Captain Rocca, comes over. Rocca and Connors exchange a few heated words. Finally, Rocca and I drive back to Ivy and Vermont to find some witnesses.

"We questioned everybody we saw, but nobody knew anything. Rocca and I go back to the hospital. They questioned me till that inspector arrived, then we were all driven to the Fifth Precinct. When they put me in an interrogation room, I told Connors to read me my rights; I wanted a lawyer. When my attorney arrived, it really pissed Connors off."

Calabrese swallows hard. "Conners attacked my story from every angle, but I stuck to what I knew happened. When he let me go, I did my paperwork, went home, thought a lot about the incident and the way I was treated. Slept a little. Then some official broad called this morning, saying you'd meet me at the morgue."

I lean forward. "How do you account for nobody else identifying another man in Piantini's car?"

Calabrese straightens his white shirt cuffs before answering. "There was this big spic squeezed into the space under the dashboard. He was wearing a light blue, short-sleeved shirt. I remember his arms were very hairy. I fired at him three times. He must have jumped from the car in route to the hospital."

"Why would an injured man leave a moving car heading for a hospital?"

"How do I know?"

"Five bullets were expelled, two hit Piantini. Three were fired at this mysterious hairy Hispanic. Hard to miss a target like that at point-blank range. And yet there was no blood found on that side of the car. How do you explain it?"

"I fired at the guy three times!" Calabrese slides his plate away with the back of his hand.

"If no bullets are found in the car, then there's the problem of no blood. If you hit the Hispanic, there should be a trace of blood. Ballistics is likely to find either blood and no bullets, telling us you hit the Hispanic, or bullets and no blood, telling us you missed."

"You know D'laska," he gives me an icy grin, "I don't give a damn what you or Ballistics find."

"You contend Nicholas Piantini fired at you with a silver .45, yet the only gun found was a black .38. And it had never been fired."

"It was a silver .45!"

The blue Chrysler is still double-parked. Calabrese and I are very different cops. I know he derives his strength from an inner compulsiveness that defines itself in street sense. From penetrating hazel eyes, he has always perceived a conniving world. A world at street level. My fault could be I'm not cynical enough.

I say, "Your report states you were in Manhattan at that hour to meet your father and brother. All three of you were to drive upstate to your home in Monticello. Was there any other reason why you were in Manhattan?"

His face hardens. "Just by asking, you're calling me a liar. Here's my answer, D'laska: when I was in Street Crime, I had city-wide jurisdiction to cover all five boroughs."

He rises toward me. "Now that I've been transferred to the Seven-One in Brooklyn, everybody wants to know what I was doing in Manhattan. It's a free country, I can go anywhere when I leave work."

"You reported for duty at the Seven-One on Wednesday. On Friday, before leaving for the weekend, you requested permission to come to work the following Monday one hour earlier so you could leave work at three in the afternoon instead of four. Correct?"

He doesn't answer.

"I assume you arranged that schedule so you could meet your father and brother directly after work and leave for Monticello?"

Moments pass. I attempt a weak smile before I speak, "You raced into Manhattan. The shooting occurred at three-fifty. Most people wouldn't have even been in Manhattan from Brooklyn that quickly, let alone be gassing up. Curiously, your father and brother weren't anywhere near that corner when the shooting occurred. In fact, they didn't arrive at the hospital until much later. I ask myself why three men, who live in Brooklyn, would want to drive into Manhattan then travel upstate when traffic is at its busiest."

I pause, then say, "You showed little curiosity about who you shot, nobody remembers you even asking his name. I find that peculiar. You saw a well-dressed man in the middle of the street, in a poor neighborhood who attempted to kill you, but luckily missed. You shot him, chased him, and when he collapsed at your feet, you had no desire to take his wallet and find out who he was? Instead, you wanted to get back to the scene of the shooting."

Calabrese sneers.

"Here's another problem," I say. "The car you followed wasn't a Cadillac. Piantini was driving an Oldsmobile Toronado. Maybe that Pontiac you claim was the second car was also something else."

"It was a white Caddie!"

"A Toronado. It's at the Impound Center."

"So, what's the difference?"

"Your story has inconsistencies, the flimsiest being why you were in Manhattan."

Calabrese attempts to interrupt me.

I gesture for him to let me finish. "I realize your reasons for coming into Manhattan, aside from meeting family members, may be very personal. I detest sitting here asking another cop questions; it's not what I do. Level with me, and I'll persuade McConnell to put this case to bed."

He's fixed—staring at some distant object behind me. "What case are you handling? I've never denied I shot Piantini." He stands. "I shot Nickie Piantini in self-defense, and I was in Manhattan to meet my father and brother. If you got a problem with that, read me my rights."

He tosses some bills on the table before attempting to leave.

"What about the Hispanic?"

"What?"

"The Hispanic in Nick Piantini's car. You think he's got a record?"

He stares at me like a man who disbelieves what he just heard.

"Don't you want to look through the mug books?"

He cracks into a cocky grin. He shakes his finger close to my face. "You play it tight, very tight, D'laska." The grin becomes a smile. "Why Homicide, not Internal Affairs?"

"My guess, because McConnell wants this tied, delivered, and buried."

TUESDAY
1:20 P.M.

SERGEANT QUINCY IS on duty at the Manhattan Station House. He's an old-timer with an inflated sense of importance and a terrible habit of spitting while talking. He motions me to the front counter. Calabrese wanders away.

Quincy shakes his chin at Calabrese. "Some cop from Brooklyn knocked off Piantini's kid. Rumor has it you're handling the case over Larry Ring. What's the story?"

"What else do you know?"

Quincy adjusts himself before speaking. "Guinea roulette. A favor for some top wop."

I walk away.

Calabrese shakes his head. "I can't believe that Irish prick Quincy is still in one piece. He screwed a lot of cops including some good friends by spreading lies to the Knapp Commission just to save his worthless Irish skin."

The elevator hums up three flights. The door opens, and we step out.

Down the hall, we enter a windowless conference room. There's a scarred gray metal table with a half-dozen used paper cups and napkins scattered over it. There's an amused smile on Calabrese's lips as he reaches for a napkin to wipe clean a chair before sitting. He looks over to me. "What nationality are you, D'laska?"

"I was born out West thirty-two years ago. I came to New York when I was sixteen. I'm American."

Calabrese sucks in his round cheeks. "Congratulations."

I sit across from him.

"You're a Giants fan I bet?" I say.

"You're a Jet's fan I bet."

"It shows?"

"All lightweights like the Jets."

"In ten years, you've worked Precincts, Mounted, Internal Affairs, and Street Crime. Street Crime your preference?"

Calabrese adjusts his jacket, straightening his shoulders and pulling down his starched white shirt cuffs. The room is claustrophobic, and neither of us is comfortable.

"My partner Gino and I did fine in Street Crime."

"Your record shows the both of you were awarded several commendations. To work that well together, you must be close friends."

"Like brothers."

"For six months in sixty-eight, you were the driver for the Chief Inspector of Internal Affairs."

Calabrese nods. "So."

"You transferred out of I.A. a few weeks before the Chief Inspector resigned and decided to run for council. Was that a coincidence?"

Calabrese gives me a fixed side profile to show his displeasure. "Yes!"

"If he didn't resign would you have asked to be transferred?"

"Why are you so interested?"

"Your record reads rather vague on the reasons why you left I.A."

Calabrese sucks in stabs of air between his small white teeth. "What does this have to do with anything?"

The door opens. A young man in his late twenties greets us with a gentle smile. He asks, "You need me for a composite?"

I say, "Work with Officer Calabrese on an identification of a Latin male, dark, middle twenties, hairy arms. Lou will fill you in."

I move to the door. "If you need me, I'll be on the tenth floor in McConnell's office."

———

TUESDAY

1:50 P.M.

FILTERING sunlight flows through the windows, outlining Suzanne Baxter's body inside her white dress as she leans over the copier machine. The view of McConnell's assistant is complimentary. When I offer my help, she gazes at me with the indifference one has for a hood ornament.

I ask to see McConnell. She faces me. She's tall, attractive with smooth, transparent white skin and thick white-blond hair pulled into a bun. When she smiles, her sharp features even somewhat, but her green eyes remain without warmth. Her one flaw is a slightly crooked front tooth between thin, pale pink lips.

"He's at City Hall," she says. "Do you want me to call the Police Commissioner's Office? I don't know if he's coming back today."

The times I've been in Suzanne's company, I've always felt secondary. Today is no exception. I run both hands through my hair. "Did he leave any message for me?"

She seats herself behind her neatly arranged desk. "No."

Frustrated, I walk to the window. Outside, a plane is slicing the sky, leaving a white, gaseous trail. I'd like to be up there. I'd like to be heading north to Montreal, to join my partner Paul, who's in Canada arranging his wedding. The plane begins to disappear, and the contrail decomposes. The gray sky zips whole again.

"Do you want to leave a note?" she says.

I open my mouth and forget what I'm going to say.

She smiles, mostly to herself. "Is something wrong?"

I find myself staring at Suzanne Baxter as if I've never seen her before. I don't think I ever noticed how stunning and shapely she is. Her complexion is flawless. I'm willing to bet McConnell's office is regularly visited just to see her.

"Detective," she repeats.

"Um...is there a phone I can use?"

She stands, still holding a manila envelope with a bold federal seal. "You can use mine. I will be in Chief McConnell's office."

I call a friend at IA. After a few minutes, his smooth voice sails through the lines. I mention Calabrese's name and his voice tightens.

He remembers Calabrese and doesn't like him. Calabrese left no friends at I.A. He was a loner, appointed by the Chief Inspector himself. Calabrese believed his only duty was as a chauffeur. He refused to do anything else. He relates how a lieutenant once gave Calabrese an incidental order to help file or something. Calabrese told him "to go fuck himself," he was a driver, not a paper pusher. The Chief Inspector liked Calabrese and covered for him at every opportunity. My friend's voice is above a whisper, "What I'm going to tell you next is all confidential." He pauses, sighs. "I will not repeat or admit what I'm going to tell you. It's very ticklish information. While Calabrese was a driver, he was never associated with any internal investigations, and he refused to be involved with any outside assignment. During the six months, he was assigned to Internal Affairs, Calabrese made only one friend, a policewoman, who he had an affair with. Later, she shacked up with a good friend of mine. Here's where it gets very curious. According to my friend, when the opportunity was available, Calabrese would hustle through the files to see who was being watched or inquired about. He would then pull the name presumably to warn the cop about a possible Internal Affairs scrutiny. Calabrese only pulled files on Italians. He used to laugh with the woman about how he would only help his own kind."

"Do you think he sold the information?"

"I honestly don't know."

I lean against the desk. "One last question. Was the woman Italian?"

With a mild laugh, he says, "Yes."

"Thanks."

"My advice: If you have something on this guy, use it to your advantage because he is certainly going to use you to his advantage."

I idly open a desk drawer. There's a snapshot of Baxter in an orange-striped bikini. She has long legs and a lovely chest. The unsmiling male next to her has long, curling dark locks and a thin, boyish frame.

TUESDAY
2:20 P.M.

CALABRESE IDENTIFIES a twenty-eight-year-old Cuban strongman named Tito Garcia. Calabrese taps the picture's edge with his finger. "This is the hairy sonofabitch that was in Nickie Piantini's car."

The make sheet states he's muscle. Three priors, one conviction for armed assault, served eighteen months in Attica in seventy-two.

Calabrese feels vindicated. We exchange glances. He sits back, his hands behind his round head. He's relaxed and gloating. "Garcia panicked. His job was to protect the Piantini kid. He fucked up, so he ran."

"That's unfortunate for you." I pause a long silent moment. "Because that's going to make it extremely hard to find Tito Garcia. And right now, he's the only one who can verify your story."

He shrugs the comment away.

"Did you identify either of the two men in the second car?"

He pinches his nose. "I didn't get a good look at them. The only thing I can say about them is they were spics too."

I move closer to Calabrese; there is uneasiness between, like two magnets energized against each other. "I'll have copies of Garcia's picture distributed to the proper precincts. Is there anything else you'd like to tell me?"

"Why?"

"I'm not satisfied with your reason for being in Manhattan. That means I have to dig further. I don't want to do that, and you won't appreciate it. If it's a woman you're protecting, I give you my word, I'll bury this case."

Calabrese stands and points a finger at my face. "Don't call me a liar again!"

At the elevator, Calabrese and I avoid each other's eyes. We're both aware of the consequences that can occur when one man puts a microscope on the life of another. The elevator door opens, Calabrese steps in and faces me. Our eyes lock before he disappears.

CHAPTER 2

WEDNESDAY, *July 2, 1975*
6:02 A.M.

THE ICE PICK suddenness of a ringing phone startles me. I bolt up in bed, and my eyes blink till they're open wide. Thousands of tiny white specks dance and vanish into the grayness. I take a deep breath.

"Yeah, hello!"

"D'laska, this is Chief McConnell. Are you awake?"

"Chief, one moment."

I place the phone on my shoulder and rub my eyes. What the fuck do they want now?

The metallic voice grows louder, "D'laska are you there?"

"Sorry, Chief, I'm just trying to wake up."

"Listen carefully. My office within the hour."

"Chief, it's my day off."

"Get there as fast as possible." His words bounce about inside my head.

The morning sun pushes its way through the cracks between the closed blinds. I can feel a tissue-thin layer of moisture forming on my skin. I walk to the window and peek out from the side of the blinds. Another hot, muggy day.

My mouth is swollen with dryness. I plod toward the kitchen.

My darts are on the table, along with a couple bags of chips and a few empty beer bottles. Last night was fun, but I lost most of the games, bought many rounds, and drank too much.

When I open the refrigerator door, a small burst of cool stale air hits me. There's an uncapped bottle of ginger ale behind the honey and Snickers bar. The soda is flat, and the candy tastes like all the stray smells in the refrigerator.

Out the window, my neighbor's black cat is about to pounce upon a frail brown bird in the small communal courtyard. One neighbor sprinkles bread crumbs for the birds. The other lets her cat loose. Such is life. I toss my breakfast into the trash and head for the shower.

———

WEDNESDAY
7:26 A.M.

SUZANNE HASN'T ARRIVED YET, so I walk into McConnell's office. He's at his desk, flipping through files.

"Sit down." His voice is stern.

I flop into a chair, rubbing my temples.

"D'laska, you look pale." McConnell walks to the coffee pot at the front of the room and fills two cups. He comes back, his coarse gray hair sticking straight out above his right ear. He looks uncomfortable in the extra twenty pounds he's carrying since I last saw him. The added weight exaggerates his features and deepens the creases in his fat face.

"You better get beyond your sluggishness. Here, drink your coffee."

He sits on the edge of his desk, assessing me as I drink. When I lower the cup to my knee, he leans forward, placing his troubled face close to mine. "Today may be the longest day of your career. Early this morning, we found out Organized Crime has put a contract on Louis Calabrese."

I place the cup on the desk and begin to pace. "It doesn't make sense," I say. "The Mafia doesn't put contracts on cops."

"This leak was provided by Chief Roberts' own personal informant inside the Gambacorda family. We have no reason to disbelieve him."

I press my palms into my eyes.

"Sit down," McConnell says. "A Mafia contract. No one can remember this happening before. A very volatile situation has been created."

"Who's involved?"

"The Gambacorda family issued the contract. We don't know if any other contracts have been ordered on any other cops. Roberts and I believe this is an isolated incident directed solely against Calabrese, but this could be a test case."

I face McConnell from across the room. "I've never worked Organized Crime. Assign this over to Larry Ring. His men know the territory. They already have informants in place. Have Internal Affairs check out Calabrese from head to toe. That's what they're trained for." I pause. "It's my day off, and I'd like to go home."

McConnell strides toward me. "Who asked for your advice?"

The statement hangs in the air, cast in bold letters.

"I'm at a disadvantage because you're not thinking," McConnell says. "This whole ugly matter is sitting squarely in your lap. Do you understand? I won't reassign you even if I see you screw up beyond belief. Don't, I repeat, *don't* think you have the luxury to dictate to me what you will investigate."

Our noses almost touch. McConnell's citrus aftershave curdles in my stomach. "If anything happens to Calabrese, I'll hold you personally responsible. You're working for me again, so start thinking clearly."

He recomposes himself. "You spoke with Calabrese yesterday. Before my telephone starts to ring, tell me what relevant information you have."

McConnell stretches on his toes, then returns to his desk. "What have you learned about Calabrese?"

"About a Mafia contract, nothing I can understand."

McConnell's short, thick fingers tap hard on the desk. "You spent time with Calabrese. What does your gut tell you? Did it happen like he said? Or did he murder Nickie Piantini?" McConnell forces my attention. "I'm waiting—courageous police work or premeditated murder?"

I bridge my fingertips and try to concentrate. "Calabrese is an independent man, distrusting and self-assured. I watched his eyes when he identified Nicholas Piantini's body. They were blank—emotionless. Yet, when I accused him of lying, he was filled with hatred. Nick Piantini is a memory to Calabrese. He's not the type who looks back. There wasn't any remorse. Calabrese isn't self-critical, he's opportunistic, and if I wanted someone to play both sides of the law, those are characteristics I'd be looking for."

"You didn't answer my question?"

Susan Baxter walks into McConnell's office. McConnell nods for her to hand over a thick brown folder sporting a federal seal.

Suzanne trades glances from McConnell to me then back again.

McConnell scratches his head. "Mike, if Organized Crime believes they have found another way to exploit their causes by using the police force, we're in trouble. Especially if the media blows this up. Suzanne and I will cover for you in dealing with the press. I want one voice handling this story. Give your detailed daily reports to Suzanne, and she'll share them with me."

McConnell's big, red face hardens. "We'll be in deep shit if we're not careful. Calabrese could be innocent, and yet the public could still see the department as corrupt. We can win and still lose. We have certain backdoor channels we're exploring concerning this mafia contract. In the meantime, D'laska you have work to do. Larry Ring, from Organized Crime, has made himself available. And I want his resources used thoroughly."

The door flies open, and a grimacing Chief Roberts takes a few steps, then stops, putting his hands akimbo. "What the fuck is this?

There's a Mafia contract on a cop's life—a cop we can't locate—and you guys are sitting around jerking off."

McConnell snatches up a paperweight and rolls it from one hand to the other. "What do you mean can't locate?"

"The Commissioner authorized around-the-clock protection for Calabrese, his house, his wife, and two kids," Roberts says. "When we phoned there was no answer, so we sent a squad car, but nobody was home."

I ask, "Neighbors?"

Roberts moves toward McConnell. "We're looking into that." I'm expecting a call." He clicks his fingers at me. "Out, college boy this is serious now."

McConnell growls at Roberts, "This is my case, not yours. D'laska stay where you are. I make all the decisions and next time knock before you come into this office."

Roberts shouts at Suzanne, "Get a hold of the Captain from the Two-Two in Brooklyn; he's been assigned to protect Calabrese." A furious Roberts turns to me. "Did Calabrese mention where he was going to be today? This guy's got brass balls. Not only did he ask to come in early on Monday, but when I talked to his duty sergeant this morning, he told me that on Monday morning Calabrese requested and received permission to have Wednesday and Thursday off."

"No, I wasn't aware that Calabrese had plans to go anywhere, but I think I know where he and his family might be and how to find out."

Roberts scowls toward McConnell.

McConnell asks, "Where, Mike?"

"Monticello and I bet his partner, Gino Guzzetta, can confirm that."

Roberts appeals to McConnell as he grabs the phone, "I'm calling Ring at Organized Crime, D'laska can work directly under him."

McConnell demands he put the phone down.

Roberts squares off with McConnell. "It's not logical to keep D'laska on this case."

I speak up, "I have other cases."

McConnell's face is beet red as he looks from me to Roberts. "D'laska stays on this case. I don't want the subject brought up again."

While Roberts and McConnell exchange more unfriendly looks, I have some curious thoughts. Calabrese had planned to take off Wednesday and Thursday after having the weekend off, making his story about going to his summer home on Monday even more improbable.

McConnell picks up the phone before the second ring. He hands it over to Roberts who relays to us, "A neighbor confirms Calabrese and his family left home last night around eight. The car was packed. She thinks they were heading upstate. There is no phone there."

McConnell moves toward the window, still tossing the paperweight. He turns his attention to me. "Okay, D'laska, what are your thoughts?"

"Assign Guzzetta to ride with me to Monticello? In the meantime, you quietly snoop to find out just where this summer home is located and keep it under surveillance until I arrive."

McConnell is a solitary silhouette against a changing sky. He asks, "How you gonna handle it?"

"Guzzetta is stationed in Harlem. Phone and have him assigned to me for the day. How much I tell him will depend on the circumstances."

Roberts bristles. "Don't say a damn word about the contract. I'll do that. Make some shit up to Guzzetta and get me on the phone with Calabrese as soon as you make contact."

McConnell walks me into Suzanne's empty office. He lowers his voice. "There's going to be a mix of personalities trying to involve themselves in this case. This assignment is your responsibility. I'm only after the truth. I'd appreciate it if you kept the waves to a minimum. I'll have Suzanne get the adjacent office ready for you."

"One question, Chief," I say. "Why me?"

McConnell pats me on the back. "That question is irrelevant." He walks away, calling back to me, "Anything you need, I will make available."

WEDNESDAY

9:40 A.M.

HARLEM IS NEVER a comfortable place to drive through, especially when the humidity is over ninety. You feel the overlay of fine brick dust permeate your skin. Every corner has a hydrant pulsing tepid water that collects into dirty pools where children play. Trash is carried by the foul-smelling water along the worn curb, past the tenement houses, past the misery, and continues below the collective gaze of indifference. The filth flows down baking tar streets and mixes with debris, creating infested garbage collages. The neighborhood reeks of apathetic neglect.

The graffiti-laden precinct mirrors the neighborhood: worn, tired, neglected, and forgotten. I pull into the fenced area behind the station house. There's a space at the far corner. Pebbles and broken glass litter the periphery of the old compound. Teen gangs like to pelt the parking lot with bottles filled with paint and stones.

I walk through the back entrance when a voice stops me in stride.

"Hey! D'laski?"

A tall, husky, broad-chested man with a smug expression and dark sunglasses approaches me. His shirt is open, gold chains rest against a wooly chest. He inhales on a cigarette, aims, and pitches it into the grill of a squad car.

He smiles. "D'laski?"

"*ka*, it's D'las*ka*."

He cocks his head to one side, shrugs, holds out his hand. "I'm Gino Guzzetta. My desk sergeant said I'm assigned to you today."

His warm voice is polished with a Brooklynese-Italian inflection. We shake hands. He has an attractive young face and sprayed-back, wavy brown hair.

"I need you to take a ride with me."

"Where are we going?"

"When was the last time you talked with your ex-partner?"

"Lou? What does he have to do with you?" He rests his large, muscular arms on the car roof. "Where are we going?"

"Lou must have mentioned that he met with me yesterday."

"That you?" He shakes his head. "Yeah, you look more like a college guy than a cop."

There's an ease in the way Guzzetta speaks, a matter-of-fact smoothness with a hint of excitement.

I ask, "Lou's upstate with his family, isn't he?"

"Yeah."

"Chief Roberts wants to speak with him. You and I are going to deliver Roberts' phone number so they can talk."

"Roberts? You're telling me my assignment today is to ride up to Monticello with you?"

"That's it."

"You being a detective sergeant, Lou must be getting a Gold Shield."

"Let's get started."

He runs his fingers down his maroon pants, straightening the creases before opening the door. Once inside, he adjusts the gold chains around his neck.

We take West Side Drive to the Hudson River. Boarded and iron-barred storefronts sink behind mounds of decomposing garbage. Vacant lots are overloaded dumping grounds. Burned-out buildings and condemned, rat-infested houses have become the living quarters for drug addicts and the homeless.

Vietnam vets, confused and intimidated by their chided return, find refuge here. All jungles blend; survival has no essential background. Prostitutes and pushers canvas their wares on the filthy streets. Their prey is eager to escape the desolate landscape for a glazed glimpse into their soul's reality.

Guzzetta's face twists while shaking his head. "It's too bad the way these people live." He unwraps the cellophane from a pack of Marlboro and flings it out the window. He taps the pack on the dashboard and smiles. "Mind if I change the radio station? I hate rock-shit music. We'll listen to the good stuff, Sinatra, Dean Martin. Ya mind?"

He finds his station and Mel Tormé fills the air.

Gino snaps his fingers, keeping lousy time with the music. "New York's the greatest city in the world, know dat D'laska?" Guzzetta's lively face is warm and smug as smoke trails from his mouth. "I remember growing up in Coney Island when it was the showplace of the East Coast. During the fifties, it was beautiful. Always things to do, the best restaurants, nightclubs, celebrities on the boardwalk. Now, it's a shit hole."

"You and Lou are both from Coney Island. Did you know each other before you both became cops?"

Guzzetta gives his last finger snap as Mel fades into something soft by Ella. He settles back after fixing some defiant strands of hair. "Lou's a few years older than me. His family ran concessions at the park: bumper cars, Ferris wheel, roller coaster, shit like that. Lou's face was familiar to me. When we met at the six-o, we recognized each other. Then we started hanging around."

He flicks his ashes into the air.

"Does Lou or his family still have any amusements left at Coney Island?" I ask.

"Na, they sold out years back before it went downhill."

"Lou's been on the force ten years, how about you?"

Guzzetta chuckles. "He always wanted to be a cop. I thought about it, but not for long. Eight years."

The scenery begins to change when we cross over 125th Street, the dividing line between Harlem's wasted wishes and Manhattan's fulfilled dreams. We ride along the river, where yachts and large colorful sails appear between the expensive high rises.

"Hey, D'laska, I'm curious why you were picked to drive me to Monticello."

"Just my turn for an easy assignment, I guess."

Guzzetta is a smooth talker. His talent lies in making one feel comfortable. He probes without setting off alarms. He is crafty in a big bear type of way. I can see where he and Calabrese would make a good team.

"Do you and Lou come into Manhattan often?"

"Na, we mostly stay in Brooklyn." His face brightens. "Ever come into Brooklyn?"

"Very seldom. I get lost."

Guzzetta laughs.

"Spend much time in Little Italy?" I ask.

"Some. How about you?"

"I enjoy eating at Fat Sam's."

"Surprising! I figure you for a steak and potatoes guy."

I lean back. "Little Italy is getting a good influx of Cubans, I notice."

He shrugs his broad shoulders. "Lice bags."

Gino is silky smooth beneath the pleasant exterior. He lights another cigarette and tosses the pack and matchbook on the dashboard.

After we cross the Tappan Zee, I ask if he goes to Calabrese's Monticello house very often.

"Once in a while."

"Is it a year-round home?"

"Na, it ain't got no furnace."

"He closes it for the winter?"

"Yeah."

"That's a pretty area."

"I don't care too much for the country except during hunting season. It's too green and quiet. It ain't natural to me." Gino points his finger to my window where a cluster of horses is running parallel to the car along a fence. Guzzetta begins to laugh again. "Lou said..." He stops cackles, then tries to talk again. "When Lou was in Mounted, he had to soak his sore ass in warm water every night. His wife, Grace, sewed a pouch in his pants where he used to stuff Kotex. I still can't believe he fucked up one of the easiest assignments on the force. Just ride through Central Park and bust hippies for smoking pot. He lost it all because he rode headlong into a television movie. He thought it was a robbery taking place, and it was only Telly Savalas chasing some actress." Gino stops, laughs, and reflects a bit more. "He was coming back from Dean Henry's office. Fuckin' Lou! I'll tell you!"

"Whose office?"

"Dean Henry." He catches his breath. "Fuckin' A."

Dean Henry's office! I tune out Guzzetta as he begins to tell of their heroics. Calabrese's file mentioned he was five miles away from his appointed beat when he disrupted a movie crew filming in the park. I remain quiet as the countryside passes. Calabrese said he was returning from buying uniform accessories. You don't buy accessories at an office. The file never mentioned whether anyone ever asked to see what Calabrese had purchased. If Calabrese was at Dean Henry's office, then he lied to whoever made that report.

Gino continues to rattle on, talking about the time he and Calabrese were assigned to crack a tough purse-snatching gang in the Bronx. Every other departmental team had failed, but Lou and Gino succeeded in arresting the gang on their first outing. He rolls his head and taps his fingers on the dashboard, bobbing along with Tony Bennett while an unsteady cigarette dangles from his lips.

"Ah, Mike, I don't want to walk into Lou's house empty-handed."

My jaw locks. "Why don't we arrange things once we arrive?"

"Italians never visit friends empty-handed, especially for a celebration like Lou making detective. Pull up at the next grocery store."

"How much further do we have to go?"

"About five more songs on the radio. Three with a long commercial. You can start the count while I run into that grocery store just ahead."

Monticello is a small community. In the summer, it derives its income from horse racing. The spill-off revenue seeps into other local businesses and judging by the names on the storefronts, a number are owned by Italians.

While Guzzetta is in the store, I reach across the dash and pick up his matchbook. It has a blue cover with raised gold lettering: *Blue Chateau Lounge, 28 Cummings Street, Brooklyn*. The back states, *An Intimate Hideaway*.

He strides out with food in his mouth, carrying a large bag crammed with groceries. He smiles, offering me a cannoli as the last remains of his disappear into his mouth.

I ask for a napkin.

Gino looks at me above his glasses. "You want my hankie?"

I ask with a smile. "What time did Lou call you after the shooting?"

His smile eclipses mine. "I may not be educated, but I am very street savvy. I would ask that question if I wanted to know two things, where was I at the time of the shooting and was I involved in any way."

"That is a valid interpretation."

Guzzetta wipes crumbs from his chest. "Just ask me what you want to know."

"What time did you leave work?"

"At four. I didn't hear from Lou at all that day. But I do watch the news."

WEDNESDAY
1:15 P.M.

CALABRESE LIVES at the end of a short rural block with few homes and no sidewalks. Trees line the road to and from his long driveway. The house is set back, isolated. There are two cars parked alongside the two-story wooden home: a late model Chevy station wagon and a new black Buick. I park in the driveway blocking any access in or out. Gino shouts for his partner as he swaggers the twenty feet to the screened door. I don't see any sign of a surveillance crew.

A surprised Lou Calabrese emerges and embraces his friend. The hug is broken as Guzzetta points back to me. Calabrese comes toward me.

"What are you doing here, D'laska?" His tone is nasty.

"Chief Roberts wants to talk with you about the Nick Piantini incident."

Calabrese removes his sunglasses and stares at me. His body is tense. Arms bent with closed fists.

"Why?"

Gino shouts from the screened door, "Hey, D'laska, want a beer?"

Calabrese asks, "Why does Roberts want to talk with me?"

"I'll bring ya one anyway," Gino says.

I survey the enclosed area. "Is there somewhere we can phone from?"

Singing in Italian, Gino joins us. He's all smiles. He puts his big arm around Calabrese's shoulder, belting out, "la...Volare, ow, woo, Volare," then takes a bite from a heel of bread.

Calabrese looks back to the house. There's a little girl behind a smaller boy at the screen door. An attractive woman in a white blouse and shorts also appears. She stares out for an extended moment as the kids disappear inside the house. "Grace, Gino, and I are gonna run into town. We'll be right back."

She opens the screen door. "Honey, there's plenty of food in the house."

He shouts back, "Keep the kids outta the driveway. Tell my father I'll be right back."

She steps from the house and lets the door slam. The sunlight splashes through the high trees. The brightness accents her smooth Italian complexion. Her features are rounded, like his, but less dramatic.

Calabrese gives me brief directions as I drive from the house. I feel like I'm another cop watching myself perform. Calabrese points to a country tavern with a neon beer sign in the large bay window. I pull into the parking area.

Calabrese orders, "Let's go make this call."

The place is a wooden rectangle encased in a white aluminum coffin. The long-haired bartender is watching TV. Calabrese and I head for the pay phone on the back wall. Guzzetta goes to the bar.

I dial McConnell's number. I'm put on hold as McConnell tries to reach Roberts at Police Headquarters. Gino hands me a beer.

Gino hurries back to the bar and brings back three shot glasses brimming with a clear liquid. He raises his glass to make a toast. "To Detective Calabrese!"

Calabrese's face gains a disbelieving expression.

Gino shouts, "Saluti!"

Calabrese lifts his drink to me with a full, exaggerated smile. "D'laska, I owe you an apology. Detective Calabrese sounds great! They are going to promote me for, ah, bravery, a lot of people could have been injured, maybe killed, if I didn't step in."

I place the receiver on my shoulder.

Calabrese hollers to the bartender, "Three more anisette! And kid, you better have 'My Way' on that jukebox."

McConnell's brittle voice bursts into my head, "Mike, Roberts will be calling within minutes. Give me your number and tell me exactly where you are. After that conversation, call me immediately. I need to know what your next steps are. You understand?"

"Yeah."

I watch two men hug in anticipation of what will be doused seconds after Calabrese speaks with Roberts. Calabrese gestures me to hurry over to them. I rest my hand on a sticky table, which teeters with my added weight. I down my shot. Its thick sweetness coats my mouth.

Calabrese answers the phone and reacts to Roberts with quick, staccato statements. Gino and I walk toward him. "What's going on, D'laska?" Calabrese says. "Roberts wants me to call him back at headquarters. He says he wants me to make sure I know who I'm talking with and that it should only be him."

"That's excellent advice."

"D'laska." He moves closer to me with cocked arms and clenched fists. "This ain't New York, so I can tell you to go fuck yourself."

"Call back Roberts."

I drop coins into the slots for Calabrese. "Hello, Police Headquarters, this is Louis Calabrese. I want to speak with Chief Roberts."

I retreat from them and walk to the window. My face is wet with salty moisture, and my heart feels like a charging piston. Outside the blue sky is netted in a sheathing of white gauze. Sweat streams coast under my shirt. I rub my eyes with damp fingers. A small squirrel runs into the sparse shrubbery below the window. He twitches his head from side to side as he stretches on his hind legs. He kneads his tiny hands together close to his mouth, rubbing them over his gray face. On the rickety wooden fence guarding the fly-swelling dumpster perches an impressive black bird with thick legs and a hooked beak. An uninspired muscular dog with short, rusty-black hair lies in the shade against a red pickup truck's rear tire. The dog stirs pricks his ears, and surveys the area. If a prowling cat were to appear, would he chance a dash for the squirrel knowing the dog might be in pursuit?

Would the dog chasing the cat give the bird a meal? Or would the squirrel just scurry safely away? So many possibilities and scenarios.

"D'laska!" An angry Louis Calabrese hurries to the door shouting to me. "You knew there was a chance of danger to my family and you made me go through that bullshit?"

"Your family is safe. The house is being watched."

"Give me the keys, D'laska. I'll drive."

"I'll drive. Get in."

Calabrese pushes me against the car. "My family is in danger. Give me the keys!"

"Get in!"

Gino makes a move toward me. "A contract on his life, and you don't say a word all the way here. You're an asshole, college boy."

"Both of you calm down and get in."

Calabrese boils over. "If my family is hurt, I'm gonna kill you, then I'm gonna kill Roberts."

They relent, and we drive back to the cottage in silence.

CALABRESE DASHES into his house while Gino hustles to the back. I hear muffled voice from inside. I survey the property. The house is situated on about four cleared acres. Nothing I can see looks ominous.

A protesting older man's agitated voice is heard coming from the house, "No, I'm not driving back to Brooklyn."

"Pa, we have to! Understand? Have to!"

"Your mother and I are staying. You go!"

"We're all going. *Now.*"

Calabrese and Guzzetta scramble in and out of the house carrying bags and suitcases. The little boy clings to his mother's leg just outside the door while the tear-faced girl pouts and trudges behind her father.

Once the gear is secured in the cars, a hard-faced, thick-chested older man slams the cottage door and tests the lock. Calabrese joins his father. The tall old man looks out at me. "He the reason we gotta go?"

Calabrese ignores the remark, directing his children into the back seat of my car.

"Gino, drive D'laska's car. Just in case we're being followed." Calabrese looks over to me to see if I'll protest. I don't. Calabrese continues, "Take D'laska's car with Grace and the kids. My father will follow you back into the city. Take the quickest route, and we'll meet back at my house. D'laska and I are gonna take Interstate 16 and ride the borderline into the city. This way if some wise guy has any bright ideas, D'laska will have a front row seat."

"What time you got, Lou?" Gino says.

Calabrese glances at his watch. "Two twenty-eight."

"Got it, like being on the streets again," Gino states.

The children wave from the back window as both cars hurry out the driveway spraying gravel. Calabrese and I turn to each other.

"Alright, D'laska, we ain't going nowhere till I find out exactly what's happening. What do you know about this contract?"

"Let's reverse the question. What do you know about the contract?"

"What? What did you ask me?"

"You killed Reno Piantini's kid."

He stares at me while his mouth twists with indignation. "Be straight with me. I don't fuck around when it comes to my family."

"The criminal underworld wants you dead. Why?"

His hard expression fades.

"It's no secret the Alessi Family controls Coney Island," I say. "That family is a baby finger to the Gambacorda organization. Maybe you owed them from the concession days. So, don't play dumb with me."

"Fuck you!" Calabrese says. "I don't owe shit to anybody."

"Maybe the Alessi family had you deliver a message to Reno Piantini."

"One more remark like that and I'm gonna kill you."

"I know you've been in Mafia hangouts. Like the Trenton Avenue Club."

Silence and muggy heat. Country sounds emerge, squawks from

hungry birds and the buzzing of flying insects on the hunt. It's going to rain, but nothing will cool.

Calabrese brings his palms together. "I need some straight answers from you."

"Maybe somebody at headquarters thinks it's outrageous to protect a cop that's a puppet for organized crime."

Calabrese paces in one of the ruts in the driveway. "Let's backtrack: They think I did a hit on Nickie Piantini? Is that what you think, Mr. Psychologist?"

"I haven't made up my mind yet."

He stops as if an invisible hand pushes against his chest. He squints and shakes his head. "They think I murdered Nickie Piantini, and the contract on my life is justified? Is that what you're saying?"

I swallow hard. I don't like this arrogant little man who all of a sudden realizes his actions have jeopardized his family.

I put my face very close to his. "You weren't in Manhattan to meet your brother and father. We both know that. Reno Piantini has been talking to the feds, that's no secret. Stefano Gambacorda isn't going to allow Reno Piantini to give up anything about his organization. So, what's so valuable that Reno can talk about it and remain in solid with Gambacorda. I have an idea Gambacorda wouldn't mind him yapping about anything that makes Gambacorda more powerful and that means Reno Piantini would have to sing about another New York family. Maybe that family is nervous. The Alessi family may want to send a message to Reno Piantini and have a local boy do the delivering."

Calabrese backs away and shakes his head in disbelief. "Is that what you believe? You are an asshole."

"I look for lies. Innocent people rarely use them."

"Oh, that was clever. Book learning shit."

"Who's Dean Henry?"

"What the fuck does he have to do with this?"

"Well?"

"Where did you get the information confirming any contract on Nicholas Piantini? There was none. Stop bluffing."

I push. "What were you doing in Manhattan the afternoon of the shooting?"

"If informants told Roberts there was a contract on me, why can't you answer my question? Didn't anybody ask who was paying me for Nickie's death?"

"Maybe you did somebody a favor, and now it's backfiring."

"If this contract is legitimate and my family is harmed, I'm coming after you."

"If the killing of Nick Piantini was premeditated, why lie?"

He sneers. "I told you yesterday, stop calling me a liar."

"Why were you in Manhattan?"

"Get in." It's said with finality.

We drive in silence back to Brooklyn.

The gray clouds have gathered, draining any color from the sky. Calabrese and I are both cops; his record shows that he's braver than I, and yet I'm not sure we're on the same side. In the ashtray on the passenger's armrest is a pack of matches, blue with raised gold lettering, *The Blue Chateau*. I slide it into my pocket.

WEDNESDAY
4:45 P.M.

"WHY ARE there patrol cars all down my block? Roberts said protection, not harassment." Calabrese's head jerks from side to side as he notices his neighbors watching cops moving inside his small front yard. Guzzetta and a thin, narrow-faced Captain approach the car.

"Louis Calabrese, I'm the Captain from the Two-Two. My men are stationed on the street, and I have cars patrolling the area. Two men are in your house. Chief Roberts wants around-the-clock protection for you and your family. I'll have a patrol car follow your parents' home, and I'll station a car at their house for the night. After that, I'll have a car cruising by regularly."

Calabrese rolls his neck in disbelief. "Captain, I appreciate what you're doing, but all these patrol cars will draw every inquisitive asshole in Brooklyn."

A group of anxious neighbors skirt the fringe around the car waiting for a moment's opening to talk with Calabrese. He keeps them at bay with a false gesture of normalcy.

The Captain points his finger and thumb like a gun at me. "D'laska, Chief McConnell wants you in his office. To prepare you, he didn't sound happy."

Calabrese joins his family in the house. An unfriendly Gino Guzzetta hands me my keys. "When you report back, convey this message. I want to be assigned to guard Lou and Grace. With me, he knows he'll be protected, and one less cop has to worry about being killed by some whacko."

"I'll pass it along."

He begins to walk away.

"Guzzetta, I have this feeling you're going to do some digging on your own. Here's my card if you need me."

He rubs it between his fingers. "If anything happens to Lou, I'm coming after you."

"Captain Roberts told your partner there's a contract on his life and if anything happens to him, you're coming after *me*?"

"Yeah, because I don't like anything about you."

I leave Brooklyn by way of the Manhattan Bridge heading north on Bowery, then west on Vermont. I want to make one stop before going back to the office.

I pull into the gas station on Vermont and Ivy, away from the pumps, and face the corner where Calabrese shot Piantini. Heavy trucks and cargo vans roll along Vermont. Traffic noises dominate the air, and you can feel the weight of the train of vehicles vibrating on the street.

I cross Vermont, staring down Ivy, a claustrophobic tributary towered upon for blocks by large, rundown apartment buildings. It's another forgotten filth stream that feeds cars into Vermont. Hundreds of identical windows view this corner. Suspicious faces now peek at me from under brown shades. From which joyless window can Calabrese's story be corroborated?

WEDNESDAY
7:30 P.M.

McCONNELL IS AT HIS DESK. "I told you to contact me immediately after Roberts spoke with Calabrese. Sit down!"

I sit, aware of how fatigued I've become. I rub my temples with my fingertips.

McConnell exchanges the pen for his paperweight. "Well, D'laska, is Calabrese still sticking to his story?"

I shake my head, trying to escape a descending lethargy.

"You look terrible," he says.

I stand and pace in front of his desk. "Calabrese likes expensive things."

McConnell sighs. "What is that supposed to mean?"

"When someone is used to more, they seldom settle for less."

"I know you're tired D'laska but talk plain."

"Calabrese joined the force at age twenty-four, six years after high school and four years after getting married, He lists jobs back through the age of sixteen. I'll bet he had a paper route when he was a kid. Between the years after high school, up until he became a cop, he was a union truck driver and a partner in his family's Coney Island concessions business."

McConnell gives me a glance of anticipation. "I'm listening."

"If you want to become a cop, you do it shortly after graduation, not six years later. Changing his career cut his paycheck, but he owns two nice homes, wears expensive clothes, and drives a new car."

"And?"

"Today, I watched Calabrese and Guzzetta interact. They're like brothers. If the Nickie Piantini shooting were premeditated, Guzzetta would somehow have been involved. I'm sure of that. He's the type of character who's a cop but wants to be a wise guy. And if he were a wise guy, he'd want to be a cop. If I were Calabrese, and I was setting up a murder, it would be Guzzetta who I would have made the hit."

"Where was Guzzetta when this happened?"

"In Harlem, working."

McConnell places the paperweight back on his desk. "What are you telling me?"

"I'm just watching how the cards fall. There are no witnesses to the shooting yet. Tito Garcia is going to be impossible to find. And I found something else out today. Does the name Dean Henry mean anything to you?"

McConnell takes in a long deep breath. "Henry is a disbarred lawyer who runs an investment realty business in Manhattan." McConnell gives me a curious look. "What has he to do with Calabrese?"

"Tell me what you know about him then I'll tell you the connection."

McConnell walks over to the coffee pot and pours two cups. "City-Wide Investment Realty is Henry's business. He specializes in putting Italian-Jewish money in the slums of Brooklyn, Harlem, and the nastier areas of the city. Henry is very slimy. Everything he's involved with is legally mottled or ethically questionable. He has strong connections and a lot of deep-pocketed clients. He tends to buy cheap properties, and just by coincidence, sells them to the city, county, or state for enormous profits. Every time he's charged with anything, it gets dropped. Your turn."

"When Calabrese disrupted the movie in Central Park, years back, he said he was returning from buying uniform accessories. He was lying. According to Guzzetta, he was coming back from Dean Henry's office."

"Calabrese lying and his connection to Henry can't help him."

We sit in silence, both deep in our own thoughts.

McConnell's says, "I'll do some checking and see if there's any solid connection between Calabrese and Henry. Until then, you better get some rest. Tomorrow, we have a ten o'clock appointment at City Hall with a Justice Department official and the head of the Mayor's Budgetary Committee."

Contempt builds inside. "Phyllis Bales-Isserlyn from the mayor's office is involved with this?"

We pass concerned looks before he speaks, "The around-the-clock protection of Calabrese is a budgetary concern for her."

"And the Justice Department?"

McConnell waits a moment before answering, "You'll, I mean *we'll*, see tomorrow."

I move to the window. Outside, the dense rain clouds haven't burst yet. Below, the traffic is still snarled. There's scattered movement on the sidewalks—black dots avoiding other black dots.

I ask, "How much did Roberts tell Calabrese?"

"Primarily, just about the contract and the protection for him and his family till this is resolved. I'm sure they've talked again since then."

"Chief, yesterday Roberts was sure Calabrese was guilty. Today, he's making sure Calabrese has twenty-four-hour protection. Roberts is playing politics and blatantly directing it for his benefit."

"Roberts can be impulsive. And he doesn't think much of you."

It's no secret that McConnell and Roberts often clash. They're motivated by different factors—Roberts is hard-headed and ambitious, he wants to be commissioner. McConnell is proud and wants the respect of his men. The engine inside my brain seems to be all static but one question squirms from just beneath the surface. I don't face McConnell when I ask, "Chief, why me? The Mafia is involved. This Calabrese is lying. Let I.A. get involved."

"Mike," he says, "you're one of the brightest cops I know. To dwell on why you were chosen won't help you."

It's not a satisfying answer. I fail at stifling a yawn. "I'm taking off."

"One more thing." McConnell swivels in his chair to follow my movement from the window. "We found out there's only one contract. Reno Piantini asked for it, and Stefano Gambacorda authorized it."

"Good night, Chief."

CHAPTER 3

THURSDAY, JULY 3, 1975
7:05 A.M.

IT NEVER RAINED LAST NIGHT. The sky just became more ominous. The dark clouds will explode shortly. Even with the petrichor filling the air, Vermont and Ivy are immune to change. The water just displaces the dirt and froths the hot streets with steam. On narrow Ivy, cars and trucks are parked a finger's width apart. Vehicles are backed up to turn onto Vermont, which has become one long snake of traffic. Horns echo in the dense, muggy air. Everything around me is too close, one continuous connection worn smooth and spiritless for blocks. The sky cracks a thunderous warning.

I squeeze through Vermont's noisy traffic on foot. The laundromat across from the gas station is empty. From the side window, there's a clear view of where the shooting took place. I walk down Ivy. The garbage lines the streets—cans, boxes, plastic bags, all varieties of rotting food and trash that animals rummage through. I notice kids hiding behind the decaying heaps on both sides of the street. A truck stops at the corner and the kids throw garbage at it. The driver hops out and yells, but it's too late the kids are scattered and gone. Cars will now drive over and mash and spread the garbage further.

At mid-block, there's a small grocery store. Most of the letters on the green, rusting Pepsi marquee are missing. The tin Heath Bar signs covering the basement grates are rolled upward. Layered graffiti an inch thick obliterates the last ancient paint job. The street-front windows are dulled by a grimy, indissoluble film.

I step up the three worn stone steps to the screen door. The loose handle is waxy and bolted. The deeply lined face shouts, "Whatta you want?"

He's in a yellowed white shirt and clutching a billy club to his side.

"Whatta you want?"

When I press my badge to the window, his resentful manner doesn't change.

"Whatta you want?"

"Police, please open the door."

Entry bells jingle. Dispirited, tired eyes greet me. The stifling room is sourly pungent with nostalgic smells. Barrels once filled with briny olives are against molding walls. The floor smells of mildewing wood under caked sawdust. Confectionery sugar from stale doughnuts lingers from a cracked glass counter where candy is displayed.

"Please, quick, I have hard work to do. What you want?"

"Good morning, D'laska, Homicide."

He rubs his forehead with arthritic fingers. "What do you want with me?"

"On Monday around four o'clock, there was some commotion on the corner. Did—"

The old man stomps his foot down on the floor. "How many times do I gotta do this? I toll all the rest, same as I tell you. I was in my store. I didn't know nothing was going on untill you cops came around asking questions."

"Did you hear the shots?"

"How can you hear, with all the Goddamn loud music these bastard kids play?"

He leans across me and opens the entrance door. Incidental rumblings sound from the brooding sky. The rains are about to begin.

"I'm sorry! Please, no come back."

The old man closes the door behind me. Trust is a forgotten concept in this neighborhood. Minding your own business is the rule for survival. And he has lived to be an old man.

I trot toward Vermont waiting for the clouds to open. The morning traffic churns, keyed for the storm. Truck brakes hiss and idling engines rumble. Voices and horns dissolve as they merge in the flux of gestating street noises. The light on this corner is disregarded as the traffic builds and vehicles edge forward.

When I'm able to cross, I enter the gas station and thunder cracks, lightning cauterizes the heavens, and the downpour begins.

I introduce myself to Vito Barone. We're alone in the oily customer area. He hands me a cup of weak coffee. We watch the heavy rainwater drain down the windows. Barone is a horse-faced man with a thin, graying mustache. The lines in his face have darkened from years of working with grease.

"Like I told the other cop, all I saw was Calabrese running across the street. I was too busy to notice anything else."

"You called in the nine-one-one. You must have seen what was happening."

"Would you like a doughnut?"

"What kind?" I say with a smile.

"There's two jellies, and one peanut left, be my guest."

"Did you ever see Nick Piantini around here at all?"

Mr. Barone lightly smiles. "I've lived and worked in this neighborhood all my life. My brother and I opened this station after the war. Not far from here, my father still lives in the house where I was raised. You look like a bright guy, so please don't ask any more questions. You know how it is around here."

He walks from behind the counter and approaches me. "I told all of you all I know."

"Mr. Barone, you're a responsible businessman in this community. There must be something you can remember."

He slips into an oil-slicked yellow raincoat. "If you want me to lie to you, I can, because I've lied to better men about more important things. Detective, put yourself in my shoes: I've got cops asking me questions and that could prompt visits from people I would rather not associate with. Okay."

He dashes into the rain. Barone is an old-time Italian with deep-rooted indifference. To him, an officer under suspicion and a dead gangster are two sides of the same hypocrisy.

Barone stomps his feet after reentering and removing the wet coat. He walks past me and dries his face with a soiled towel.

I ask, "If Piantini, hypothetically speaking, ever came here to gas up, do you think he would be alone or with somebody else? A big guy?"

Barone shakes his head, "I told you before I don't know nothing, and I'll tell that to any judge who asks."

Sometimes it's not what you're told but how you listen that's important. I study Barone. He's a tough man with a mule's sensibility.

"Mr. Barone, a man's career could rest on your testimony, maybe his life."

Barone's face twitches. "If I have any problems with my decision I'll talk with a priest. Who do you talk to? Better think about it because you seem to have a problem."

"Did Calabrese get a free tank of gas that night?"

He moves to the coffeepot and pours himself another cup. He glances at the service bays avoiding the question.

I ask again.

He answers with his back to me, "He paid me later."

"That night?"

"I think so."

"Remember how much?"

He turns around. "What difference does it make?"

"Mr. Barone, I am not the enemy. Did he get a couple bucks' worth or did you fill his tank?"

"Who can remember?" he says, anxious to change the subject.

"When Calabrese ran across the street, you were putting gas in his car. At some point, afterward, you must have marked down how much he owed you?"

Barone swallows hard and bites his lip. "Things got hectic."

"Shortly afterward, did anybody come into your station and ask where Calabrese had gone?"

"Nope."

"A tall older man and a younger man. Might have looked a little like Calabrese?"

Barone shakes his head. "I don't think so."

"It must have been late when Calabrese got back. Did you two talk?"

Barone forces a smile and nervously blinks. "Not really, I was busy. All I remember is giving him his car keys, and he left."

"Then he must have paid you for the gas?"

There's a slight uneasiness in Barone's manner. I press him further. "Funny, he didn't mention anything to you."

"Listen, Detective, you told me you're not the enemy. So, this conversation is over. I've got customers to attend."

"One last question were there many keys on Calabrese's ring?"

He regains himself. "Just car keys on a big Giants key ring."

"Did you ever see Calabrese before?"

"I told you everything I know."

"I'll probably stop by again, Mr. Barone."

"I won't remember anything else then either."

THURSDAY
8:40 A.M.

AT THE FRONT DESK, Quincy's eyes widen as he watches me pass. Out of breath, he catches me at the elevator. "What's happening? Rumor has it, you and McConnell are going to some big meeting today."

"Quincy, I need some information."

"Yeah!" He wipes his lips with a red handkerchief.

"I need to know who made the real decisions in Mounted in sixty-eight?"

He snickers with a gelatin smile. "What's in it for me?"

"I owe ya."

He just looks at me. "My son's selling candy for his school, count you in for four bars?"

"Deal."

"Twenty bucks first."

THURSDAY
8:45 A.M.

Suzanne Baxter wears a white blouse and a straight gray skirt. The blouse is loose but doesn't conceal her full chest. She's tall but not slender. Not heavy either. Solid is a good description. She stands beside her desk, sipping coffee while gazing out the window. Her right knee rests on the cushioned swivel chair.

Suzanne greets me by turning her head. "Hello, Detective D'laska." She continues to watch the rain tap against the window.

"Terrible out, isn't it?" My voice seems loud though I'm sure it isn't.

"Dreadful. The adjacent office is ready for you. You need to give me a list of supplies you'll need."

"Thanks. Please call me Mike."

"Sure." She continues to gaze at me. Her attractive white face has little makeup. It seems like a beautiful cut of alabaster sculpted to complement her cold green eyes. She reaches for her glasses and sits.

My temporary office is small. One window looks down on an overflowing dumpster. The hard rain pelts at the rotting piles, fraying the edges, soaking the centers. Nourishing the attraction for insects and maggots to feed.

McConnell is ready for me. He hands me a coffee. His suit looks uncomfortably tight. There's no way the buttons and the holes will ever meet. He has gained too much weight, and it doesn't become him. His face is less fatigued than yesterday, but the worry remains.

I sit facing his desk. He looks over to me. "A few things before we leave. Calabrese has been temporarily reassigned from the Seven-One to Brooklyn Headquarters. We do not require him to maintain a schedule. Hopefully, this will keep him closer to home and easier to protect. He has already voiced his opinion against having a special unit around him. He prefers patrolmen dressed in civilian clothes to watch him and his family. Do you see anything odd about that?"

"He feels more comfortable with men equal in rank with him."

"Later today, I want you to meet with Larry Ring. They filmed Nickie Piantini's wake. Have Ring familiarize you with some of the characters we may be dealing with. Here's Deputy Commissioner Mulvaney's phone number. She wants to speak with the investigating officer. Call her and set up an appointment."

He hands me a card with her number. "I know what you're thinking—you don't need the Knapp Commission queen sniffing around. It can't be helped. I tried to deter her, but I couldn't. You know how persistent she can be. Don't let her surmise anything, just have a quick, patronizing talk with her and keep her on our side. Or else every talk show in New York will be discussing your case."

Mulvaney is a dreadful deputy commissioner, self-righteous and sanctimonious, all bluster and innuendo and no common sense. Mulvaney's name and poison are synonymous to all non-Irish men on the force.

McConnell gulps what's left in his cup and stares at me. "Lastly, Calabrese is an old friend and customer of Henry's. A few years back, Henry invested heavily in the gold market. He caught the peak and pulled out just before it nosedived. He made a fortune for himself and some of his investors. Calabrese wasn't that lucky—he lost about half a million dollars in profits and his initial investment of thirty thousand."

"A cop from Coney Island begins to amass half a million dollars in less than three months, and he just lets it ride. Most cops would have taken one day's profits and run to the bank."

I walk to the wastebasket and drop my cup.

McConnell says, "If Mulvaney gets a hold of this innocent, or guilty, Calabrese is cooked."

"Does Roberts know?"

"Not yet. But you can bet he is working behind the scenes to find reasons for Calabrese to be guilty and you to be found incompetent." McConnell checks his watch. "It's time to leave for City Hall."

THURSDAY
9:32 A.M.

McConnell and I watch the rain spill across the windows while being chauffeured to City Hall.

I ask, "What's the Justice Department doing arranging meetings the day before July Fourth? Isn't today like their Christmas Eve?"

He's meditative for a moment. "Any day is a good day for surgery, and those boys do magnificent work. They punch their arms into your ass and push their way up, eliminating every organ in their way. The cleansing is over when they can see their fingers dangling from your mouth. Then they peel you away, and the shell is discarded. In their defense, they don't play favorites. I trust you'll do the right thing at this meeting."

I doubt McConnell knew what he was going to say before he expressed it. The indictment's force now seeps through him. This can't be his first contact with them.

We watch the rain.

He gives me a bitter smile before speaking again, "The Captain from the two-two phoned me this morning. Calabrese isn't overly cooperative with some of the men guarding him. Twenty-four-hour protection and he's bitching."

McConnell crosses his legs, wiping the damp window before continuing. "Roberts was at his house last night. He told me Calabrese gave the same story he related on Monday. He avoids most other questions. Is he the same with you?"

"He's not a trusting man, if that's what you mean."

We remain quiet.

"When you're used to more, you seldom settle for less. Isn't that what you said yesterday?" McConnell pauses. "Last night your statement just rolled around and around in my head."

THURSDAY
9:58 A.M.

Our footsteps echo as we walk on the tiled hall floors. There's an eerie quality that pervades large corridors in old civic buildings. It smells like the musty classrooms of my youth, that unique scent of tarnished authority. We take the elevator to the fifteenth floor.

The stenciling on the office door reads *Phyllis Bales-Isserlyn, M.B.A.* Below her name is *Budgetary Committee*. McConnell knocks, and a tall woman with thick, frosted hair opens the door. She leads us into an inner office, then exits.

The attractive woman who walks toward us with an outstretched hand looks like she would have two surnames. Her tailored suit is flattering, purchased no doubt in a tiny uptown boutique with a fancy French name.

Ms. Isserlyn has a broad, determined mouth with downturned corners. Her eyes are almond shaped and waste little time lighting on any single image. With a proper introduction, she turns McConnell and me toward a light-haired, square-jawed, well-built, and handsome John Gage from the Justice Department.

At the table where Gage is seated are four decorative coffee cups with a small pastry tray at the center. We all participate in light New York chatter before Isserlyn checks her watch. In a perfected manner, she summons our attention like Mother Superior to three adolescent schoolboys. "Detective Sargeant D'laska, I think we were all impressed with your determined police work in solving the Lafayette Hotel rapes and stabbings."

Wasn't what I expected but I respond by nodding my head. "Psychopaths can have patterns. Once we figured out what they were, my partner and I captured the offender."

Gage speaks up. "Excellent work, D'laska. I read the complete case file. You thought it through, used logic, reason, worked hard, and solved a tricky case."

Gage is using the old warming tactic. A compliment to set one at ease and ask leading questions. No matter, I understand the rules of chess and police work—think like your opponent to outsmart him.

Ms. Isserlyn clears her throat. "Mr. Gage has some information to share with us."

Gage is a confident red, white, and blue, dot the i's and cross the t's, man. He is tall with very American blue eyes. His inflection has that distinct quality of importance. He removes papers from a manila envelope and carefully sets them in front of us.

As Ms. Isserlyn gets comfortable, the hem of her skirt secures itself to the chair's seat, tugging the fabric up to her lower thigh. My eyes travel the length of her tanned, exposed leg.

While my attention is divided, Gage begins, "Louis Calabrese has ended many long months of serious negotiations between the government and Mr. Reno Piantini. We have painfully gone to great lengths to secure Mr. Reno Piantini's valuable testimony against major drug dealers operating in New York and their overseas connections that are exporting narcotics into the United States. Very critical information. He was to surrender himself to federal authorities shortly, but now that looks doubtful. We have lost all contact with Mr. Piantini. It looks like the government's hard-pressed deal has crumbled. Officer Calabrese has seriously set the government's cause back."

Gage says to me, "Detective D'laska, the Justice Department is very interested in your findings. You will remain in contact with me." He juts his chin. "Here's my card with a number where I can be reached twenty-four hours a day."

I let his card hang in the air for a moment before pinching it between my fingers. "Mr. Gage, do you have any intelligence linking Calabrese with organized crime?"

"Deputy Inspector Ring is doing our local correlative work. I was led to believe you are working closely with him?"

"I'm meeting with him this afternoon."

My eyes slide back to Isserlyn. The distraction is gone. Gage arches his eyebrows. "What can you contribute to help your government's efforts to bring Mr. Reno Piantini back to the table?"

I take a breath. "Like?"

"Is Calabrese working for a rival Mafia family?" His voice is like a drill, finding its way to a critical nerve.

Gage and I exchange glares as I ask Ms. Isserlyn, "May, I have some water?"

McConnell offers his cup to her.

After taking a sip, I ask Gage, "Was Reno giving names for a lighter sentence on the Zicaro murder?"

"That's classified."

I ignore his detour and continue to think out loud. "If Reno Piantini can go to Stefano Gambacorda and get a Mafia contract on a New York City cop, I would say they're on good terms. So, if Reno isn't going to spill his guts about Gambacorda or his organization, what information is he going to give you?"

"Detective, there are things I would love to share with you, but at this time, I have told you as much as I am allowed to convey. You realize narcotic use is climbing quickly. We need to curtail its entry into the country."

"Was Piantini going to turn in dirty cops he's dealt with through the years?"

Gage's eyes crawl to Isserlyn, who is standing. He says, "I can't answer that either. Detective, I must admit you do ask the proper questions. We should get together for a drink sometime. Please begin, Ms. Isserlyn."

"Gentlemen," she says. Her red blouse presses against her small pointed breasts.

I interrupt, "Thank you, Mr. Gage, there must be more information you can share. I do want to help, but like all good investigative work, I need a firm basis of intelligence."

Gage gives me the look of an opponent whose pawn has been

taken. He is not alarmed but didn't expect the move. "We are willing to share all the background necessary. But you must admit, your reports are vague. Maybe informally, you might have more to express."

I look to McConnell whose expression is blank.

Isserlyn begins again, "The City of New York is facing dire financial problems—"

"Excuse me!"

Isserlyn gives me a paralyzing stare.

I say, "Mr. Gage, you still want Reno Piantini. Doesn't that mean more concessions on the government's part?"

Gage pinches the bridge of his nose. He says, "That's not for discussion here. Now, as a psychologist and a police officer, what are your observations about Calabrese?"

"Maybe we should meet and exchange information about Piantini and Calabrese?"

Gage smiles. "We should. Now, Ms. Isserlyn, please continue."

"May I, Detective D'laska?" Isserlyn's tone is like nails scraping across a blackboard.

I stretch my legs under the table and sit back.

Isserlyn smirks as if to cut away any further interruptions. "My only purpose at this meeting is monetary; we all know I've been appointed by the mayor as chairwoman for his Budgetary Committee. New York's purse strings have been cut. The mayor, the Committee, and I feel that so volatile a police case could be costly. If this killing of an underworld figure prompts a gangland war, do you realize what extra expenses the city will have to incur? More police, more firemen, more city employees. If this officer is guilty, I can't see wasting needed money for a long-involved investigation to prove what the evidence seems to state. Time is money, and we are very short of that precious commodity. Detective D'laska, have you found anything to prove Mr. Calabrese is innocent?"

Isserlyn's tone has that air of privilege. That perfected knack for making people seem insignificant, like a surgeon inflicting snips of pain only to impress upon the patient the unequal relationship between the two. "Detective, I am speaking to you."

I run one hand then the other through my hair. "Ms. Isserlyn, I have found absolutely nothing to show that Louis Calabrese is guilty."

Her nostrils flair before speaking, "I have read the briefs concerning this investigation. Purportedly, Nicholas Piantini fired the first shot from less than four feet away and missed. The gun found in the victim's car had never been fired. I believe if you're a criminal, from a criminal background, knowing how to shoot a gun would be a prerequisite for using it. Don't you agree?"

Isserlyn doesn't wait for an answer. "Don't you agree with what I've just presented would be enough for the grand jury to indict Calabrese?"

"Ms. Isserlyn," I say, " All I know is we should give Officer Calabrese the courtesy his good record deserves."

McConnell says, "Ms. Isserlyn, leave the police work to us. Before we start pointing fingers, let's get the facts."

Gage asks, "Has Ballistics found any bullets that can confirm Calabrese's story that he even was fired at?"

McConnell moves his tight lips from side to side. "That report may be on my desk at this moment."

"I refuse to write a memo to the federal government," Isserlyn says, "who is bailing us out of this crisis, saying we are spending their money on a prolonged investigation concerning the death of a mobster by a dishonest cop. This careless incident has already caused the eroding of a Justice Department investigation."

To McConnell, her words are like coarse sandpaper over an open wound. "Ms. Isserlyn, we can empathize with you. We are feeling the budget crunch, but money shouldn't interfere with justice."

"That is true, Chief McConnell," she says. "My office also wants to get to the truth. This investigation will be directed under the auspices of one office. What we don't want are several city arms working simultaneously, duplicating information and increasing costs. The mayor and the commissioner want you to continue to be personally in charge. Chief Roberts will provide support as needed. Chief McConnell, your office will act as the coordinating mechanism. Patrolman Calabrese and his family will continue to have around-the-clock protection. Cooperatively, federal and city monies will be available to pursue further negotiations with Mr. Reno Piantini. Detective, you will continue to handle only this case."

She cuts short any questions by wishing us all a productive day.

Before leaving, Gage takes McConnell aside.

Isserlyn says to me, "How much longer do you see this investigation lasting?"

"Truth exists on no timetable that I know of."

She moves to her desk. "Here's my card. I want to be kept informed."

THURSDAY
 11:15 A.M.

OUR DRIVER MOVES INTO TRAFFIC. The heavy rain has become a light drizzle.

"What's on your mind?" McConnell's says.

"This case has Calabrese's name on it, but it's not about him. It's about ambition."

Moments pass, he looks over to me. "What this whole city believes makes no difference. You, D'laska, determine whether anything has to be proved in court."

"How deeply is Gage involved?"

"I'll take care of him, but do not underestimate him or Isserlyn." McConnell's big Irish face confronts me. "Mike, get this done as quickly as possible."

"Chief, none of this makes sense to me. There's something either you're not telling me or you're in the dark about also."

"This is a case that needs an intelligent cop with good investigative skills and that is you."

The answer is unsatisfying.

Before leaving, I turn to McConnell and ask for two favors. I want daily copies of all reports submitted by all patrolman assigned to

Calabrese. Also, I want my partner, Ainsworth, attached to this case when he gets back to work on Monday.

McConnell opens his door but stays seated. He takes in a deep, weary breath and rubs his fingers across his chin. "They may not like pulling two cops from Homicide. But you and Ainsworth are a proven team."

THURSDAY
1:00 P.M.

Deputy Inspector Larry Ring of Organized Crime waves me into his office. He's a powerfully built man in his mid-forties. On the wall behind his desk are numerous boxing trophies. His nose has been broken a couple of times and blunts to the right. He combs his graying hair straight back. Ring has earned the right to brag. His arrest record is enviable. He's brave, energetic, and dedicated. He's been shot at more times than other cops have used their guns at the firing range. He leads me into a screening room.

While watching Piantini's funeral, something catches my interest. They don't stand out, just two punks leaning against the entrance at the funeral home. The film moves on, and Larry Ring points out bosses and underbosses, influential gangsters, local wise guys, tri-county mobsters, and national representatives. Again, the camera pans the two men watching guests pass through the opened doors.

Ring looks at me with disbelief when I ask him to rewind the film so I can examine the still where the two men are in view.

He rolls back to the men. The picture is fuzzy, but I recognize them.

"Who are they?" I ask.

"I can find out easily enough. Why?"

"Tuesday morning when I was meeting Calabrese, those two were double-parked outside the morgue."

In the dim light, I can make out Ring's face as his head moves from the screen to me. He shakes his head. "They're more than likely Cuban nothings. I've pointed out every major Mafia figure, and your only interest lies in these two nobodies?"

"Cuban?"

He snickers. "Trust me. From what I hear, you're pretty smart. It must take all that schoolin' to specialize in psycho cases. If I were in your area, I'd be lost. I couldn't think like a nut job."

Ring pours coffee into two cups, setting one down on the empty chair next to mine. "Forget those two. Here's what you have to work out: go over Calabrese's background with a fine-toothed comb. I think somebody got to him. I'm willing to bet a fairly known name put out some big money to give a warning to Reno Piantini not to sing to the feds. I'll do some nosing around. You hang loose. Do some backchecking." Satisfied with his comments, he rocks on his heels.

I say, "The two Cubans and see if a dark blue Chrysler is registered to either of them?"

Ring's smile mocks me. "You're not listening to me!"

I face him. "Where will I find them?"

"Are you looking for a connection between those Cubans and Tito Garcia? Maybe Calabrese is setting up Garcia. They could have conspired together to kill Nickie, now Calabrese is sacrificing him 'cause Garcia is a dead man on the streets."

"Garcia was the muscle for Nickie, wasn't he?"

Ring fingers the vertical scar that runs along his ear. "You've done some homework."

"Let's get back to those Cubans."

Ring folds his arms across his thick barrel chest. "They sprinkle themselves throughout Little Italy. They'll mix at some Italian spots. Marlowe's, Three Deuces, and a few other joints. If you like to dance, try Juan's Caribbean Club." He smirks before he continues, "Cubans, Italians, and Orientals all live in that area. A lot goes on in the back rooms of many a storefront. If I were you, I'd be cautious about where I stick my educated nose."

He waits for me to react; I remain impassive.

Rings rolls on his heels again. "Get back to me later. I'll have information on those two Cubans."

I ask. "How would Piantini go about killing Calabrese?"

"If Piantini sent those two to the morgue to kill Calabrese, he'd be dead."

"Who do you think will benefit the most by Nickie Piantini's death?"

"Now you're asking the right questions." He rewinds the film till centered on the screen is a tall, handsome man in his early thirties. He has a narrow face, blue eyes, and straight, sandy-brown hair. Ring points to the image. "That's Claudio Cellini. A definite player. In a few years, that bold son of a bitch will be a powerful man. He's a carbon copy of Nickie, without the family tie. Claudio made it up the hard way. He used to run numbers, then they gave him a small book. The book expanded and with that expansion came inroads into loan sharking, carjacking, and drugs. His stature gained momentum as he became more successful. He and Nickie were rivals, and Nickie was losing. Recently, Cellini started to legitimize himself by buying into established bars and investing in real estate. He's very shrewd."

I remember Olearczyk mentioned Cellini when I asked him the same question. "Hypothetically, do you think Calabrese could be mixed up with Cellini?"

"I've never heard Calabrese's name mentioned on the streets, and you know how names tend to get passed around."

"Calabrese did Cellini a favor when he killed Nickie, didn't he?"

"Nickie had his father behind him, and that contained Cellini's ambitions. Now there's nobody in his way."

Ring starts the projector again. "Watch the film, because we know Reno Piantini was definitely at his son's wake, yet he can't be spotted. If your purpose is to protect Calabrese, start memorizing faces."

"The Two-Two is assigned to guard duty. My job is to clear Calabrese or hand him over, and yours is to cooperate."

"If Reno Piantini sent men to the morgue, why is Calabrese alive?" Ring's tone is mocking.

I've been expecting the question, but I have no credible response. I watch figures on the screen pass, knowing those two Cubans have a connection with Reno Piantini and Calabrese.

The reel ends, and Ring looks directly at me. "You need me involved with this case."

"Why do you think I was given this assignment?"

He taps a pencil against his palm. "I've thought about that. You have the credentials, but this should really be my case. I suppose McConnell had something to do with the decision."

I smile. "I was chosen because I'm the best detective to solve this case."

Ring holds the door open for me with an unmistakable smirk on his face. "You never told me whether you think like a madman?"

Looking at him, I whisper, "Maybe, and maybe that's my advantage."

THURSDAY
4:30 P.M.

THE RAIN SUBSIDES as the sky helplessly fights to loosen itself from the clouds. I drive back to Ivy and Vermont. I remain seated, staring at the sight of the shooting. Ivy looks like one long trash bin. Apartment windows line each side of the street, with nervous eyes looking out from the edges.

I pull in traffic and circle the block once, then a second time slowly. It's going to be near impossible to get anyone to talk. This neighborhood lives under a dome of either fear or indifference. Kids emerge from the butted buildings. They're playing on the wet streets, tossing firecrackers, giving defiant looks to the impatient drivers who lean on their horns. Their deafening music boxes held close to their heads.

My car moves forward, but everything remains the same. No witnesses will emerge; finding Garcia will be near impossible, so that leaves the two Hispanics, probably Cubans, in the second car.

I cross over Vermont and pull into Barone's gas station. Something has been bothering me. Yesterday, in Monticello, when Calabrese twirled his keys, there was no Giants pendant on the ring.

Barone sighs with annoyance as I open the door. I'm not a welcomed guest. He gives me an uncompromising look. "I know as much now as I did this morning."

"I've been thinking about gas tanks. How much would it cost to fill up a brand-new big Buick?"

"Cops coming in and out of here don't help my business. Ten bucks maybe."

"So, Calabrese could have owed you that much?"

"Na, half that for his car." He faces me. "What do you want?"

"What make car does he have?"

"A red Javelin."

"He owns a red Javelin?"

"Yeah."

I block his path to the bays. "Do you remember what Officer Calabrese heard that caught his attention?"

"Look, D'laska, you can ask me questions here or downtown. My answers aren't going to change."

My hand moves up to grab Barone's shirt, but I stop. I figure the scowl on my face conveys how I feel. "Did you see the actual shooting?"

"No." His voice brims with irritation.

"Did you get a look at the two men in the second car?"

"No!"

"Why are you so jumpy, Mr. Barone? You have something to hide? Should I be looking into your background?"

He glares at me and says nothing.

"Cooperating with the police isn't a crime."

"That's cute. How fucking naïve do you think I am?"

I point across the street. "Do many kids usually hang around that laundromat?"

Barone crosses his arms. "Who notices?"

"Kids are kids," I say. "Maybe every once in a while, cops are called to break up some minor disturbances at that laundromat.

Maybe a crotchety senior citizen watching from one of those windows gets annoyed when gangs gather on that corner."

"This morning I gave you coffee and doughnuts. I'm not serving supper."

"Have you seen Calabrese?"

"No."

"Who else was working on Monday?"

"The pumps? Just me. And next time, come with a subpoena or something."

"I'll come with a search warrant and a couple of Irish cops to rifle through everything in this station."

"Look, I've answered all your questions."

"Not honestly, Mr. Barone."

In my car, I stare at the corner. Red Javelin, black Buick, expensive clothes, impressive jewelry, a house in the city, a cottage in the country, a thirty-thousand-dollar loss, all on less than fifteen thousand a year—is he a cop or a magician?

My thoughts pivot from Calabrese to Nickie Piantini. I jump out of my car and walk to the scene of the shooting. If Nickie Piantini conducted business on Monday, wouldn't it have been Garcia doing the collecting and Piantini sitting in the car? Garcia is the muscle. He should have been collecting the drug, gambling, loan shark, or whatever money was owed to Nickie. At the least, Garcia would have been with Nickie at the second car if they were involved in a business transaction.

Calabrese said he heard Nickie yelling, "Give me my money," and that's what attracted his attention.

Garcia never got out of the car—that means Piantini knew he could handle the situation. Nickie wasn't worried the men in the second car could be a threat to him. He was angry, yet felt self-assured and confident about what he was about to do. That encounter was strictly between Nickie Piantini and the men in that second car.

Thunder draws my attention. The sky lights up and thunder cracks. I head for my car thinking about Nickie's reasons for being at that second car alone. Why weren't the two passengers brought to him? They owed him money. Garcia is paid to collect money. Why wasn't he collecting the money on Monday afternoon?

Light rain creates liquid harlequin figures, elongated and slippery on my windshield, then recreated over and over as the water beads and draws down.

Nickie's emotional state interfered with his reasoning when Calabrese approached. Instead of reacting rationally, he pulled out his gun and shot at Calabrese. He shoots at a cop. Why? That only brings heat on him from both the cops and the mob.

I start the engine and the windshield wipers whoosh, giving me a clear view of Vermont and Ivy. According to Calabrese's story, Nickie surprised these two men; he cut them off and rapidly approached them. Calabrese heard Piantini shouting, threatening them for his money. Apparently, they didn't have it. Nickie became angrier, more emotional, out of control, and fired at Calabrese.

The sky opens, and the hard drops pound on the car.

THURSDAY
6:30 P.M.

RING KEEPS me on hold for five minutes before he tells me to wait for ten more. He gives me the names of the two Cubans who were at the morgue and at the wake: Sergio Diez, who owns the Chrysler and Manuel Vasquez. They have priors for armed robbery, carjacking, and extortion. They're bottom-rung boys trying to make their way up the ladder. Ring is as amicable as a hungry dog wearing a loose muzzle. Full reports will be delivered to me.

I set down my pencil and paper and gaze around my living room. From behind the couch, I remove a large piece of heavy poster paper. I print the name Louis Calabrese in the left corner, beneath it: Gino Guzzetta—best friend. Dean Henry—unethical investor, friend.

Below I jot,

Notes:

Dismissed from Mounted under questionable circumstances. Left I.A. Under questionable circumstances/affair/rifled files.
Has money.
Lying about why he was in Manhattan.
On the other side of the poster, I write:
Nicholas Piantini.
Beneath that:
Reno Piantini—father, Mafia henchman, murderer of Mario Zicaro.
Stefano Gambacorda—head of organized crime. One-time rival of Zicaro.
Tito Garcia—protector and muscle for Nick Piantini.
Sergio Diez, Manuel Vasquez—two-bit thugs in the Gambacorda family.
Beneath the names, I jot,
Notes:
Mafia contract.
Justice Department.
In the center, I write,
Cubans—second car.
and lastly,
John Gage.
It's too early for the puzzle to have a defined picture, but the border is interesting.

THURSDAY
10:30 P.M.

BROOKLYN IS MUGGIER THAN MANHATTAN, more confining. The earlier downpours have subsided into drizzle from a dark, overcast sky.

From the outside, The Blue Chateau blends into the concrete surroundings, another business in a row of businesses. Drugstore, Realtor, optician, discount appliance store, one small shop after the other down the block.

The Blue Chateau is without decorative fanfare. Outside there is a tasteful blue neon sign in one of two tinted windows on either side of the entrance.

The dimly lit place has a robust crowd, but not so thick I can't move around. The bartender has a friendly smile and clean Italian looks. He places my beer on a Blue Chateau coaster. I'm impressed with my cozy surroundings. Chocolate carpeted walls. Velour booths. Smooth jazz hums through the speakers. I can barely make out an archway leading into a dark back room. There are people scattered around the horseshoe bar including two smartly dressed, dark-haired women. The bartender plays with a white towel while pacing behind the bar.

He pours what's left from the beer bottle into my glass. "Another."

"No TV?" I ask.

He smiles at me, glad to talk, "Na, not even during Monday night football."

He snatches up another beer from the cooler and sets it down beside a clean glass.

I glance around. "What time do things pick up?"

"We're fairly quiet till eleven."

"A friend of a friend told me about this place." I take a sip of beer. "Gino, know him?"

"Yeah, Gino and Lou come in," he says. "Eh, you a cop too?"

"Friend of a friend."

He looks down the bar at two dark-haired women. "Connie and Donna are good friends of Gino and Lou."

I take a gulp of beer.

"What's your name?" he says. "I'll introduce ya."

"Mike. And get the ladies a drink on me."

The less attractive of the two women is smiling at me.

When the bartender returns, I ask, "Bet you're a nice Italian boy from the neighborhood."

He laughs. "Eh, you got it."

"What kind of a crowd do you get in here?"

He opens his top button and loosens his tie. "We cater to a low-profile crowd. Professional types."

I lift my glass to the smiling dark-haired woman. He whispers to me, "You're doing well."

It's no secret most bartenders love to gossip about their customers especially when they're bored. I swing my stool around. "The back room looks private."

"Yeah, hidden and dark. Balcony seats without the trouble of a show."

"Is there a back entrance, if you don't want to be seen at all?"

"Just an emergency exit," He says. "Check it out before we get crowded."

Couples filter into the Blue Chateau. Few come to the bar. Guys have taken seats around the horseshoe. Women in pairs stroll past.

He returns after talking with one of the waitresses.

"A guy named Tito ever come in here?" I say. "Kind of hairy?"

"Ain't nobody named Tito come in here. No way!"

The dark-haired woman watches me. The bartender notices and gives me a grin. He jerks his head. "If I were you, I'd take Connie. She's not as pretty as Donna, but her body's better. And she's the one who's smiling."

I call him as he begins to walk away. "What kind of professionals comes in here?"

He steps back, bringing his shoulders up and making a praying gesture with his hands. "Class guys with money—not jerks who wear cheap suits off the rack."

"A nice Italian crowd."

"Naturally!"

I slide off the stool and head toward the ladies.

They welcome me with ease. None of us are awkward. Connie and I begin talking trivial nonsense after the introductions, and frequently at the same time. Neither of the women is bashful, although Donna remains on the fringe. She's not interested in me. I'm a distraction for Connie. Donna chain smokes while watching the door.

The place fills. Near the bar, small pockets of people chat. The women and I share laughs and drinks. Connie and I have much in common, at least that is the way my lies are falling. She's unemployed at the moment, Donna cuts hair, and I'm in Vice. When Connie steps from the stool, she presses her chest into me. Our faces become very close, and our arms wrap around each other's waists. The difference between a drug and a poison is the dosage. I need to gather information. "Connie, how long have you known Gino?"

Connie asks Donna. She shrugs her off, directing a column of smoke my way.

Connie giggles. "Donna and Gino had a thing last year."

I say to Connie, "How about Lou? Was he your date?"

Both women laugh.

"What's the mystery?"

Donna scrutinizes me. "How well do you know Gino and Lou?"

I remain with a dumb look glued to my face.

Connie says, "Ya know, aside from Gino's cousin Marty, you're the first person who's ever come here to meet Lou and Gino."

I give a broad smile. "Lou and Gino always talk about how friendly this place is."

Donna bursts out laughing. "Connie, remember that night we all went to Atlantic City. Kitty and Lou, me and Gino, you and your ex, and Fat Dean with that Puerto Rican girl."

When Connie stops giggling she looks at me. "Lou is out with Kitty right now. I was talking on the phone with Kitty when Lou arrived to pick her up."

I contain the alarm that goes off inside me.

I ask, "Lou and Kitty are together right now?"

"Probably at a motel."

Connie's face comes closer to mine. "They'll be here in a little while, and maybe we'll be at the motel."

"Lou and Gino will be here?"

Connie says, "Lou and Kitty, and Gino and his date."

Both women continue to laugh. Before assessing all the new names, I try and figure out how Calabrese got out of the house. He wanted patrolmen. I understand his reasoning now, establishing camaraderie with men of his own rank, confidences are gained, a small favor requested, Guzzetta his best friend will protect him. Bang, the dynamic duo of Street Crime are back to their tricks.

"Marty has dark hair?" I say. "A mustache, I think? I bumped into him and Gino at the track once."

"That's Marty. He's a gambler," Connie says.

"What's his last name? I forget."

Donna exhales smoke my way. "Floriano."

"Bartender, we need a round of drinks for us."

He pours, and we toast to better days, but Connie corrects us, "To better nights!"

Donna looks at her watch. "The son of a bitch didn't show. I knew he wouldn't."

Connie kisses my cheek, then says to Donna, "Mine did."

I'm like a persistent dentist. "How long has Lou been going out with Kitty?"

Donna swishes the Black Velvet in her glass and drains the liquid. Placing the empty on the bar, she asks, "You know Lou's married?" There's an edge to her voice.

"Of course."

Connie asks if I can name the seven dwarfs, distracting my thoughts with a soft embrace. Feeling like a combination of Doc and Dopey, I decide to push my luck further.

"I met Kitty once. What's her last name?"

Both women look as though I just became a pariah.

Connie steps back from me. "Why?"

"Just wondering." I try sounding amusing.

Donna looks over to me, smoke coming from her mouth. "Who are you? I can smell you're a cop, but you're not here to make friends. You're after something."

Both women exchange anxious glances, excuse themselves, and swiftly head for the restroom.

The bartender comes over. "What happened?"

"They'll be right back," I say. "I'm in a spot. What's Kitty's last name?

His eyes go directly to mine. "If you don't know I ain't tellin'."

"It just slipped my mind."

The bartender moves away to wait on another customer. I feel like I'm the only naked person in this place.

I drop money on the bar. As I reach the exit, Connie catches up and pulls me into the coat room. "What's going on? I got to know? Look, did Lou's wife send you here?" Her eyes enlarge with fright. "Are you a friend of his or what? Lou ain't got a great sense of humor. Know what I mean?"

"I'm here to help Lou Calabrese. Answer one question."

She tries to step away. I hold her by the arms and ask, "How long have Kitty and Lou been going out?

"Maybe a year."

I take a deep breath before asking. "What's Kitty's last name?"

"You are an asshole!"

"The name?"

"You a cop?"

"Yes. "I'm not here to get anybody in trouble. What's her name?"

Donna laughs, "The name, hows this, her husband is Frankie "The Saw" Jacovino.

My head begins to spin, and it's not from the booze. Calabrese, the cop, is fucking the wife of a convicted mobster.

I tell myself not to act surprised—this is just another facet in a string of all things absurd. The name Jacovino is synonymous with organized crime in New York. Who is Louis Calabrese? There are many puzzles with all the pieces scattered, edges torn, and I bet quite a few missing.

I let her go. The world is rotating but I feel like I'm in super slow motion and I'll never catch up with myself and place my feet on solid ground again.

When the door closes behind me, I try to disassociate myself from my surroundings. Calabrese isn't shacking up with any woman from just any Italian family, but a woman whose husband's family name is branded into the texture of New York crime. A perverse laugh growls in my head. It's Connors setting fire to my brain.

This convoluted grotesqueness must all be part of some bizarre Italian logic. Kitty's husband, Frankie was put away for armed robbery, but inside information says a year before his prison sentence, Frankie murdered an undercover cop who had hard evidence against him and his brothers. The cop was found in pieces. His head and limbs had been sawed off.

I watch my reflection in the storefront windows while walking; it's tilted and contours to every angle. It's ugly, speckled with dirt, and it seems to cling to me.

―――

FRIDAY
1:30 A.M.

I OPEN the door to my apartment and flick on the kitchen light. The potato chips are hiding beneath a *Time* magazine on top of the TV. Flopping on my couch, I contemplate all the pieces that don't fit. This day started with an old grocery store owner on Ivy who didn't say a word and ended with two women in a Brooklyn bar saying too much.

I make a mental note to add the name *Kitty Jacovino, lover, wife of a jailed mobster* to my board.

Louis Calabrese loves his family but jeopardizes them, loves his job but compromises it, shoots Nicholas Piantini, but doesn't feel he owes an explanation.

Is he a murderer? And what about Garcia? Why wasn't he by Nickie's side at that second car?

CHAPTER 4

FRIDAY, JULY 4, 1975
7:30 A.M.

NOT AGAIN! I listen to each successive harsh ring becoming louder and more irritating.

"I'm not here," I shout, reaching for the phone. "Yeah!"

"Detective Sergeant Michael D'laska?" The voice is female but neither familiar nor appealing.

"Yes."

"This is Deputy Commissioner Ruth Mulvaney."

Suddenly, I seem to be wide awake. "Yes, Deputy Commissioner, what can I do for you?"

"I would like to meet with you between eight-thirty and nine-thirty on this lovely Fourth of July morning. I want to discuss this terrible Nicholas Piantini shooting."

I conjure up my best faux sincere voice. "Deputy Commissioner, thank you for calling, but unfortunately I've made previous arrangements for this morning."

"Where will you be starting your day?"

There's no way I'm starting my day with her.

"In Brooklyn," I say.

I can hear her breathing into the phone. "Detective D'laska, it is imperative I speak to you before two o'clock tomorrow afternoon. I'm a guest panelist on a television special about crime in this city. We're taping the show tomorrow. That's why we must discuss this Patrolman Calabrese and his connections to organized crime."

"Deputy Commissioner, there are absolutely no ties between Calabrese and any criminal activity. Nothing. I think discretion would be the wisest course of action on television."

"Yes, you're right, we shouldn't discuss this over the phone. Tomorrow morning at nine."

"Ten. It's Saturday."

"God bless you."

"Bye."

I drag myself to the window. Jiggling the strings, it's a blue-tinged, muddy-colored morning, which will mature into a slow-baking, hot brown day.

I let my head drop back on the pillows. I don't need Deputy Commissioner Ruth Mulvaney interfering in my investigation. I already have that happening with Ring and Roberts. If Mulvaney uncovered as little as I know about Calabrese, she would have him responsible for every unsolved mob-related murder in the city. She's not vindictive; she's just simple-minded, believing Jesus lives in her soul and guides her actions. Therefore, she's never responsible when she's wrong.

Mulvaney's husband was a sergeant killed in a nasty drug bust years ago. She maintains he was set up by fellow officers because he couldn't be bought. A few months after he was gunned down, his partner quit the police force and moved to Miami where he operates restaurants that are supposed fronts for drug smuggling. In 1974, after serving two years on the independent Knapp Commission to investigate allegations of departmental corruption, Ruth Mulvaney was appointed to one of the few civilian police positions. As deputy commissioner, she's a relentless, puritanical crusader for her interpretation of justice.

I skip through the police directory, then dial.

The Sixth Precinct. It's time to hear what the other captain who questioned Calabrese has to say. After being transferred around, I get Captain Rocca on the phone. He asks if I can be there within the hour and to bring bagels.

FRIDAY
9:08 A.M.

THE DUTY SERGEANT leads me into Captain Anthony Rocca's neatly arranged office; the sun bathes through two large, clean windows, brightening the moderately sized room. The walls are unadorned except for a few commendations. He welcomes me with a firm handshake placing a padded chair in front of his desk. I hand him the bag of bagels.

"Mixed?"

I nod.

He looks into the bag and with a smile takes out a sesame seed bagel. Rocca isn't attractive; his facial features are compacted in the center of his face.

He grimaces. "No cream cheese?"

"I'll take a plain one."

"Want it toasted?" he says. He's wearing a pink shirt with an American flag pinned to his collar.

"Sure."

He finds the bagels and walks across the room. When a timer rings, he brings me a small stoneware plate with the bagel, a plastic knife, a napkin, and two pads of butter as well as coffee with condiments.

I take a generous bite.

"Thanks for bringing them." He chews like it's his first meal.

I summarize my involvement, then ask him to relate his story.

His smooth, warm voice rolls from a round jaw as he sits back in his chair. "When I arrived, Nicholas Piantini had already been taken into the hospital. A crowd had gathered outside; the standard inquisitive types as well as some cop haters chanting obscenities. Captain Connors had already set up an extensive perimeter of men to keep the people away from Nickie Piantini's car and the blood stains in the street.

"Connors was pissed. He was badgering Calabrese to tell him what he wanted to hear. Calabrese was pretty hot himself. It seemed to me that everybody, especially Connors, wanted a bad guy but there wasn't one. Only this agitated cop who was being accosted with questions and accusations. The harder and meaner Connors became, the more belligerent Calabrese grew. It was ugly—two cops screaming at each other in front of a hostile crowd.

"Reporters were arriving, sticking microphones in everyone's face, creating on-the-spot stories about what had happened."

"Why did you personally drive Calabrese back to Ivy and Vermont?"

"I wanted answers. It seemed reasonable to me if we gave Calabrese a moment to compose himself, the explanations would surface."

"Did it work?"

"Yes, it did!"

Disliking Rocca would be difficult. He's a man who exudes a confident, trustworthy, and warm persona.

I walk to the window; there's not much of a view, just a fenced parking lot. "When you asked Calabrese why he was in Manhattan, what was his reply?"

"I didn't have to ask. He volunteered a plausible explanation."

"Plausible?" I turn toward him, disbelieving what I just heard. I close my mouth and swallow, almost frightened to ask my next question. "That he was in Manhattan to meet his brother and father? That story?"

"Yes! Don't tell me your interest lies more in why he was there rather than what he accomplished."

"Why do you look so skeptical?" he questions, walking past me on his way to the coffee pot. "More coffee?" he adds.

I shake my head trying to assess his comment.

Rocca sighs deeply. "Maybe Calabrese was in Manhattan to screw some broad, as Connors suggests. That's none of our business. He killed a shit like Nickie Piantini in defense of his own life. We owe him the courtesy of some discretion. Who cares why he was in Manhattan?"

Rocca strides back to his chair. I tap hard with my fingers on his desk; I capture his full attention. "Calabrese is lying about why he was in Manhattan, and he's lied to superiors about his actions in the past."

He cocks his head. "Do you want to know why you're here?" Rocca puts his hand on his hip as his voice rises. "Because Connors lit up the old Irish brigade. No little guinea is going to make a fool out of him. He must have called every Irishmen in the department. He started a big fire under their asses to make them assign someone. It restores my faith in McConnell that he assigned a D'laska. I know you're not Irish."

He takes a sip of coffee, and a strange callousness comes into his face. "Is Deputy Commissioner Mulvaney involved?"

I bridge my two first fingers together and place them against my lips. "Aren't you sounding as prejudiced as you're making the Irish out to be?"

Rocca says, "Mulvaney will stick a cattle prod into your heart while preaching, 'Jesus loves you.'"

"Finish telling me about Calabrese and the ride you took back to Ivy."

Rocca becomes impatient with me. "Does it matter? One week before this incident, Calabrese was in Street Crime. That man went wherever he wanted, at any time. He was a twenty-four-hour cop. No one ever questioned his motives. With one change, a transfer to a precinct, his integrity is in jeopardy. Calabrese and I both knew at that time it didn't make a damn bit of difference why he was in Manhattan. The only thing that mattered was that he was there, doing a cop's job."

I lean forward. "What about that black gun found in Nicholas Piantini's car?"

Rocca's face softens. "Connors tried to ram that gun down

Calabrese's throat when he was interrogating him. They went 'round and 'round for hours. Calabrese kept insisting that Nicholas Piantini fired at him with a silver gun, probably a .45. The gun found under the driver's seat was a black .38. If Calabrese would have said, 'What's the difference, I don't know,' or anything to indicate it didn't matter, Connors would have arrested him. He read him his rights, you know. That's when I called to make sure an inspector was on his way."

Cautiously, I state, "The reports say the black gun had never been fired. If Calabrese had flinched, Connors would have contended that Calabrese shot Nicholas Piantini in cold blood."

Rocca stands, putting his hands into his pockets. "It was ugly." He removes one hand and opens his top drawer. He hesitates before reaching for a cigarette. "I'll have to quit again." He lights up, smoke trails while he walks around his desk. "Connors assumed that because Calabrese wouldn't take his shit, he was guilty.

"Connors hates Italians; he hates Calabrese. Connors is a relic, part of the old Irish guard who held the Police Department in their fists. Didn't you notice the Knapp Commission was primarily Irish and Jewish, fucking Italians and Puerto Ricans?"

I want to keep Rocca focused, but everything seems to have an ethnic ring.

"Hypothetically," I ask, "if Calabrese would have admitted being in Manhattan to meet a woman, would Connors have backed off?"

He takes a deep drag from the cigarette. "Christ could come down off the cross and join Perry Mason in Calabrese's defense, and Connors still wouldn't have believed him. Remember, Mulvaney and the Knapp Commission found a lot of dirty cops in the Fifth Precinct, most were Italians. Connors was never chastised for that, but his career was over. He's never going to get a nice cushy Irish job at headquarters."

He watches me wag my head. "You're saying this whole investigation is based on ethnic prejudice. Calabrese is a victim; a lying victim who's above suspicion."

Rocca straightens. "Check the records." He squeezes his hands together. "Corruptible behavior gets translated as an ethnic flaw only if your roots don't weave back into the department's historical framework."

Rocca waits for me to respond, but his game is too controlled for a quick response. I remain in thought for a long moment before speaking. "You didn't question Calabrese's father and brother because you didn't see a need." I piece it together as I'm talking. "Calabrese's word was good enough for you. Connors, on the other hand, didn't question them because he felt it was useless—they'd lie to protect him."

"That's about it."

"Calabrese was questioned for around six hours."

Rocca shrugs. "Calabrese's story never deviated. Then, Connors and the inspector started in about Italian social clubs and Mafia figures. That's when Calabrese realized he was getting railroaded and he was smart enough to demand a P.B.A. lawyer."

"They were trying to tie Calabrese to organized crime, that's what you're telling me?"

Rocca, dismayed that I'm surprised, smiles. "Connors wanted Calabrese to spend the night in jail, so he could beat the shit out of him."

"Pretty strong words."

Rocca strides to the window with his coffee cup fitted into his hand. Yellow sunlight streams into the room.

I string together my thoughts. "What do you make of the contract on Calabrese?"

Rocca walks toward me. The implications of the remark weigh on his face. "All the more reason to believe him."

At the door, he looks confidently at me. "Think about this. If Calabrese were black, the NAACP would be tearing down City Hall. If he were Jewish, his Rabbi would have had this inquiry ended the next day. And if he were Irish, a Gold Shield would be handed out at a momentous ceremony. Calabrese is Italian, and the papers are really cautious about making him a hero."

I nod. "I'll be in touch."

"Thanks for the bagels."

I say to the duty sergeant, "I need to use a phone."

He points to a desk behind him. "Go ahead."

A question has been rolling in my head since last night. It may take a while to get anything on Kitty Jacovino, but her husband's record might give me some quick information. I dial Central Records. After being jockeyed about, a bored operator goes through Frankie Jacovino's file. He relays Kitty works in Manhattan at Macy's in the sportswear department. Unfortunately, Macy's is closed today.

I call the Two-Two and ask for a list of the men assigned to watch Calabrese, their schedules, and their files.

The Desk Sergeant relays some men are nervous. They realize Reno Piantini is a murderer and how easy it would be for them to be killed alongside Calabrese. One officer refused to be assigned because he thought Calabrese's house would be bombed.

Before hanging up, I ask what time the report says Calabrese went to bed last night.

"Around ten," he says.

FRIDAY
3:00 P.M.

THREE DEUCES IS LONGER than it is wide, with three wooden archways separating the eating area from the bar. There are the typical posters of New York on the faded plastered walls. A long case, crammed with trophies and plaques, hangs above the liquor bottles. That's the only sign of any athletics unless you count the five loud men playing liar's poker at the corner of the bar.

Three Italians are in casual polyester with opened shirts and gold jewelry. The fourth is a tight-framed Latino; a sinewy, disagreeable-looking man clad in black sweatshirt and slacks. The fifth member of the group is a thin, good-looking man, meticulously dressed in designer clothing. His light olive skin is tanned, his playful eyes are soft blue separated by a pinched nose. I remember him from the film of the funeral. Claudio Cellini is the one all the attention is directed toward.

The least threatening of the group, a chubby Italian whose colorful shirt is several sizes too small, is the brunt of amusement. He's poked from time to time and flinches when one of the others attempts to punch his forearm. The chubby fellow and the Latino who files his nails are the primary targets of all the verbal abuse.

The tables in the restaurant area are empty. On the opposite end of the bar, four guys were discussing the Mets' loss to Houston last night. The barmaid is a hard-looking woman whose voice is pregnant with barroom raspiness. Her shape is oval, fitted unattractively into tight jeans.

My steak and dandelions sandwich are in a sticky, plastic basket.

She points to my glass. "Another beer?"

The players' voices grow louder and more boastful with each round of drinks.

Four other men stroll into the bar. One is Hispanic. They're welcomed with animated Italian gestures, handshaking, and embraces. Claudio drops twenties on the bar and calls the barmaid over. "Get everybody in the place a drink."

She obeys like a well-trained dog, turning over a shot glass in front of me. She says with a false smile, "Ya got one coming with Claudio."

A loud dispute between the newly arrived Latino and the largest man of the original five breaks out. They swear and theatrically point fingers. The big man wraps his hand around the smaller Latino's throat. The Latino growls in the big man's face. Claudio snaps his fingers. There's immediate posturing, and the pecking order reestablishes itself.

The Latino digs into his pocket and throws a fifty into the money pile. The other Hispanic scowls while vigorously filing his nails. All the gamblers make the trip to the men's room coming back making nasal noises. Claudio makes the trip last. I follow.

I stand at the only urinal when Claudio swings open the toilet stall door and struts out wiping his nose. He combs his hair in the mirror.

I take his place at the wash basin as he removes paper towels. I rinse my hands. He turns his head toward me, widening his eyes. "Did you drop something?"

I glance at a fifty-dollar bill beneath the sink. I say between clenched teeth, "Doubtful."

Cellini is as slippery as he is good looking. "There are two fifties, I think. Why don't you look?"

"No, thank you."

He asks, "You must be new at the Fifth Precinct?"

For a moment we stare at each other, then I push open the door and walk to the bar.

The barmaid's eyes are dilated, and everyone is animated, talking fast with little regard for content.

Two more men join the group with added fanfare. A dark man wearing mirrored sunglasses and a well-defined Hispanic in a tank top they call Andre.

The smell of corruption is always a nauseous odor. Two wet fifties, one hundred dollars. How many cops would have stuffed the quick money in their pockets? Who couldn't use an extra hundred for the mortgage, the car payment, the kids, and on and on? Money, always the soiled but effective stimulus.

I leave cash on the bar. I face them, taking a mental picture. Claudio smiles, his straight, white teeth showing. He winks to pepper the insult.

FRIDAY
5:13 P.M.

I RECOGNIZE THE NAME, P. Wrobel, on the tag of the sergeant at a desk. He was the first man to speak with Calabrese outside the hospital. He's in his mid-twenties, soft-boned, light complexion, and short blonde hair. I approach; his manner is friendly and accommodating. He leads me to a small lunch room where a few men are reading the paper.

Peter Wrobel repeats the same story in his report. When he finishes, I have him clarify a few points.

"You arrived when Nicholas Piantini was lying in the street. Where was Calabrese?"

"Moving toward him, crouched with his gun in hand."

"Captain Connors persisted in questioning Calabrese as to whether he was in Manhattan to see a woman. How did Calabrese react?"

"Calabrese must have told Connors three or four times to go fuck himself."

"Connors didn't like that, did he?"

"Not at all."

I lean forward. "Were you with both captains when Calabrese was questioned at the hospital and at the precincts?"

"I kept an eye on Calabrese when they sent him out of the room."

"Did it seem to you that Calabrese knew the victim?"

Wrobel leans back and sighs. "Officer Calabrese didn't seem to care who he shot."

I lower my voice, "You know that Calabrese has a contract on his life. You were the first man on the scene with Calabrese—you observed him, you questioned him, you dealt with him. I want to ask you one important question."

Wrobel's face tightens. "If you're going to ask me if I think Officer Calabrese murdered Nicholas Piantini, I don't know. He acted like no cop I've ever seen. Ranting and raving about being in Street Crime, how important he was and disregarding everybody. If Captain Rocca hadn't arrived, Calabrese would have been arrested."

I fall back into my chair. Wrobel has the face of an honest man who couldn't lie with any confidence.

"One last question," I say. "Was there an immediate follow-up with possible witnesses? I would like a list of those people and their statements."

"I'll dig them up."

When Wrobel leaves, one of the officers in the room lowers his paper and begins to speak, "I was there."

I turn my head toward him.

"At St. Vincent's, my partner and I responded to the ten-thirteen. That cop was a maniac. I don't know nothing about the shooting, but I do know that cop didn't give a shit about anything except making sure everybody knew he was from Street Crime. Then I heard later that he wasn't even assigned to Street Crime anymore."

An indefinable feeling nags me. I imagine the shooting taking place, frame by frame. Nicholas Piantini gets out of his car while Tito Garcia stays behind. Piantini rushes to the second car; he's threatening the driver. What would Garcia be doing? Calabrese appears from nowhere shouting he's a cop. Piantini fires. What does Garcia do?

Wrobel returns with the reports, and I make myself semi-comfortable before going through them.

FRIDAY
8:30 P.M.

AFTER LEAVING WROBEL, I stop at the station where Quincy had left a manila envelope with the desk sergeant. There wasn't any candy, and I realized from reading the memo that Calabrese's promotion to Mounted was legitimate. Relatively easy assignments like Mounted are usually favors. But it doesn't appear it was for him. The recommendation came from a respected, old Irishman who now has a meaningless desk job at Headquarters.

The Innfield Pub is practically empty, a few guys playing darts while their wives drink white wine and chat in a booth.

Two men at the bar are separated by a vacant stool. One's a regular; he waves to me. The barmaid's name is Britt. She's shapely, never wears a bra, and is quick-witted. I think of her as Bambi with fangs, lovely face but lethal mouth. She's also a stubborn Red Sox fan, and that's tough to take in New York.

I pour golden liquid from the green bottle into a tall glass. Tiny bubbles form at the sides, and white foam appears on top. I stare at my money on the bar. I pick up a dollar bill and think back to the liars' poker game at Three Deuces. I scrutinize the serial numbers.

Britt sashays toward me and asks if I need anything. "Another beer. And get yourself something, Britt."

She steps back, watching my face break into an overwhelming smile. "What—what is it?"

I snap my fingers joyously, then snap them again. "It's the Fourth of July—give us a shot of bourbon. I just put two and two together!"

She smiles. "Sounds good to me."

We toast, and the warmth of the drink butterflies going down. Gambling is personal! Gambling is very personal. They gambled together, Nickie Piantini and the two Cubans in the second car. Nickie was somehow saving face Monday afternoon. They didn't owe him professionally from a bet on a game if that were so Garcia would be doing the collecting. This was a private transaction—this was Nickie's own money, but bigger than that. Nickie wanted to make an example out of them for something they did to him. They tricked him, or they gambled with him, and he loaned them money, or they just outright cheated him. I'm close; I know it. He knew those two would be traveling down that particular street. Why? Do they live there? Work there?

Britt asks if I want another. I decline, but I give her that I-could-be-interested-in-sticking-around-till-you-get-off look. She gives me that never-gonna-happen smirk!

CHAPTER 5

SATURDAY, JULY 5, 1975
11:30 A.M.

SUZANNE SURPRISES ME. I didn't expect her to be at work.

She's reading a file; her head is tilted down in deep concentration with the metal drawer pressed against her chest. Her left calf is parallel to the floor where her shoe is waiting for her foot to return.

"Deputy Commissioner Mulvaney is gone," Suzanne says.

"How long ago?"

"Forty-five minutes."

"Did she leave a number?"

"No, but I have numbers where she can be reached."

"Was she pissed?"

Suzanne fails to suppress a yawn. "What do you think?"

She pushes the heavy drawer closed. She faces me sideways, stretching her arms forward and then upward, twisting her waist. Her nipples point through her sleeveless white blouse.

I'm talking mostly to myself, "I was at the Impound Center...I forgot about the appointment...What are you doing here?"

She flops down in a chair. "I had some work to finish for Chief McConnell. I'll be out of your way in fifteen minutes."

Without her professional, standoffish presence, I'm not sure how to react. She looks down at her legs knowing I'm impressed with the view.

"Mike," my name sounds strange, wooden coming from her mouth, "how could you forget you made an appointment with Ruth Mulvaney?"

I sigh and walk past her toward the window. "I must have blocked her out of my mind."

She comes to the window, standing a few feet away.

"McConnell isn't going to be pleased," I say.

"If it's any consolation, Chief McConnell can't stand her." She smiles politely, and her crooked front tooth catches on her bottom lip. She walks to her chair, stretching her arms again. "I need to join a health club."

I'm not sure what I want to ask, but I feel compelled.

I realize anything I say is going to sound silly. I smile, wondering how stupid I look. "Suzanne, would you like to have dinner with me at Fat Sam's Italian Gardens tonight?" The moment the words leave my mouth, I know they're wrong.

"What?"

"I have to do some snooping in Little Italy; another intelligent pair of eyes and ears would help." I surprise myself. The words just roll with sincerity.

"Does this have to do with the Calabrese investigation?"

"I need to scout a few spots, and I'd enjoy your company."

She laughs. "My company? You don't know me."

"I'm adventurous. And I'd like you to join me. More observation than real work is involved."

"What time?"

"Later. I have a lot of things...things I must do. About—"

"What can I do to help?"

I clear my throat. "Are you serious?"

"I think so, yes, before I join a spa, I want a great meal. Now, besides Mulvaney's number, what else?" She picks up her pen.

94

"Run me off a list of female officers assigned to Internal Affairs in 1968. Background check on Claudio Cellini. A file on Frankie Jacovino—he's serving time in Attica. Ring's office should have this information. And, I need a favor. An authorization to have Nicholas Piantini's gun released to me."

Looking up, she gives me a grin. "What would you have done if I wasn't here?"

"I have no idea! Give me an address, and I'll pick you up at eight."

She hands me two pieces of paper. The first has Ruth Mulvaney's numbers. Glancing at the second, Suzanne explains, "I've also written my phone number in case you get lost."

I call Macy's. After being transferred a few times, I get a kindly manager who gives me some disappointing news: Kitty Jacovino worked from one to nine on Monday.

SATURDAY
12:30 P.M.

CALABRESE'S BROOKLYN neighborhood is a carbon copy of itself. Two family houses with tiny front yards and narrow driveways.

I pull up behind a shiny new red Javelin. A window curtain flutters when I close the front gate. A loud warbling catches my ear. I look over, and a patrol of brown birds are casually chattering on telephone wires. The birds aren't what holds my attention though—it's the wires. Four lines running into Calabrese's house.

I press the bell, and a serious-faced young officer comes to the door. We enter a large kitchen from the entrance way. The room is clean and neat, smelling of fresh coffee. From the basement door, Calabrese's young daughter appears and looks directly at me. She cheerfully says hello and runs from sight.

Grace Calabrese recognizes me. Her sensitive expression changes to a hesitant smile. "My husband went to the hardware store with his brother, our son, and Officer Donofrio. He should be right back. Lou was tinkering in the basement, and he needed something."

"How do you like your Javelin?"

"Please, sit down. Have some homemade cookies." She's uncomfortable, fidgeting with her hands while speaking with me. "Lou takes the red car to work. I prefer the Buick, it has power everything."

I bite into a cookie with sesame seeds surrounding it. "It must be hard to go about your normal business with these men in your house."

She sits. "It's alright."

"I guess some are old friends of your husband?"

She wraps her hands around her cup. "I guess."

It's evident that their marriage is based on old-world sensibilities and has two distinct aspects—their life together and this unaccountable private life. I doubt if Lou has shared much about his profession with her.

I take another cookie. "Excellent!"

She nods with pride.

"Grace, what kind of car does Lou's brother drive?"

"Jerry drives our old Buick. When Lou bought the new one, he gave the old one to Jerry."

"How old is it?"

"Nineteen seventy-three, I think. It's black too."

"Mommy?" The playful voice comes from one of the other rooms. Grace and I exchange glances before she excuses herself.

I toss the last of the cookie into my mouth. I walk to the basement door and follow the wooden steps into a large family playroom.

No phones are visible. Searching the walls, I find phone lines leading into a small enclosed space. Inside is a small office with a blue trunk and an antique roll top desk. The drawers are all locked. Three phones sit atop the desk. Two are disconnected. None have an identifying number.

I return up the stairs.

The living room is comfortable, full of Italian ceramics and porcelain. The young officer watches from the window. He's solidly built, ex-military I would guess from the way he carries himself.

I approach him. "There are three phones downstairs. Two aren't working. Do you have any idea when they were disconnected?"

"No."

"Have you noticed a 1975 dark blue Chrysler hanging around?"

"No, sir."

"Jot down this plate number, BK 1510."

"What's the connection?"

"It's just a hunch. Pass along the information."

"You want the car stopped or followed?"

"Followed. Here's my card."

He slides the card into his top pocket without looking at it. I pop my head into a few rooms; the house is spotless and orderly.

SATURDAY
1:09 P.M.

CALABRESE'S FACE tightens when he sees me at his kitchen table talking with his wife.

"What's up, D'laska?"

Grace stands. "Coffee, honey? Jerry? Tom?"

Donofrio answers, "I'll have a cup, Grace."

"Soda for me." Jerry opens the refrigerator door.

"I'd like you to take a ride with me," I say to Lou.

"Why?"

"I want to show you something."

He rolls his head and grins in the direction of his brother, Jerry, and one of the officers he requested to protect him, Tom Donofrio, "I'll change." He nods to his wife, and they both leave the kitchen.

Donofrio looks like his file picture. A simple-faced man with heavy features and a forehead that's beginning to slide down his thick nose. Jerry Calabrese is around thirty, about six-two and over two hundred pounds. Full trimmed black beard and a bright twinkle in his dark eyes.

I can sense Donofrio's familiarity with Calabrese's family. He drops his hand on Jerry's shoulder before speaking to me.

"Detective sergeant from Homicide?" He has that superior attitude that binds those who speak before thinking. "Ah, how come you got this instead of Organized Crime?" He dunks his cookie in his coffee and tries to catch the soggy mess in his mouth before it blots to the floor.

I stare at him. "Where's Calabrese's little boy?"

He sighs, putting another cookie in his mouth, spitting some of it out when he starts talking, "Upstairs at his grandmother's."

"Who's up there with him?"

He gives me a spiteful grin, cursing under his breath. Then, as if to prove something to Jerry, he smiles at me. "Uh, the kid's alright!"

Lou Calabrese reenters the room. "What's going on, D'laska?"

Donofrio feels more secure with Calabrese in the room, puffs out his flabby chest, grabs a handful of cookies. A few fall to the floor.

"Goin' upstairs," he says with a mouthful.

Calabrese leans against the sink. Jerry sits at the table. Lou takes a gulp of water, spilling a few drops on his hand. "You have anything to ask my brother?"

Jerry's round, boyish face drains of color.

"How's your car running?"

"What?"

"You have one car, a Buick?"

"Yeah." His voice is weak.

"How's it running?"

"Good." He looks over at his brother.

I sit next to Jerry at the table. "When did you, your father, and brother make arrangements to meet at Barone's gas station? On Sunday?"

Jerry's blank face tries for an appropriate expression but it's too late, He's not a skilled liar. This is all a charade, and Calabrese and I are both aware of it.

Jerry chooses a crooked smile. "Yeah, it was Sunday night, my brother called me after dinner."

"On Monday, did you and your father ride in your car?"

"Yeah."

"You came into Brooklyn, got your father, and then were you meeting or picking up your brother?"

His face screws up. "What's the difference?"

"Just answer."

"Yeah, my father and I were meeting my brother, then we were going to Monticello."

"Did you have a full tank of gas?"

He looks bewildered. "What?"

"If you were driving to Monticello, did you stop to get gas before coming to meet your brother?"

"No, I didn't get gas."

"Lou was going to drive then?"

His eyes search his brother's face behind me. "We hadn't decided. I think so."

Lou Calabrese walks behind his brother and rests his hands on the back of his chair. "That's it?"

"One question for you. When you went back to the gas station, to pick up your car around one in the morning, how much did you owe Barone?"

He lets out a laugh. "I don't remember."

"Do you remember, when you pulled in, where your gas gauge was?"

"No! No, I don't."

I run my hand through my hair as if confused. "Well, if you were going to meet at a service station, and you were gassing up, I assume you were the one who was going to drive. So, I figure your gas gauge had to be about half before you'd buy more. But I'm curious how you knew when you decided earlier to meet that you'd need to gas up. A dirty filling station is a strange place to meet. I would have arranged to meet at a coffee shop or a bar. I hate the smell of fumes on a hot, muggy day."

Lou Calabrese shakes his head. "See, Jerry, this is an educated cop at work. Worried about gas tanks, gas fumes, meeting places, and whether I pay my bills. Goddamn impressive, isn't it?"

Grace enters and kisses her husband on the cheek before we leave. Outside, the sun shines brightly in a nearly cloudless sky.

SATURDAY
2:15 P.M.

Calabrese yells at me, "The car impound! What are we doing here?"

I answer sarcastically, "Solving mysteries."

The duty policewoman and I wait patiently for Calabrese to approach the desk. She hands Calabrese a plastic bag containing the contents from the Toronado's interior. He snatches the bag and drops it on the counter. "What am I supposed to deduce from this?"

I pick it up. "I want you to be aware of a few items. This loose change was inside the center ashtray, a Marlboro box with five cigarettes missing. All the cigarettes are dry and stale. The box also contains two joints. It was inside the dividing console, along with cassettes and racing forms. Sports sections from numerous newspapers were also found folded on the floor in the back. A nail file was found under the passenger seat. All the ashtrays were empty, except on the passenger's side, which had this half joint tucked between the holder and the rim of the tray. There were more belongings in the glove compartment, and, of course, the black gun, which was found under Nick Piantini's seat."

The policewoman hands me Nickie Piantini's car keys.

"Let's go outside," I say.

We walk along the cracked blacktop like we aren't together, past rows of cars parked on either side.

"Do you gamble, Lou?"

Unaware I've stopped, he swaggers past Nick Piantini's Oldsmobile.

"Hey, Lou." I hand him the keys. "Start it up." We stand facing each other under the hot sun. He spits on the ground. "Why?"

"Just do what I ask, please."

"You're getting on my nerves."

"Just turn the key?"

Calabrese leans inside the car, puts the key into the ignition, and starts up the car. Loud Latin music flows as Calabrese flinches away.

I smile and say, "If you're a bookie, and there's a baseball game along with horse races at three tracks, would you be listening to this Spanish station? There were six cassettes in that bag back at the desk, all rock and roll. Pull free the one that's sticking out from the radio."

Barely keeping a lid on his temper, he pitches it to me. I catch it and toss it back. The cassette tape hits his arm and falls to the ground.

Aggravated, but determined, I bend forward to pick up the cassette, presenting it for him to read. "It's Frankie Valli!"

Pushing me aside, he attempts to walk away.

Without hesitation, I turn him around by the shoulder. "Wait!"

Glaring at me, he clenches his fists.

I ignore his hostile manner. "Nick Piantini's car was towed here from the hospital. Nobody has touched that radio dial. Nobody! An Italian listening to a Latin radio station? Extremely unlikely—listening to an Italian icon from New Jersey? Absolutely. Now add everything up: Spanish music, nail file, and half a joint on the passenger's side. We have just given your story credibility."

Calabrese approaches me like an anxious panther about to pounce. His head twists from side to side.

I continue, "There was a second person in this car. A second person who changed the channel as soon as Nicholas Piantini jumped out of the car. A simple reflex, changing the station. Tito Garcia did just that when Nickie left."

"And I already identified Tito Garcia."

White sunlight roars down. There's glaring light reflecting from rows of chrome and metal bouncing at us from all directions. We bake for a few more moments before I walk back to the impound center.

Ten minutes later, Calabrese joins me.

He asks, "Where to now?"

I slowly roll up Ivy toward Vermont.

I leave the car running about two car lengths from the corner, blocking any would-be traffic on Ivy. I tell Calabrese to reenact all the events that took place on Monday.

He describes the details precisely as he had before. When he finishes, I blast the radio and hand him a pad.

"Stand across the street on the sidewalk. Watch the windows in the apartment building behind me. Note any movement. I'll do the same for your side."

His voice is strained, "D'laska, there's something wrong with you. You're not a cop you're a... I don't know what you are."

A car stops behind mine. A horn sounds, again, then again. The driver begins to shout. The apartment windows have some movement, not anything distinct, shades fluttering, the rippling of a curtain. The horn is in sync with the driver's aggravated shouting. Kids run up the block toward us. A second car pulls up. People from the laundromat press their faces and hands against the large yellowed window. Another vehicle arrives. Horns, shouts, music, dogs barking, kids hollering, tension tingles in the air. Dark slices of life are now visible at the windows. The attendant pumping gas at Barone's across the street switches hands to get a better angle. An old man shades both his eyes to see the commotion while walking past. Mothers with babies appear on stoops.

A hulking fat man from the third car begins to walk my way. "Hey asshole, move your fuckin' car before I do." Calabrese begins to respond. I remain still, jotting notes on my pad. The lanky black man from the first car joins the fat guy. "Hey, asshole!"

They come toward me their fists clenched and shouting more obscenities. The woman from the second car opens her door. "Ya jerk!"

Two kids run to my car and begin to dance, fueling the carnival atmosphere. Calabrese runs around the first car. His badge stops the two angry drivers in stride. They swear as he directs them to their cars.

A seething Calabrese comes toward me. The kids back off, though more have gathered. "D'laska, what are you doing?"

"Solving a mystery!"

We drive across the street into Barone's gas station. I look over at him with a cool smile. "I have to make a phone call."

He shakes his head in disbelief. "You want me to join you to see if anyone can identify me?"

"I'll be right out."

No one is inside the station. On the glass counter next to the register is a green ledger. I scan the bays where mechanics are busy. I don't see Barone, and the other attendant is at the pumps. I flip through the pages quickly. July, nothing. My eyes run down the lines. June, Calabrese! Calabrese. Four plate numbers are scribbled above the name. June account, fifty-six dollars, and twenty cents. I stare at the black numbers between the green lines. The last entry is in pencil for June thirty, seven dollars. Barone's voice wafts through the air, getting louder. I close the book as he enters the room. He doesn't look like he's happy to see me. He places the book under the counter. I nod at him. "Need to use your phone."

He doesn't say a word, just looks out the window.

An emergency dispatcher comes on the line, and I respond. "Hello, this is D'laska, Homicide. I need copies of all calls reporting an incident at the corner of Vermont and Ivy in the last ten minutes. Vermont and Ivy. I'll pick those up later today."

I walk out into the hot, hazy sunlight, I stretch my hands up to the sky. My fingers become transparent pink.

Poking my head in the car window, I ask a bored Calabrese, "Seven dollars sound about what you paid Barone on Monday?"

"What's the point?"

"The truth is the point."

He says, "Why the bullshit on the corner?"

"I'm tracking down that Pontiac you saw."

"Why are you a cop?"

"Change the world!"

It starts with a grin, breaks into a chuckle, and the more he thinks about it, the louder his laugh gets. I join him.

SATURDAY
3:49 P.M.

CALABRESE and I walk up the steps to his house. Donofrio is at the table eating a sandwich, mayonnaise oozing from the bread. Grace kisses her husband. I move toward the basement door.
 I catch Calabrese's attention. "Where are you going, D'laska?"
 "Let's talk downstairs."
 Donofrio says loudly, "I'll meet you guys in a minute."
 "You're doing fine guarding the table."
 He glares at me.
 Calabrese leads us into the basement. We sit across from each other at a long table. He pours red wine into two glasses. He takes a gulp. "I'm listening, but I want you to know, I don't give a shit what you say."
 I take a sip of wine. "The day of the shooting, you were driving your little red Javelin. It doesn't carry much, and it's uncomfortable, especially for two big men like your father and brother. I would say your father is an impatient man. Not someone who would enjoy sitting in traffic for two hours to get out of the city then ride another hour or so to Monticello.
 "I did some checking. Your brother works mornings and attends brokerage classes in the afternoon. He would have to skip class. I ask myself why three men would open a summer home on a day that's an inconvenience for all of them and not bring any furnishings, groceries, nothing you would assume would be needed. I ask myself, what were you going to do there? Meet at four, get there at seven. What's the purpose? This house is spotless. I'll bet your wife would prefer to clean your Monticello home before moving in."
 I rub the glass between my palms and give him a moment to think before I continue. If I'm rattling Calabrese, it's not showing. An arrogant grin is glued on his face.
 "When I was up there at Monticello, I noticed the shrubbery had

been trimmed recently, and the lawn was cut. Opening conveys work to me: taking down shutters, putting up screens, hosing down the exterior, cleaning gutters, maybe some touch-up painting. I noticed a pool in the backyard. That must take a day to clean alone. Inside that house, it would probably take a meticulous woman, like your wife, a week to get everything cleaned and in order. Monday, you were going to open it up, but you didn't. Curious on Wednesday you're living in a warm, clean, comfortable home."

He says, "I hired someone to clean the joint. I can show you the receipt if you want."

I ignore the lie, and continue, "Barone told me your key ring has a Giants logo. When we drove together from Monticello, your keys were not on a Giants ring. That got me thinking. You usually use your Javelin for work and leave the big Buick at home. Odd that Barone would remember your key ring and not how much you owed him. Strange you don't remember how much gas you put in your car that day." I pause. "How am I doing so far?"

"Just great." His expression fills with patronizing boredom. "You got Barone and me old friends. Please continue."

I plant my elbows on the table. "This part has nothing to do with gas. It has to do with intelligent police work. I'm going to take the notes we jotted down on the corner a little while ago, along with the reported nine-one-ones from the commotion we created and match them with the nine-one-ones at the time of the shooting. Then we should be close to either a witness or a license plate number for the second car, maybe both."

Calabrese's sarcasm spills out, "You're quite a thinker!" He takes a long gulp of wine. "Anything else?"

"You were absolutely right. Garcia was the second man in Nick Piantini's car, but you weren't at Barone's to meet your father and brother. That's pure bullshit. You've been to that gas station before. You and Barone are linked in some way, and I'm going to find out how."

"Fascinating."

"Calabrese, your life is unraveling. You have numerous skeletons in your crowded closet. I'm continuously tripping over them, and I don't like that. In fact, every time I turn around, I find something out about you I don't like."

He stares at me. "Know what I think about your little analysis, Mr. Criminal Psychologist? Cops." He pauses. "Cops have something inside them. Something which makes them stand out. They're privileged. They have pride. You may have smarts, but you don't have balls."

I look directly into his eyes. "I have balls enough to ask you again, what were you doing in Manhattan?"

"I was meeting my brother and my father. We were going upstate to Monticello. And all your college insight can't disprove that." Calabrese spits in a sewer grating. "If you're not going to read me my rights, get out of here."

"A contract out on your life and you play tough guy."

Calabrese's face lights with self-importance. "I have no problem throwing you out of my house." He does his exaggerated Italian swagger to a battered basement door, pulling it open. Sunlight rushes in. "Goodbye."

I face him. "You are far from innocent!"

Thin clouds have appeared. I feel like I'm stuck in a black void asking questions in a foreign language nobody can hear.

SATURDAY
6:04 P.M.

IN MY OFFICE, I rifle through my messages: call Ainsworth in Montreal, I'll do that. Roberts wants a status check. Screw him, screw Ring. Interesting, Isserlyn called. Screwing her, that's a thought. Mulvaney called twice.

I decide not to call anybody but my partner. The rest can wait until tomorrow.

I received copies of all 911s reported today and the complete record for Monday, June thirty. Going through tapes is tedious.

Hundreds of calls are recorded hourly. The shooting produced twenty-six calls. The second car is always identified as a Chevy, not a Pontiac like Calabrese described. The license plate is given five times with three different sets of numbers. Three elderly voices called in more than once within five minutes. All the stories describe what happened after the shooting—none before. Nobody reported what Calabrese alleges caused him to respond. No report confirms that Nicholas Piantini was shouting into the Chevy. Seven nine-one-ones called in today were by people who responded on Monday; three by the same individuals who called more than once. I know people in that neighborhood sit at the edge of their windows and watch the street from the narrow space along the shade. Someone in one of those windows on Ivy saw everything.

Suzanne left me two notes. The first is official: *The files you requested will be ready tomorrow at Organized Crime.* The second sheet is handwritten: *The papers authorizing Nicholas Piantini's gun to be released are typed but without a signature. If the meal and the company are satisfactory, I'll sign it later.*

I fan the papers wondering why I asked her to dinner.

SATURDAY
8:01 P.M.

WATER DRIPS from my hair as I dry it. My bedroom is strewn with clothes. I can't decide what to wear. I feel clumsy. Cologne spills down my arms.

The telephone slips from my wet hand once, twice.

Finally, I dial the right numbers.

"Hello."

"Suzanne. Mike. Sorry, I'll be there in thirty minutes, okay?"

"Fine, I had a feeling you'd be late. I'll wait downstairs in the hall so you won't have to search for a parking space."

I guess I should wear a tie. How about dark slacks and a pullover?

No! Blue striped oxford, black pants, and no tie. My favorite sports jacket has stains on the sleeve. The gray herringbone should be given to the Goodwill—it's that old. There it is, at the back of the closet—perfect for a night out in Little Italy. My black, pin-striped suit and red pocket handkerchief.

Why am I so nervous? This isn't a date. But I am attracted to her. I scan my dresser mirror. Toilet paper sticks to my chin where I cut myself shaving. I'm covered with moisture. Who cares what this woman thinks? In the cupboard behind the dusty box of Quaker Oats is a bottle of Smirnoff. I take a mouthful. Now I'm close to ready for Suzanne Baxter.

SATURDAY
9:15 P.M.

FAT SAM'S doesn't take reservations, so Suzanne and I wait at the crowded bar. It's a sizeable, noisy room, cramped with small tables. Plastic grapes and sepia photographs of stern-faced Italians decorate the walls. An army of employees wearing black and white slither through the restaurant. Italian spices tempt our nostrils and remind us how hungry we are. The room is a collage of movement: people, tables, mouths, glasses, chairs, arms, all moving without regard. I'm pressed into the corner of the bar; she's cramped beside me, leaning against a street map of Palermo.

Suzanne's oval face is close to mine. Her skin is cream over sharp crystal. She's all pointed edges, coated smooth like a cubist sculpture dipped in white butterscotch. When she parts her thin, pale lips, her crooked tooth appears. I doubt Suzanne could be intimate while her icy green eyes are open. They're too clear, too remote to view anything with emotion.

She's aware of the glances coming her way as we're shown to our table.

"I almost forgot this is business," she says. "What should I be watching for?"

"Just enjoy yourself."

The place is a mix of families, couples, old timers, tourists, and locals. It looks like an Italian wedding where everyone is related.

Suzanne tenderly taps my folded hands. "I'm not an ornament, so don't use me as one. What should I be watching?"

"I'm not anticipating anything in particular. Maybe just a second surprise. Enjoying sitting across from you is the first."

She purses her lips and wrinkles her nose.

The portions are large, and the food is exceptional. My only suggestion is to upgrade the music from Mantovani to Sinatra.

Suzanne and I adapt, but we're not complete.

"Where to next?" her tone is playful.

"Someplace quiet and intimate. Pieri's!"

When I ask for the check, the waitress politely tells me it's already been paid.

"What?" I look around, and everything is the same, people eating, people serving people, people drinking, and people in a rhythm of motion. "Who?"

Suzanne's smile vanishes. The bewildered waitress eases from our table and walks away quickly.

"Wait! Who paid for this?" The customers in the immediate vicinity stare. Suzanne bows her head.

I leap up to follow the waitress. She stops and talks with a table of customers. I anxiously wait a few feet away. She notices my approach and comes toward me. Her voice is a whisper above the restaurant noise.

"A man about half hour ago gave me fifty dollars. He told me not to expect a tip from you 'cause 'you're a cop.'"

"What did he look like?"

"I can't just stand here. I've got customers."

"I *am* a cop. What did he look like?"

She scurries away, and I follow. She disappears behind swinging doors. My hand goes to push open the door.

"Excuse me, is there a problem?" The voice comes from behind me. It's tough, yet warm. A man over two hundred eighty pounds with light brown eyes grins at me. "I own the joint. Please, move away from my kitchen, or they'll run you over."

Fat Sam has his hand out for me to shake. The waitress, comes through the door, avoiding me and turns to him.

He asks, "Do you need her?"

I become aware of my surroundings. "I'm sorry. May I buy you a drink?"

Fat Sam's voice turns soft and friendly, "Let me buy you one. Mind if I join you at your table."

While we walk back to Suzanne, I search for a familiar face. I bump into a busboy clearing the table. All I can hear are restaurant noises, dishes, silverware, glasses, chatter, and laughter. All the faces have a common aspect now. I'm trying too hard. Why pick up a check? A warning? A message? I've got to call Calabrese's house. I excuse myself, pointing out our table and telling Fat Sam I'll join him in a minute. I jockey about to the phones. I've got to slow my thoughts. Think more clearly. Premature action always results in apologies. Who am I a threat to? Have I put Suzanne in danger? No, this is some type of signal for me personally. I return the receiver to its cradle. As of this moment I have had no confrontations. All I have done is to compile information. This is a gesture directed to me. I walk back to the table.

Fat Sam looks comfortable talking with Suzanne. "Welcome back. Your girl is very charming, and I think she likes me."

He has a rolling laugh like a department store Santa.

Suzanne takes hold of my wrist. "Everything okay?"

"Sure. Fat Sam, I need a small favor."

"Just ask."

"I'd like to speak with our waitress."

He doesn't flinch; his softball face stays full of hospitality. "Sweetie get over here."

She approaches sheepishly.

Fat Sam rubs his big belly. "Three Sambucas and coffee. When you get back, Detective D'laska wants to ask you a few questions."

When she returns her young face is pale. She stands behind Fat Sam with her hand under his on his shoulder.

I ask, "Was he old, young, dark hair, light hair, attractive, Latin, Italian?"

She looks down at the floor.

Fat Sam pats her hand. "Tell him what he wants to know. Don't worry about it. Come, on girl."

"A handsome Italian man."

"Describe him."

"Tall."

"Go on."

"Light brown hair, nice clothes."

"What color shirt."

"White, silky white."

"Thin, round, or flat face?"

"Handsome. Can I go now?"

"Alone?"

"I don't know. He came from the bar I think."

Fat Sam dismisses her, and we all drink a toast. Suzanne's face blossoms into light reds and soft pinks. Her lips glisten as she gasps to catch her breath.

Fat Sam chuckles as he holds his stomach while wiping his wet forehead. The restaurant catches up with his laughter, looking our way, pointing forks and nodding their heads.

We stand, Fat Sam pecks Suzanne on the cheek and shakes my hand. "Next time, I will personally make you the best fettuccine alfredo you have ever tasted."

Outside, the humid evening air sticks to us. Suzanne puts her arm through mine while we walk down the crowded street. Saturday night in Little Italy is a thoroughfare of impatient pedestrians wandering in all directions.

"Do you want me to take you home?" I ask.

"No, I'm in for the whole program. Where next?" She presses herself against me to avoid couples walking past. I feel her beneath the dress; she's soft and hard at the same time.

People with loud voices race along the sidewalk trying to avoid the trash spilling over.

A bulging tuxedo-clad bouncer opens the door for us to enter Pieri's Lounge. It takes a moment for my eyes to adjust to the darkness. The bar is traced in the faint orange light. I have my hands-on Suzanne's waist as we both sink into the carpet. Serious-faced men are scattered at the bar. Thin silver strips of metal delicately outline booths across the room, but I can't make out if they're occupied.

I order. "Smirnoff on the rocks, with a wedge and light Bacardi and soda for the lady."

Wes Montgomery fills the room, and a very polite, male-model-type bartender sets down our drinks. Suzanne and I touch glasses.

"To the rest of the evening," I say.

We taste our drinks.

She finds the lime in her drink and twists the citrus into the liquid. "Who bought us dinner?"

Our faces are close; I attempt to kiss her.

Suzanne's eyes flash *no* in ice-cold terms as her hand darts to block my face. "Don't! I don't want to spend the rest of the evening with someone questioning whether he'll be getting laid later."

I feel that ridiculous helplessness after an embarrassing faux pas. "I'm sorry, I just..."

She self-consciously leans toward me. "Come here." Our lips touch lightly. It's quick and indifferent, like kissing a relative. She sips her drink. "Now, what's going on?"

"It's ten-thirty, two more stops, one business, one pleasure and..." I lower my voice, "I'm not going to explain a thing to you in here.

"Enjoy your drink," I say. "Look and listen. Bars are notorious for picking up information."

"Does that mean you're not going to pay attention to me?"

"I have a game. I bet you can't name the seven dwarfs."

She stares blankly at me. "I'd rather kiss you again."

This time there are tongues, mine at least. Very pleasant.

In the dim bar light, Suzanne's face is all fragile glass.

The place fills. As patrons enter, diamonds and gold sparkle then quickly disappear into the darkness.

Suzanne and I have another drink. "What are you thinking?" she says.

"Two things: one, funny how acute your hearing becomes when you fully concentrate and two, I think you're lovely."

We finish our drinks. Suzanne kisses me; it has promise. Her tongue rests while mine sponges the rum from her mouth.

SATURDAY
11:20 P.M.

"MICHAEL, you've got to be kidding," she says.

Marlowe's is for the non-claustrophobic. It's a reflection of the stalled traffic and condensed neighborhood. Waves of bodies elbow to make room where there is none. People occupy every tile on the floor. Drinks are carried so close they're impossible to tilt without hitting someone. Suzanne keeps her lips pursed while we edge slowly across the room to the back of the club. Her hand is on my shoulder, my hand is over hers. The music slams into the crowd from every direction and bounces off the walls, attacking again.

She sticks her mouth in my ear when we stop. "Every friggin' guy in here has felt more of me in the last minute than you have all evening. I hate these places."

"Wait here, I'll squirm to the bar."

The bartender's pupils are larger than half-dollars. His body is in constant motion, mixing, ringing the register, and attending to selective screams. Directly down the bar is Claudio, wearing a silky white shirt. He's surrounded by adoring women, carefree loud Italians, and cautious Cubans. The bar area before them is a large cluster of drinks, cigarettes, shot glasses, and money. I've seen enough. It's time to shed Saturday night in Little Italy.

Outside, Suzanne shakes her head. "Thank you. That place was horrible."

I hold my car door open, our faces become close again, kissing close, but I sense her displeasure if I should try.

After a few blocks, I turn toward her. "While we're driving, let me explain what I've gathered because at the next spot I want to forget about everything except enjoying ourselves."

Suzanne crosses her legs toward me. "Deal, as long as the next place isn't like the last."

"This is my theory. The dinner was bought by a hood named Cellini, to intimidate me. Fat Sam stayed at our table to advertise us." I pat her knee. "Pieri's is the perfect rendezvous spot. The conversations were in whispers and what little I did overhear is hard to piece together. Finally, come closer, I have to catch up with the guys in Marlowe's."

She moves as close as a bucket seat provides. "The two guys behind us at Pieri's mentioned that name, Cellini. Who is he?"

"He's an ambitious man who's more important now than when Nickie Piantini was alive. I'll know more tomorrow when I get those reports from Ring. Now, are you ready for the blues?"

"What does Cellini have to do with Calabrese?"

"Aside from being Italian? I don't know yet."

SUNDAY
12:09 A.M.

It sounds exactly like I remember: gritty, brash, from tight guitar strings. The blues crawls inside your soul. Colored lights splash the band on stage, leaving the tables in darkness. I caress Suzanne, playing her according to the lead guitarist. She feels me negotiating and doesn't hinder my predictable movements.

The band breaks. Suzanne relaxes and rests her back against me.

"Enjoying yourself?"

"Both you and the band are playing very well."

"Do you want to sit through another set?" I remain as stoic as I can in expectation of her answer.

She whispers, "Not especially?"

"Shall we hit another spot?"

"I don't think we need to, do you?"

SUNDAY
1:15 A.M.

Her apartment is white and orderly, uncluttered and very tasteful. A large bookcase hugs a wall. The proper number of glossy art magazines rest on a glass coffee table. She hands me a cognac, we tap glasses, and she offers me one of the huge white pillows on the thick light green carpet.

"I don't see a television," I say.

"In the spare bedroom. I try to avoid it."

"How do you spend your evenings?"

"Do you know anything about art?"

"I know what I like."

Her face brightens. "I like colors that slice a canvas. Colors that jolt. Colors that dissolve all your petty thoughts and create a cold neon flash of clarity. I cherish that big canvas above the stereo. Black lashes on a large white background slapped hard with a thick, texturized, red streak. I love slashing colors, don't you?"

I grin that stupid grin of polite but utter incomprehension.

"Colors that stab and cut, slash and pierce are like a catalyst, triggering deep, hungry emotions inside me. Art is my entertainment."

I point to it. "Is it famous?"

She turns her head in my lap, looking up. I can smell her flesh through the clothes. "Only to me. I went to a private art school in San Francisco for more than four years, but I never finished. Do you know who Franz Marc is?"

"Does he do beer commercials?"

She slowly rolls away from me. "Give me your hand, I'll show you my favorite artist's work." She leads me the few steps into her bedroom and flicks the light switch.

Bold strength is captured above her bed. A powerfully muscled silver-blue horse commands attention on yellow, among determined mounds of reds, greens, and browns. The blue horse, with bowed head, has a presence, a strong, controlling charisma. Bleeding colors lyrically spill him in un-corralled desolation. The solitary horse a vibrant statement of forceful independence.

She is prepared for my move. Though the embrace is close, I can't seem to fit her into me. Our fingers fumble, running into cloth, buttons, and zippers. We clumsily palm flesh we wish to be gentler with. I pull her closer and feel her breasts compressing into me. My nostrils inhale her; she is tightly in my arms, yet she feels remote. We quickly strip ourselves, ignoring the awkwardness of viewing each other, pretending we're not thinking how absurd this ritual is. I watch her long white legs step away from her black panties. We devour that final second of approval, our eyes filling with anticipation.

The blue horse dissolves with the light, but I still sense its presence. She twists and maneuvers with me. Large and full, I press her breasts into my face. She is everything I have ever craved. I feel her seeping into me. She is beautiful flesh poured over alabaster.

My mouth travels from her lips to her breasts, down her stomach to just above where I want to be, I linger with kisses, my head looks upward, green eyes look down at me. She lifts her thighs up for me to indulge, and I do. I am exactly where I want to be, doing exactly what I am doing. She is warm and complicit. Her legs spread wider, and her hand finds my head when I find the spot she is willing to let me explore. I feel her eyes on me, the hunter as prey. Her leg swings over my head, and she is on hands and knees before me. One must embrace temptation to become gluttonous. If this is a danger and I'm a fool, I am a willing one. My mouth makes its way to where it was, she seems more ambitious now, more a participant and I hate knowing that she knows I am enjoying myself. I am covered by her, and I can't get enough. We find a rhythm, but suddenly she tightens and rolls to her back.

I back away, stand, and gulp whatever was in the glass beside her bed.

She gives me a grin. "Need a chaser eh? Hand me the glass." She takes a long gulp and hands it back to me. She can see how hard I have become but makes no move to touch me.

Suzanne gets comfortable on the bed once more while eyeing me. She's all white flesh that I'm devouring. As I attempt to lay on top of her, she pushes me on my back and straddles me. I am inside her, this isn't a sprint, it is Suzanne imagining herself in a pastoral landscape. Like riders on a carousel, we go up and down.

I'm the instrument, and she's the performer. I raise my hands to her breasts and play with the nipples. When I attempt to bring her close to kiss she ignores the advance. Her fingers dig into my upper chest. I have no idea if this is pain or pleasure. I only know I want more of her, more than she can ever give. She moves faster, twisting and gyrating, my excitement peaks. I want to hold myself, but that is impossible. I neither sigh nor say a word as she feels me emptying.

"Don't move." She says as she tries to bring herself across the edge, but it doesn't happen.

Suzanne rolls off me and the white sheet comes up to cover what's below our waists. I attempt a kiss, but she turns her head and my lips slide across her warm cheek.

At the click, light condemns us. I try to avoid her eyes. "I'm sorry you didn't climax." It's a lonely statement.

"Men are predictable." Her tone is matter-of-fact. I'm another casual attraction tried and discarded.

I dig for my voice. "Mind if I get something to drink?"

She holds my arm for a moment, first tenderly then adding more pressure. "Wait!" she says, "Gently bite my nipples."

Suzanne lifts the cover to expose her lower body. She holds my neck tightly, away from the two images in the mirror. Her sharp fingernails crawl along my shoulders then I sense them slipping inside herself. I feel her probing.

There is no longer a pretense of a sexual unit. I had mine, now she is delivering hers. I grab her breasts and squeeze them hard as I run my teeth over her nipples. "Harder," she commands. Her hand moves quicker. I can feel the vibrations from her body. She creates a feverish rhythm with herself. As her whole body tightens then shudders, a long moan follows. She is still for the moment.

I feel Suzanne's fingers moving inside once more, then they crawl slowly along my back, my face, then into my mouth. "Thought you would like to know what it tastes like."

I roll away and put my feet on the hardwood floor. I feel the flush in my cheeks and a concrete sense of impotence turning inward, against myself.

I stand. Stopping to lean against the door frame; I tilt my head toward her. She's enclosed in a tight, icy smile. "You lied to me." Her words permeate like acid. "We were supposed to work together, but we didn't. You used me after I asked you not too." She throws her head back, and her voice grows more contemptuous, "You derived such macho pleasure in condescending to me, fondling me, using me in those bars. All night, till we walked into this bedroom, you held control. How do you enjoy its taste?"

There she is, a white spider on white sheets below a blue horse. It's incredible how ugly a beautiful woman can become. Her face remains contorted. Her arms rest on her spread knees, the space between her legs a reminder of how intense the artwork and the subject remain.

"Very calculating."

She gives a mocking laugh. "You're not a bad lay!"

"I'm sorry, Suzanne?"

She laughs a bit harder. "That's what I love about art—it's never sorry."

"Well, I'm neither art or artistic."

She widens her legs, watching me watch her. "Paint me with your tongue again. I liked that."

"Will that make you any less a bitch?"

Suzanne joins her hands behind her head, pushing her chest out. "I was waiting for that. I prefer the word cunt! I like the sound of that word. It has such power when men use it." Tilting her head, she further admires Franz Marc's creation.

I retort, "The horse is only colored paper."

Now, her laughter really begins. "You're not that dumb!"

I take a step toward the bed, she halts me with a grimace. "What are you trying to prove?"

"I don't like being used."

There is silence, cold silence, like silence after an explosion. I walk into the kitchen and open the fridge door, nothing to drink except skim milk. No thanks. I unscrew the honey jar and take a finger full. I sit in the dark, drumming my fingers on her wooden table. I try to distinguish the fine line between selfishness and understanding. I suck the honey from my finger and realize there are no lines, just degrees of intent, and countless interpretations of that intent. Every word, every action has a bitter, astringent underside.

"Michael!"

The prisoner is summoned.

I step into the bedroom. She's recoiled and beautiful.

Her voice a tool, "I'll make you a deal. You shower first, this way you can leave while I'm in there. Next time, you will treat me as an equal, and there will be no misunderstanding."

"Which is the real Suzanne?"

"Would you like to find out?"

The flawed tooth digs into her lower lip, and her big, green eyes stare at me. I want to shred that obscene painting and become the object of her needs. I stare at the darkness between her legs. It's an excellent view, and I'm a fanciful addict on exhibition. Aren't all men fascinated addicts when it comes to a vagina?

After a shower, I return to the bedroom. Suzanne is still nude, still beautiful, still beneath the blue horse and still in control. Her words pour over me, "You didn't answer my question?"

With her venom racing through me, did she think I could resist? "What's the point?"

"You're a bright man. Figure it out."

"I'm tired of saying I'm sorry."

"Then tell me next time you won't use me."

Silence again. Suzanne closes her legs. A smug, expectant expression glued to her face.

"I want to taste you again," I say, my eyes exploring every inch of her.

Her legs fall open once more; she stares down, then gazes up coyly. "The paper authorizing the release of Piantini's gun is signed."

She comes forward, our lips touch, and I can't resist sliding my finger inside her, feeling her muscles contract. When I break the embrace, I bring my moist finger to the tip of my tongue.

SUNDAY
2:21 A.M.

I TRY to think logically when she closes the door behind me, but all that comes to mind is the thought of being with her again.

I walk to my car running, my finger beneath my nose. I have this notion Suzanne tries to use sex as a vehicle to achieve some kind of artistic triumph.

I feel restless, and there's unfinished business. I need to confirm who bought dinner. Sometimes, things fall into place—there's Mr. Claudio Cellini, in an expensive, silky white shirt opening the door of a racy silver 240Z for an attractive brunette in front of Marlowe's.

CHAPTER 6

SUNDAY, JULY 6, 1975
6:15 P.M.

AT ORGANIZED CRIME, a lieutenant directs me to a cubical within the brightly lit detectives' area. I sit uneasily on the hard chair, ready to go through the files.

The Cubans—Diez and Vasquez are loosely linked with the Gambacorda organization. They are young, active, hard-working soldiers, eager to move up the ladder. Of the two, Diez is more ambitious. They work directly under the organization's focus, unlike Garcia, who Reno probably chose to protect his son.

Next file. Frankie Jacovino is from Queens. He has been in and out of jail his entire life. Recently, he was convicted of armed robbery. Kitty's father is also doing time. It's hard to see any connection with Calabrese. Italian criminals don't encourage their wives to have affairs with married cops while they're in jail. I would bet Kitty's in-laws are in the dark about her seeing Calabrese.

I place my feet against the cubicle desk and lean back, shaking my head. Why would Calabrese get involved with the wife of an alleged cop killer? A cop having an affair with Kitty Jacovino would be like painting a target on yourself. Maybe I just don't understand Italians. Perhaps, I'm not that big of a risk taker.

I can't find the list I requested about the females in I.A. in 1968. I know there weren't many. I begin to pace. It was easy to get the information I wanted about Barone. The trick was to go there when he wasn't around and frighten his help into talking. An accessory to murder charge opens the tightest seam.

When I was there earlier, Barone's nephew pleaded not to mention anything to Barone about showing me the ledger. Calabrese and Barone have been doing business for years. Calabrese owns a so-called courier service in Manhattan. Every Friday between three and four o'clock, his three vans gas up as does Calabrese in his Javelin. Last Friday he didn't show—his drivers were there, but not Calabrese. He showed up on Monday for no reason. The nephew told me Calabrese was in earlier today asking for Barone. When he wasn't in, he called him.

So, Calabrese wasn't at Vermont and Ivy to meet his family or Kitty Jacovino, or to supervise the gassing up of his business vehicles. Why was he there? Am I wrong could this be premeditated murder like every other cop is telling me?

I finger through Cellini's file. From the side window, I can see a red haze silhouetting the skyline as the sun begins its descent. The street is quiet. I gaze back to the open file. Cellini's everything Ring told me—he's come up fast and smart. In three years, he's been in jail overnight just once for suspicion of drug trafficking. Three times in a matter of hours for auto theft and bookmaking. Everything dismissed.

SUNDAY
8:30 P.M.

николай

NO MATTER what brand of draft beer they're serving at any airport, it always tastes like they're pumping it from the nearest urinal.

Ainsworth's plane is thirty minutes late. Leafing through a discarded Sunday paper at the bar, I find three columns on the shooting and the Mafia contract. Calabrese is mentioned by name. His courageous police background is spotlighted as are his numerous citations. The story goes on and on about the drain of money spent to control crime, mentioning the Knapp Commission. Mulvaney's name is singled out, more about injustices to city employees. Questions of who's in control: mobsters or city officials? A lot of the traditional mudslinging. It plays heavily on Reno Piantini' s year of eluding capture, while inside sources say he's hiding in Little Italy. There's rhetoric about a subverted system and so forth.

I toss it on an empty table and order another beer. Ainsworth's voice is loud. "I knew where to find you." We shake hands warmly. I ask, "How was Montreal?"

"All the wedding arrangements have been made. Small and informal."

"How's Clare?"

"Beautiful as ever and wait until you see the maid of honor. Very French, very sexy, and divorced."

SUNDAY

9:15 P.M.

AINSWORTH LISTENS AS I DRIVE, rambling through the whole story from Roberts, Tuesday morning, the Impound Center with Calabrese, Barone's nephew, and finally, the newspaper article.

He soaks up my ranting, my nervousness, my frustration, and he allows me to hear myself. When he knows I'm nearing the end, he runs his slender first finger down his long thin nose. He says, "The Mafia rarely targets anyone who isn't connected to them."

I ask, "Then why isn't he dead?"

Paul smiles. "With people like Gambacorda, two chief inspectors, likely the commissioner, and the Justice Department involved, there are probably secret negotiations taking place."

I shake my head in frustration. "Nothing makes sense. Cops have killed more important mob members than Nicholas Piantini, and there's never been a contract before."

"I know one thing: when the Mafia wants to kill someone, the potential victim usually spends most of his time in church or with the D.A. Something's not right. Calabrese doesn't act like a man whose life is in danger. Yet Gambacorda wouldn't issue a contract just to draw media attention."

Paul faces out the opened window, taking in a deep breath. "Normally in a case, you find out why, and then concentrate on who. The old means, motive, and opportunity come together to give suspects. You've uncovered a sizable amount of suspicious information against Calabrese, but it doesn't seem to have any direct relation to the shooting."

"He is a paradox," I say. "The harder I dig, the less guilty he becomes. Yet he's not an innocent man."

"It's like squeezing a balloon."

There's silence for a minute. Then Paul says, "Suzanne Baxter, huh? She is not my type, I like my women warm and friendly."

It's not something I want to comment on. I brake quickly to miss a trio of scavenging dogs.

Ainsworth fumbles through his bag. "Here, I got this at duty-free." He lays an imperial quart of Russian vodka between us.

"What's the game plan for tomorrow?" he asks.

"In the morning, run down the three sets of plate numbers for the Chevy reported at the scene of the shooting. Second, Calabrese should try to see Barone again. I'll check who's on duty at his house tomorrow. I want you trailing him."

Paul's contemplative for a long moment before speaking. "If Calabrese is innocent, the best thing he has going for him is you. If I discover a motive, I'm burying him fast."

I lean back, not wanting to see the expression on his face. I've viewed it too many times in the last three years. Paul mistrusts his intellect—he depends on his instincts.

Outside his apartment building, Paul leans inside the car window. "You ever been to Montreal?"

"Once for the Canadian Grand Prix. About five years ago. I had fun."

The yellow street light behind Paul silhouettes his head and shoulders. He's lanky, seemingly put together with bones too big and skin too thin. "Yeah, it's a nice town. Clean, provincial, low crime rate. It isn't New York, though."

I give him a friendly smile. "Paul, Clare's a wonderful woman. You're doing the right thing. She'll get used to the city again. Plus, working for the airlines, you've got it made."

He flips his bag over his shoulder, momentarily blocking the light. He nods. "Yeah, I know I could do a lot worse. I could be remarrying my ex."

―――

SUNDAY
11:20 P.M.

My house is messy, and tonight's not the time to clean it up. I relax on the couch. My imagination transports me back to Suzanne's bedroom. I'm tempted to call, then the phone rings.

"D'laska, you really did it this time!" McConnell shouts. "Mulvaney called me yesterday and was on TV today. My office tomorrow at nine sharp."

CHAPTER 7

MONDAY, JULY 7, 1975
7:35 A. M.

THE RING DOESN'T STARTLE me. I've been up for a while listening to the quiet drizzle and mentally rehearsing what I know I'll forget to say later this morning.

"Yeah!"

"Mike. One plate number fits, but it was reported stolen weeks ago."

I ask Paul, "The other two plate numbers didn't pan out?"

"Nope."

"We need to find a witness, then."

"Figure out a way to keep Calabrese home till one o'clock. I've got some digging to do till then."

"Get back to me later."

I bounce my finger on the black nipple and dial the Two-Two. The Desk Sergeant is indifferent about helping. I direct him to have Calabrese remain in the house as Chief McConnell will be calling. He informs me Donofrio is on duty so Calabrese can do as he pleases.

Nothing is exciting in the refrigerator for breakfast. In the freezer, there's a frozen chocolate banana with nuts behind the rock-solid venison that Ainsworth gave me last Thanksgiving. I let the banana thaw while I shower.

MONDAY
8:45 A.M.

QUINCY GIVES ME A MOCKING SMILE. "How much trouble you in, D'laska? We have a pool going, guessing where McConnell is going to assign you next."

I ignore his remarks. "I expect make-sheets today. When they get here, send copies to the Two-Two in Brooklyn."

He wipes the saliva from the corners of his mouth. "If you want to buy more candy, I think I can find an envelope Ainsworth left for you."

My stomach curdles as I toss a ten on the desk.

He gives me a hideous, wet smile. "Twenty dollars, please. You want the chocolate with nuts."

Ainsworth's short note is folded in the motor vehicles report. It merely states: *1) Do not trust anybody. 2) Buy us more time.*

MONDAY
8:50 A.M.

SUZANNE DOESN'T GIVE me much of a greeting when I walk into her office. "They're waiting for you."

"Who?"

"Ring and Mulvaney."

I say, "You never asked Ring for that list of women's names, why?"

She hesitates, then says, "I was told you might request it and not to give it to you."

"From who?"

"Chief McConnell. I remember it was right after he was off the phone with John Gage from the Justice Department."

"It's just a list of names."

Suzanne shakes her head. "You better go in."

"I need your help?"

Her green eyes sear me. "Again, you need my help. Maybe, I need your help. I don't want to lose my job."

"I guess I am expecting too much."

"Yes, you are. This Calabrese case has consumed this office, and now that I've slept with you, it makes matters even more complicated." She moves away and sits at her desk. "Everybody but McConnell wants you removed from this case."

"I don't seem to satisfy anybody."

MONDAY
9:00 A.M.

THE CONVERSATION IS INTERRUPTED as Suzanne leads me into McConnell's office. Perfume and cigarette smoke are prominent in the room. Three chairs are arranged in front of his desk. Ring gives me a waxed grin, and Mulvaney waits for me to introduce myself before shaking my hand.

For some time, we rehash the incident. I'm asked to explain Calabrese's background; every minor infraction is examined. All his commendations and awards are glossed over. Interruptions come at will.

Ring's conversational but directed speech is well orchestrated, emphasizing how Reno Piantini's killing of Mario Zicaro made Gambacorda the most powerful gang lord in New York. Ring gives graphic descriptions of Reno Piantini's criminal history and influence. He concludes with his own credentials of why it might serve all concerned if this assignment was handed over to his department. He is frothing for a public splash, and this case can offer that. I can't trust him, but I will continue to use him if I survive.

Deputy Commissioner Mulvaney, a round woman in her late forties, carrying an extra fifteen pounds in her midsection and rear. Her face is lightly freckled, clean Irish looks with an innocent smile. She nods to each of us. "Gentlemen, I am an expert on the cancer of corruption. These four years, I have spearheaded the campaign to eliminate depravity from the Police Department. I know one cannot review someone's record to find out if he's a bad cop; one has to scrutinize the individual. Cops, like criminals, are clever. We must investigate habits. That is what will reveal true character. Does he have strong moral convictions about God, country, and his family? We all know I have been criticized for my views, but I have never been wrong about people without strong beliefs".

Mulvaney stands as we all lean back. "If Louis Calabrese is guilty, which I believe he is, I think justice should work quickly to show the people we do not allow criminals in police uniforms. The evidence is clearly against this man. We must work together and let justice triumph."

Pleased with her point, Mulvaney pans our plastic smiles for encouragement. "Now, I realize the Police Department is obsessed with protecting their own, and I find that admirable. We must come to terms and admit that being too careful and too protective can cause needless pain."

Mulvaney beams with satisfaction, she waits for Suzanne to set the coffee cups down before she directs her attention to me. "I have also done some investigating into Mr. Calabrese's background." She pauses. "Detective D'laska, in your brief description, you have failed to tell us of his best friend, Officer Gino Guzz...Guzzetta and his family's criminal ties."

McConnell wipes his hand over his mouth. Ring gloats.

Mulvaney shifts her weight from one stocky leg to the other. She makes eye contact with me, then proceeds. "Detective D'laska, you have presented a credible assessment of this officer, but I understand you're a brother in blue, blinded by what you want to see."

Mulvaney's tone is like infested water, sickly warm. "After the shooting, Officer Calabrese was defensive, arrogant, and obstinate. Is that the way an innocent man acts? You see, Mr. Nicholas Piantini was supposed to die at the scene, not in St. Vincent's Hospital." She smugly waits for an acknowledgment.

I say, "Deputy Commissioner Mulvaney, have you ever been involved in a shooting?"

"Of course, not." It's said with pride. She was an excellent choice for a civilian cop.

I place a pencil behind my ear. "Let me give you a sketch, Mrs. Mulvaney—"

"It's Deputy Commissioner."

"Deputy Commissioner Mulvaney, excuse me. Once a gun is fired at another human being, your instinct takes control. Survival overcomes reason. The situation is very traumatic. The after-effects ripple inside your body. Your heart is pounding in your ears, your eyes are burning, and you rerun the shooting over and over in your head. Which scares the hell out of you."

I glance at McConnell before continuing. "You didn't just put a stamp on a letter, you fired a gun. You may have just killed somebody. You're a little rattled, somewhat unfocused. Dazed. You begin to understand you're alive and someone else may not be. You have shot, maybe killed, someone. And you better have a good explanation because you could go crazy reasoning with yourself or schizophrenic listening to the shit I've heard you say this morning."

Mulvaney shakes a finger at me. "Don't try that psychology stuff with me."

McConnell roars, "Stop this." There's dead silence. Uncomfortable, self-absorbed moments pass while he composes himself. "Deputy Commissioner Mulvaney, if you've got something to say pertinent to why we're all here, say it." He faces me. "Your disrespect is uncalled for."

Mulvaney composes herself with the air of an exorcist and the sincerity of a politician. "It is evident to all this murder is a calculated move by organized crime to infiltrate the department from within. Calabrese and his partner are traitors. This Guzzetta had to be investigated and judged by a panel before being admitted to the force. His father has been in prison as have other members of his family."

McConnell's tone is tempered. "No one is guilty by association, which goes for both Calabrese and Guzzetta. I understand your zeal, Deputy Commissioner, but from what Mike has related, there is nothing that connects Calabrese to any corruption. Please stick with facts."

Mulvaney's says, "If there was no crime, why was Calabrese obstructing justice by refusing to answer questions? Instead, he called a P.B.A. lawyer, who incidentally, represented him before and happens to be Italian."

She clears her throat and gives us all a warm Irish smile. "Facts sometimes hinder justice, and justice would be better served if Detective D'laska were relieved of this assignment and it was given to Lawrence Ring and his unit."

Mulvaney draws out time by straightening a religious medal that has lost itself in the folds of her blouse. McConnell says, "Deputy Commissioner, I appreciate your interest in this case, but I've spoken with the commissioner at length about this assignment. D'laska stays with this case."

Ring clears his throat. "With all due respect, my department is better equipped to deal with the circumstances of this case."

McConnell is sarcastic. "Circumstances? He's investigating one man. It's called police work. Plain and simple. Your department has no jaw hold on good police work. Now, I want cooperation among the departments. Teamwork isn't a new concept."

A quiet moment passes.

McConnell sighs. "This case remains my responsibility, and I'll handle it appropriately."

Ring is not pleased, and he makes himself heard. "We all know this investigation has been mishandled from the beginning. Why is the head of Patrol leading the investigation? Why isn't a more experienced officer involved?"

It's time to drop a bomb. "I... ah...Chief."

McConnell's looks my way. He is not smiling.

"I've substantiated Officer Calabrese's story."

Ring openly smirks. "Chief McConnell, I'm taking my inquiry over your head."

McConnell reacts bitterly. "Anytime, I'll meet you at the commissioner's office."

"I'll be at the New York attorney general's office."

I take in a breath and proceed. "There was another man in Nicholas Piantini's car, Tito Garcia. That's been confirmed. The second car was a 1975 Chevrolet with two Cuban passengers. We have witnesses who saw the incident unfold. Calabrese is telling the truth."

Ring reacts as if a hammer just landed on his toes. "What witnesses? From where? The apartment buildings? We've talked with those people. This is a farce."

Ring does not close the door behind him when he storms out.

Mulvaney puts a notebook into her large pocketbook. "This is very unfortunate for you, Chief McConnell. I have heard nothing hear today that leads me to believe this officer is innocent, and I am inclined to believe Larry Ring that there is some type of cover-up involved. You will excuse me, but I must see the mayor. I guarantee there will be an investigation into this whole affair and the wrong way it has been handled. Goodbye."

McConnell folds his hands into a prayer gesture and rests his chin on them.

I walk across the room, open a cabinet, and take out a bottle of Irish whiskey along with one glass. I pour my friend and mentor a drink. It is gone immediately.

McConnell rubs the glass between his palms. "What exactly do you have?"

"I have a warrant to pick up Garcia, and I have witnesses."

"Do you have any leads on Garcia?"

"Not yet."

"How about the driver and passenger in the seventy-five Chevy?"

"Paul's working on that right now."

"You've got shit." He takes in a deep breath. "This case is yours because I thought you could handle it. With your insight, I thought you could cut across the crap and answer the one basic question you're avoiding. I need an answer, but I'll take your opinion. You said earlier Calabrese is telling the truth. Does that mean he's innocent?"

The silence hangs heavy. McConnell adds, "I thought so."

I rebound. "It's not that simple."

"You're supposed to be the best. You're supposed to be an expert in deciphering what's pertinent, disregarding the useless, measuring information, and seeing your way clear to the truth. Your reports are sketchy, which means you're either holding back or you have nothing. Don't bullshit me, which is it?"

"I believe Calabrese was telling the truth about Garcia riding with Nickie Piantini. Witnesses will confirm—"

"How close are you?"

"I'm putting the pieces together."

McConnell shuffles through some papers. "Tell me about...Diez and Vasquez?"

"They may have been at the morgue to kill Calabrese on Reno Piantini's orders."

He glances at me. "Have you questioned them?"

"No."

"Why?"

"The contract on Calabrese isn't a secret?"

"We should bring them in for questioning," McConnell says, red-faced.

"No! Reno Piantini isn't going to use them again."

"How do you know?"

"Piantini is going to settle this himself."

McConnell bows his head and closes his eyes. "Talk to me, D'laska."

"I need more time."

McConnell comes around and leans against the edge of his desk.

He waits for me to look up into his small, tired eyes. "I can't keep this train that wants to run down Calabrese detoured forever. If he's clean, prove it fast, then get the hell out of the way. You have no idea what is at stake, especially for you."

"For me? I'm investigating a case you personally selected me for. I didn't understand why then and I am still confused about it. But that's history. Do I have your word—you are one hundred percent truthful with me?"

"Tell me what you have."

"Nicholas Piantini being at Vermont and Ivy had something to do with gambling. I'm sure."

He says, "Neither Ring nor Mulvaney is kidding. What proof do you have?"

I crack a weak smile. "I promise, I won't let you down."

———

Suzanne makes quick and commanding strikes at the typewriter. There's a large manila envelope with McConnell's signature below the Justice Department seal. She hands me a folded piece of paper. "Please don't get caught with those names."

"Don't worry." I place my hand on her shoulder.

She tilts her head to me. "Paul Ainsworth called. You're to meet him at Three Deuces at noon. I don't know if this is important, but Phyllis Bales-Isserlyn wants Chief McConnell..." She notices the light on the phone base. "He may be speaking with her right now."

I remember how Suzanne posed on that bed with her spread legs. I shake the image but not the hunger for more of her. "Thanks, I think you are...are...beautiful."

Her green eyes search my face.

I let out a long sigh. "Oh, I need a complete file on Martin Floriano and Police Officer Gino Guzzetta. Please call Calabrese's house and tell Officer Donofrio that Chief McConnell won't be able to reach Calabrese today."

———

MONDAY
12:05 P.M.

. . .

AINSWORTH SITS at a table against a wall in Three Deuces. Some of Claudio's mob eat lunch several tables away.

Ainsworth pushes a chair out for me. "What happened at the meeting?"

I ease myself down. "Mulvaney and Ring are frothing for my blood, I can handle that, but I know he is holding something back from me. I know it."

"Why wasn't this given to Ring and his crew in the first place?"

"Not important!"

Ainsworth hands me a menu. "I don't have much time. What's good?"

"Steak and dandelions."

He makes a face. "Steak, no weeds."

When the waitress leaves, Ainsworth starts talking, "I questioned the people who identified themselves on the nine-one-one tapes."

"Did you find a witness?"

Ainsworth gives the mob boys a hard look and continues, "On the surface, I struck out; off the record, if we need her, one frightened woman can be pressed to talk."

"Did she substantiate Calabrese's story?"

"Somewhat. Nickie Piantini gunned his car from a parking space, forcing the driver of the Chevy to slam on his brakes. That's what attracted my witness' attention. Funny, Calabrese heard shouting and not brakes squealing."

"Go on."

"Piantini ran to the Chevy, slamming the door on the driver who was about to run. Nick was shouting loudly about money. Get ready to pat yourself on the back. The woman said it sounded like the two men in the Chevy had stolen money from Piantini." Ainsworth pauses. "We both know you don't steal money from someone like Nickie Piantini."

"You're right, Paul. It's stolen like in cheating."

Ainsworth catches the punks stretching their ears to hear our conversation. He stares at them.

"Your witness confirms Calabrese's story?"

Ainsworth says, "No, not really. A neighbor lady knocked on her door. When she got back to the window, Calabrese was backing away from Nickie's car. The shots had already been fired. She saw the beginning, heard the shots, and watched the Toronado speed away."

"Did she see a second person in Piantini's car?"

"She can't be sure."

The waitress sets down our food.

Ainsworth and I catch comments coming from the other table. They're loud at times, talking about how slimy cops are. They amplify their importance and spout their ties to power. Two more men join them; there's six now.

I say, "Nickie Piantini was at that corner to surprise those two Cubans. That means he didn't know exactly where to find them, but he knew where they might be driving. Did anybody you talked with notice how long Piantini was waiting there?"

"No. Do you think the two Cubans in the Chevy helped set up the shooting?"

"They're the key."

Ainsworth nods toward the other table. "Think they can help?"

I pop the heel of my sandwich in my mouth. "Target the non-Italian. His name is Andre."

Ainsworth glances at his watch. "I have to get a magazine to read while waiting for Calabrese to show up at Barone's."

"You ready?" I say.

Ainsworth taps the leg of Andre's chair with his foot. Anxious muttering shuffles through the group. Ainsworth turns Andre's chair to face him. "What's your last name?"

"Who wants to know?"

Heads cock, fists close, and arms are ready to swing. I watch one hand wrap around the neck of a beer bottle. Nervous anxiety spreads like electricity. I clamp a fist around an arm sliding into a pocket. My other hand rests on my gun.

Ainsworth presses his finger into Andre's cheek. "ID, shithead."

"Fuck you."

Andre's chair falls backward. The most muscular of the five leaps up. Ainsworth juts his elbow into his neck sending him against the wall. I swing around, holding Andre's shoulder. Ainsworth chops the muscular guy in the upper chest and throws him into a chair. The men at the table vacillate, wondering whether to react. Footsteps come toward us from behind.

I shout, "Police!"

The barmaid's voice is hostile, "From where?"

"Get back behind the bar."

"You can't just come in here and beat up my customers. I'm making some calls."

I squeeze Andre's neck. "You gotta a last name yet?"

"Fuck you."

Ainsworth lifts Andre by the shirt and presses him against the wall. "Name and ID. And Andre, pal, give me one good reason and you're out the front window." Ainsworth tosses his wallet to me.

"Andre Gabriel." I search further.

Ainsworth says, "How well do you know Sergio Diez?"

Andre flinches but says nothing.

"Where can I find Tito Garcia? You think about it. We'll see you again, very soon."

Ainsworth throws Andre into the table. Glasses and dishes shatter on the floor.

As we walk out, Ainsworth shakes his head. "Not bad."

"Call me at the Innfield Pub after eight."

MONDAY
2:38 P.M.

DOWN THE STREET FROM CONNORS' station, kids bounce a ball against a crumbling warehouse. They play in the condemned remains and listen to loud music from a radio King Kong would have a problem carrying.

I interrupt a sergeant at the counter who's dealing with two dowdy women clamoring in Italian. "Where's Peter Wrobel?"

He shakes a finger above the women. "Back."

I spot Wrobel filling a cup of coffee.

"Wrobel." He turns.

"Remember me, D'laska, Homicide. Talk to you for a moment."

He urges me into a cluttered back office.

I say, "At what time did Calabrese call the P.B.A. Lawyer?"

His mouth opens, and the wheels inside his boyish head begin to turn. He searches, but his face remains blank.

I coax him. "How long a time was it between when Calabrese requested a lawyer till he arrived?"

"Good question. I don't know exactly."

"Calabrese was interrogated intermittently during that day. When he wasn't being questioned, you were watching him. What time did he use the phone?"

Wrobel is handsome and muscular, not a strategist. I take a different route. "Did Calabrese ask you if he could use the phone?"

"No."

"Do you remember him using the phone?"

"I don't think so."

"Were there phones he could use?"

"Yes."

"Did you overhear him say he had to call anybody?"

"I really don't recall."

"What time did the lawyer get there?"

"Around nine."

The door swings open, a granite-faced Connors leers at us.

He shouts, "What the fuck are you doing here again?"

Wrobel's face loses its color.

I ignore the question and ask Connors, "What time did you allow Calabrese to call his P.B.A. lawyer?"

Connors slams the door after Wrobel swiftly leaves. "What are you doing in my precinct?"

"What are you afraid of captain? That Calabrese could be innocent?"

"Mulvaney called me this morning to tell me the mayor is personally transferring you to the Bronx Zoo, you'll be shoveling elephant shit for the rest of your career."

"I am getting used to snakes, but I prefer giraffes; they seem to be above everything."

Connors comes very close. "I told McConnell to keep his lap dog, wop-loving, college parasite's fuckin' face outta here. My men don't got no time to clean up after some dirty cop."

Connors begins to open the door, but I slam it closed. Our faces are so close, his putrid breath stings my nostrils. "Connors, you're a disgrace."

"You wop-lovin' son of a bitch, you listen to me. The bastard's guilty, and tomorrow you'll be wiping those giraffes' asses. Get the fuck out of my way!"

Connors erupts from the office, cursing loudly down the hall. I hear my heart beat through my temples. I arch my head against a clapboard wall and push my hair from my forehead. Timidly, Wrobel shows his face at the door.

I ask, "You said nine o'clock, Wrobel?"

"Yeah. Everything okay?"

I frown, thinking out loud, "It takes at least an hour to get through to the P.B.A. office and another hour to explain why you called. Even if he got a hold of someone immediately, he would still have to clarify why he needed a lawyer. When did he call?"

"What?"

"Nothing. Thanks, Wrobel."

I walk up the stairs to find Olearczyk. He's not pleased to see me. His cheerless eyes skirt to the other detectives in the room. I can tell I've been marked with Internal Affairs red. You know, Ring had a great question this morning. What the fuck *am* I doing here?

"Hi, Flip."

"What can I do for you?" There's little sincerity in his voice.

"Know anything about Andre Gabriel?"

"Don't know him."

We study each other.

"Listen, D'laska," he says. "I told you before, I don't want to get involved. Especially now, with Mulvaney nosing around. You say you're from Homicide, but you ask the same questions I.A. would."

Olearczyk gulps what's left of his coffee. He whispers, "Sources say Calabrese is a good cop. Drop this now before those Irish cocksuckers with easy jobs at headquarters have you up on charges."

I ask, "Mind if I have a seat?"

"Yes! Do you think Nick Piantini arranged to get himself shot just to incriminate Calabrese? Bury it."

"How much has Cellini benefitted from Nickie's death?"

He grumbles, "Cellini has..." he stops, then faces me to finish "...his income and territory have increased, and his future is very bright." He pauses. "Listen, this is the end of the favors. Mulvaney's involved now. I can't afford to lose my job."

I offer him my hand, but he doesn't accept it.

MONDAY
4:50 P.M.

S<small>UZANNE STARES</small> out the window while absently turning a spoon in a container of yogurt. Half of her face is shadowed.

"The files you requested are on your desk." She hesitates a moment, then continues, "Captain Connors called Chief McConnell earlier. He's lodged an official complaint against you. The commissioner and the mayor's office have also called."

"After they called, did McConnell make any calls?"

"Yes, he did, to John Gage and Phyllis Isserlyn."

Some rattling happens inside my head. "Did McConnell then call the commissioner or the mayor's office?"

"Not immediately. I don't know; I was busy."

I whisper, "You're a beautiful woman, Suzanne."

She stares out the rain-streaked windows. I place my hand gently on her shoulder. Her whole-body arches as if being threatened. I touch the nape of her neck with my lips and retreat into my office.

Below the single window is the overflowing dumpster. The wind swirls loose papers into the moist air for the rain to beat down. Calabrese had reason to be nervous and frightened at the hospital.

After Connors cornered and badgered him for answers, Calabrese lost his self-control. He knew he needed to secure his alibi. Calabrese lied to Connors, but he had to build a credible case for his lies. He had to call his brother; his father is too brittle to have understood the subtlety of the situation. Calabrese needed to explain to his brother what to say and where to show up. He required his fabricated story substantiated. I always come back to the same question. What was Calabrese doing in Manhattan? Eliminate that he was meeting his mistress and his business and what's left—to meet someone else, or to kill Nickie Piantini.

I rub my fingers into my temples. When did Calabrese know he was going to need an attorney? A call to a P.B.A. lawyer requires a lengthy explanation. What are the odds he would get the same P.B.A. lawyer who supported him and Gino for excessive violence two years before to defend him? Who called the lawyer?

I open the envelope Suzanne gave me. Here is another loose end of Calabrese's sordid life. It's a short list of I.A. females. Matching places, dates, and Calabrese's preference, one name jumps out, it's maiden Italian and married Jewish. Funny, I have met her, and I'm not surprised. She's assigned to Homicide, just Calabrese's type, earthy looks and glib in a loose way. Her husband's also a cop. Calabrese's affairs all seem to be with women whose husbands carry guns.

I tear the paper to shreds, not exactly knowing what I'm going to do with the information. I despise everything about this case, especially now that I know who McConnell spoke with before he called his immediate superiors. The world may be closing in on me, but I'm too obsessed to care.

MONDAY
7:46 P.M.

. . .

Before I finish my first beer at the Innfield, Britt hands me the phone. Ainsworth says, "Mike! Something's up! Get someone to call Calabrese and keep him on the phone till you can meet me around the corner from his house. Guzzetta is also waiting there."

I throw some bills on the bar. "I'm on my way."

MONDAY
8:16 P.M.

I spot Ainsworth and park a distance away. He picks me up. We circle around and pull over.

I say, "I had the Desk Sergeant call and ask a litany of questions about Calabrese's background. They should be done by now."

"Guzzetta is waiting in front of the house."

"What did you find out today?"

"I trailed Calabrese for three hours around half of lower Manhattan. He went into eleven different office buildings. He never carried anything in or out. I shadowed him into The Lyman Building. He went into some offices and... Wait, Calabrese is ducking into Gino's car. Here we go."

We follow far enough behind to be safe. The light drizzle and gray overcast sky working in our favor.

"Looks like we're heading to Coney Island."

"Degenerate city," Paul says. "When I was young, coming to Coney Island was a major event of the summer. That was before all the hippies and junkies started hanging around. What did you find out on Guzzetta?"

"His father was picked up years ago for bookmaking. His family is still connected. He has relatives who divide their time between jail and social clubs. His cousin, Marty Floriano, is an arrogant, reckless, and very ambitious wise guy. Floriano's best friend is Richie Stone. They're the bad boys of Coney Island. Rumor has it, Floriano and Stone murdered a neighborhood rival. He was found dead in the trunk of a car just outside Long Branch, New Jersey. Stone's arrest record goes back to reform school. Two years ago, he beat a bad battery and armed robbery rap when the only witness disappeared. Last year, Floriano and Stone were picked up for assault. They walked away clean."

Paul's face fills with disgust.

I continue, "Floriano and Stone are under the watch of Gino's uncle, the head of the local construction laborers' union. The uncle operates from the Trenton Avenue Social Club. Floriano and Stone are figured to be connected with extortion, auto theft, and robbery. Probably drugs. They're dangerous because they're hungry for recognition."

"How does this tie in with Calabrese?"

"Who knows?"

Red brake lights appear on Guzzetta's car.

"Slow up," I say.

They park, and we pass the car. From the back window, I can see them going into a dimly lit diner.

"What now?" Paul asks.

"Go in and grab a hot dog."

———

MONDAY
9:25 P.M.

PAUL HURRIES back to the car with his head down to avoid the blowing rain.

I ask, "Well?"

"Henry is in there. They're all in a booth talking about buying and selling real estate. Henry was doing most of the talking, he's very smooth. Then a black guy joined them. Calabrese and Guzzetta are in the restaurant business. They own that diner and a pizzeria on Tribute Street in Brooklyn."

"Are you shitting me?"

"They're selling the diner to the black guy for eighteen thousand."

"There's more. Guzzetta and his cousin Marty are getting into the bar business together. They want Henry to find them a spot near the Union Hall. Here's the last tidbit, with the money from the sale of this diner, Calabrese is buying another apartment building. I don't know how many he owns already."

What does it all mean? Where is the connection that ties this all together?

I look over to Paul. "What's Henry look like?"

"About two hundred fifty pounds, expensive Italian threads. Rolex on one hairy wrist, thick, gold links on the other. Big mother diamond pinky. The three of them look like ginzos all decked out for New Year's Eve in Little Italy."

"What does Calabrese know about the contract on him that I don't? He doesn't act like it bothers him at all."

"I don't like Calabrese, and I don't like what we're finding out. Whether he's innocent or guilty, if we report any of what we're discovering, no other cops will trust us. They'll think we're tied to I.A"

"Finish your earlier story."

Paul's mouth twists. "Calabrese was collecting envelopes in office buildings. White business envelopes with money in them."

Every crime has a flaw. This case is a series of faults running parallel to a singular incident that may be a crime. We sit and stare at the continually changing liquid patterns on the windshield.

Paul is restless. "I've had enough, let's confront them."

"Not yet."

"I'm not sacrificing my career for those two pieces of shit in there."

"If Calabrese isn't worried about Reno Piantini murdering him, do you think he'll be panicky when we confront him?"

"Did you ever think about this: what does he think you're doing?"

I crack a grin. "Calabrese is too cocky to take me that seriously."

"What does he take seriously?"

"Paul," I say thinking as I'm speaking, "if you were Reno Piantini, what would be stopping you from killing your son's murderer?"

"Go on."

"Knowing you were going to kill Calabrese or knowing that not killing him would be beneficial?"

"I'm listening."

"Piantini knows nothing will return his son, so he may be looking at other options."

"Using his kid's death to his advantage."

"Why not?"

Paul points with his chin. "Here they come."

MONDAY
9:45 P.M.

LOU AND GINO emerge from the diner. They wave to Henry as he gets into a big white Caddie.

Gino rolls into light traffic heading deeper into the Italian heart of Coney Island. Pressed between two old vacant wooden structures is a small storefront business. The dark shades are permanently drawn, and there's a faded yellow sign in the window, *Trenton Avenue Club. Members Only*. We watch Calabrese and Guzzetta straighten their suits before entering.

Paul's face sours. "Had enough?"

"Look at it from Calabrese's perspective. He obviously has underworld connections. Maybe he's trying to set up a deal for himself."

Paul hits the dashboard with his fist. "We're not saving Calabrese from Piantini; we're protecting him from Mulvaney and Ring. I can't see doing that any longer."

"I'm only interested in one thing: finding out whether Louis Calabrese committed premeditated murder. Everything else is bullshit."

Ainsworth's jaw tightens. "It's your case."

"If Calabrese is guilty, he could be trying to cut a deal. If he's not guilty, why not set up a meeting with Piantini? We both know that could be arranged in that social club, especially by Gino's uncle."

"That could be suicide."

"I know why Calabrese isn't dead. Reno Piantini is assessing his options. This case continually changes with perspective. Things are loosely connected but not necessarily interwoven. I believe this case is all about deals. Everybody involved has a deal going, everybody except us. We're the hostages, possibly the scapegoats."

"If Reno Piantini kills Calabrese, it's our fault," Paul says. "We didn't protect him. If Calabrese remains alive and guilty, Mulvaney will make sure we're also guilty. If he's innocent of murdering Nickie Piantini but guilty of something else, we'll be the pricks who found that out. Then we're I.A. Let's get a drink."

I face him. "Not yet. We're going to pay a visit to Andre Gabriel."

"Why? He's not going to tell us what kind of deal Piantini's contemplating."

"As long as the truth is unknown, every kind of deal is possible. The truth is the only deal killer."

"What the fuck does that mean?"

I speed, the drizzle flapping off the rain as it splats against the windshield. *Swish, swish* the windshield wipers clear away the view for a moment. I've stumbled onto the underbelly of the law; the element nobody knows for sure, but everybody surmises. The phoniness, the deal-making, the types of knowledge that make your insides convulse. That good and evil are the same concepts wrapped in different snake skins. This is the casual conversation of drinkers in neighborhood bars. Bits of injustices trickle down. We hate believing it's true, but we despise being naive. When we shout for justice, it's always done in a crowd, never alone in front of a mirror because the words would stick in our throat. We all have to believe our reflection doesn't lie.

MONDAY
11:05 P.M.

. . .

Ragged gray clouds choke a dull half-moon. The rain has stopped but the night air remains clammy. Foul odors emanate from sewer grates as we cross the wet street in front of Andre Gabriel's apartment building. The stairwell stinks of old clothes and rotting wood.

Andre Gabriel opens the door of his dingy apartment. His eyes widen like black pits. His naked, well-cut chest tenses. He's wearing slacks opened at the belt and two-inch heels. Ainsworth pushes him into the living room. I snap the lock and set the chain. He cries out while stumbling backward. "What you guys want?"

Ainsworth threatens him with a nasty smile. "Did you give our questions much thought?"

Sweat begins to appear on Andre's face.

Ainsworth asks, "You familiar with the self-exclusive rule?" He points in the direction of the kitchen. Ainsworth jabs two fingers into his neck and Andre stumbles backward into the kitchen.

"Tito Garcia and Sergio Diez?"

Andre's mouth barely moves. "I... want my...lawyer."

"Listen, fuckhead," Ainsworth's says, "we're not here, so you don't need anybody, understood? Who drives a new white Chevy with stolen plates?"

"I... want...my lawyer. I'm a citizen."

Ainsworth forces Andre into a chair. "One more time, start talking."

"Fuck you, pig."

Ainsworth cuffs him tight to the chair, pulls his head back, stuffs a rag in his mouth, cups his chin, and places two forks between his legs and starts to squeeze.

His eyes roll as pain resonates through his body.

I remove the gag. "You ready?"

He shakes his head, sweat streams down his face. "Please, please God!"

I step back. "I'll give you sixty seconds to collect yourself."

I walk into his putrid-smelling bedroom. On his dresser is a round mirror with two long lines of cocaine. Next to the mirror is a half-smoked joint, and inside the top dresser drawer are baggies and ties. Underneath a pile of photos of nude young girls in compromising positions is two ounces of cocaine.

I stroll back into the kitchen where Ainsworth is telling him a cruel story about how boiling water can be poured through a funnel to puncture an eardrum.

I squeeze Andre's jaw. "We're going to play a new game. I'm going to dump some of this expensive cocaine from this big plastic bag into this smaller baggy, then I'm gonna place the bag over your nose, so all that powder covers your nostrils. Every time you try to breathe, that shit will go up your nose and block the passages, and your stomach will begin to convulse. You'll have to puke, but it's going to be difficult with a rag down your throat, and a bag pressed into your face. So, you'll have to swallow it. Your heart will burst soon."

"Wait! We can make a deal."

"Hold him, Paul."

The cocaine builds up, blocking his nostrils. Ainsworth holds his head tighter. I press the bag into his face with my palm. He chokes, writhes, his eyes begin to bulge larger than the sockets that hold them. With an oversized metal spoon, I swat his crotch.

His foul perspiration blends with the dense air to fill the apartment with a pungent odor.

I feel no compassion. I'm a hypocrite, one step beyond control. Some would say this has to be done. A cop does what he has to, mainly to save another cop. It's all rationalization. I'm over the line. I'm as filthy as this pig I'm punishing. I bring the spoon down hard, and Andre Gabriel begins to convulse.

When Gabriel looks two seconds from death, Ainsworth removes the gag and cuffs, then drags him to the sink where he runs cold water over his head.

He wants to cooperate now, gasping wildly for air. He starts rambling in Spanish and English, anything that comes into his head; he mentions the name Filippo numerous times. He just keeps on talking. He thinks he's giving us all he knows. He thinks he's informative, another good Cuban-American helping the cops. He thinks it's over when Paul throws him into a far corner. He thinks it's over when he sees me pocket his drugs. He thinks it's all over. But it has just begun.

I nod to Ainsworth. "Time to leave."

Outside Ainsworth grabs my arm. "I don't understand. Why are we walking away he gave us a lot of shit, and he only sounded half-ass sure of some guy named Filippo? We had him where he would have given us anything we wanted."

"Oh, he still will."

"How?"

"Forget about Andre for now. I'll get what I want from him later."

He gives me a long, concerned look. "I've never seen you act this way."

"They're not fucking us. Not before we have all the information."

We face each other over the car's roof.

I say. "Go into Brooklyn, start at the Blue Chateau. Find out all you can about Floriano and Stone."

"Shouldn't we be trying to find out who this Filippo is?"

"Leave that to me. Let's rendezvous at the Innfield at three."

"Where are you going?"

"To meet Gabriel."

"What!" He steps backward, flinging his arms in the air. "So, you're going back up there?"

"No, I'm going to Marlowe's."

TUESDAY
1:40 A.M.

"IF YA GOT BAD LUCK, bad luck, bad luck..."

The music inside Marlowe's is late-night loud. This crowd is different from Saturday, more elastic, more the same, one large amoeba feeding off itself. Conversations inside conversations, across the bar, around the bar, over the bar. Drunk, laughing, partially drunk, stoned and stiff, stoned and loose. This isn't a night for strangers. I push my way to the bar.

I'm inside a small circle of jewelry and tight, open shirts. This group looks to the bartender, whose job it is to serve me and tell me to move. Smartly dressed, Claudio Cellini is at the opposite end, surrounded by swarthy complexions and attractive young women. The bartender persuades me to move; I'm outside the ring of exaggerated tones and loud voices.

There's a hand on my ass. "Hi!?" She's smiles, "You're new."

"I'm looking for you."

She laughs, stops, then laughs again. She places her arm around my waist and feels the gun under my jacket. The color drains from her face as her arm falls. My expression is concrete.

She asks, "You're a cop, right?"

A large group of men cheerfully parade out of the restroom with nasal problems. I'm in a sewer of piss-heads. A bar full of fuck-ups, proud to be around the trash that keeps them running on the illusion of a charmed life. There are cops in here, too, I can feel them, sponging from the excess, taking a modest share, nothing serious, just a taste.

She taps someone on the shoulder. "Know this cop?"

A stocky figure tilts his head to her ear. "What?"

I face an ugly Italian with one long black eyebrow.

He asks sarcastically. "You a cop?"

"I heard Tito Garcia is in Florida. Thought you might know where?" I'm correcting those answers Andre Gabriel gave me.

The ugly Italian becomes uglier. He calls to the bartender, "Give him a drink." He turns to me. "What's your name, man?"

"Mike."

He can't understand why I'm not following the rules. This conversation isn't supposed to be happening, not in here.

"Two Cubans from the Bronx ever come in here. They're friends of Nickie."

He looks to the waiting bartender, then to me. "What you drinking?"

"Vodka, rocks."

He nods. "Top shelf."

I say with a friendly grin, "They drive a white Chevy."

He sips his scotch. "My cousin is a detective in Lower Manhattan, maybe you know him?"

I continue to correct Andre's information. "What time do the Cubans generally arrive?"

His irritation finally breaks the surface. "There are cops in here, ask them!"

I notice the bartender is at the other end of the bar whispering to Cellini, who grows a broad liquor smile and motions with his chin in my direction.

The ugly Italian turns his back to me. I tap his shoulder. "You never answered my question."

He grimaces over his shoulder. "I'm telling you for your own good, fuck off."

I close my hand over his muscular forearm. "Turn around and step away from the bar."

He has the smirk of a man about to swat a fly.

I tug his arm. "Let's talk over at the back wall."

He squares to me, his amused buddies looking on. I open my jacket slightly, but my gun's not what makes him begin to move. It's something more profound, more threatening. He looks into my eyes and sees nothing—not justice, not compromise, not bravery, but a man capable of anything.

"Listen, buddy, I think you should fold your cards and leave."

"The two Cubans, they gambled with Nickie, maybe on the afternoon he was killed." A hand squeezes down hard on my trapezius muscle, turning me. Two cops flank me. I just know they are. One is dressed in a dark leisure suit and sporting numerous gold chains. The other is wearing a tight tee shirt, his biceps are larger than most waists. Nothing stops me. I take the ugly Italian by his floral polyester and pull him closer.

Biceps grips the back of my neck. "Let's discuss this outside."

The night air has a wet slipperiness. Puffy clouds hide what's left of the moon. We walk to the side of the building. The nearest streetlight is broken. I cautiously step away from them.

I point at the unamused cops. "When your friend answers my

questions, we can all go inside again. I'll buy the round. Maybe all of you know a guy named Filippo?"

Biceps lets out a long sigh, "I am extending a courteousness to you because we're both cops. I don't want to know where you're from, who you know, or what you're doing here. I just want you to leave without making a scene."

If a match is lit, the atmosphere will explode.

"It's a lovely evening, I like this place, and I need to finish my conversation with our Italian friend."

The two cops take the ugly Italian aside. They mumble, gesturing with their hands and spitting at the ground. I become aware of myself, my hands, my arms, my chest, my legs. I'm not nervous. I just need answers.

Biceps approaches me. His voice is alcohol gruff. "As a professional courtesy, I've decided to overlook your rudeness." He looks back to his friends, then continues in a low voice, "First, I'm gonna give you some information. Filippo used to stay over on Prince near Ivy, but he moved back to the Bronx. Second, if you want information about spics, go to a fuckin' spic joint. Now, I'm gonna give you some excellent advice, go back to wherever you fuckin' came from and don't return."

I harden my jaw. "What's Filippo's last name?"

He crosses his arms, putting his hands under his biceps making them even more prominent. "I don't think you're quite getting what I'm saying. Now, good night."

"You figure Garcia's in Florida?"

He gives me an icy grin. "Florida's a good place for spics." He brings up both hands, rests them on my shoulders, then squeezes my trapezius muscle, the pinch brings me to my knees. His grin is now a full smile as he applies more pressure.

They leave me on the sidewalk and with arms around each other walk back into the bar.

After a moment, I walk back into the bar. The music is liquid brain level. The crowd is a little more drunk and obnoxious. I push myself to the center of the bar between two stoned ladies in low cut blouses. The bartender brings me a drink and points to

Biceps. "From your friend, he told me to say you're done for the evening."

I pick up my drink and swirl the clear liquid. I unbutton my jacket for the start of round two. Andre Gabriel, looking half dead and crazed, has arrived.

Cellini listens to Gabriel. He nods; he rises on his toes then extends his hands, stretching his fingers. Cellini's cooked eyes search the people at the bar; they pass me, then crawl back and focus. He finds his drink and raises it to me. He leans over and takes hold of the bartender. The bartender avoids many customer calls and comes to me. He finds a level slightly above the music. "I was told to make an exception and get you a double on Claudio."

"This bar is very friendly," I say with a broad smile.

Cellini is wearing a starched black shirt and a cock-sure grin. Andre is at his side; he's jittery, with nervous eyes and a twitching mouth. He avoids looking my way.

The music blares on, "...Lord, I'm going downtown...I'm just lookin' for some tush...I'm just lookin' for some tush."

The place is a sea of movement, heads bob, the falling crest of the evening. It's the almost-last-call scramble-for-partners time, last-chance romance. Cellini's corner has all the attractive choices. I take my glass and ease myself in his direction.

One of Cellini's dollies scampers between us. She's no neighborhood girl—Long Island is written all over her stoned, blue-blood face. Her lips are curdled and twisting as she goes through her small purse. She cups a little brown bottle. She yelps as I force her hand open by squeezing her wrist. The cocaine vial falls on the bar.

"Who the fuck are you?" she shouts.

Immediately, I'm between my cop friends.

Cellini snaps, "Get him outta here."

The cops keep me sandwiched.

I shout in their faces, "Move!"

Biceps is livid. "You're leaving."

Seemingly, for the moment I acquiesce, the cops relax, and I swiftly move, punching Cellini in the gut. He doubles over. I pull his head back by his hair and lift him by his pants. The immediate vicinity is frozen, stunned. I use him as a shield to push into the crowd toward the exit.

I shout to the doormen, "Open that fuckin' door, or he goes through it." They respond immediately.

I throw Cellini into the trash cans at the side of the building. He jerks up. Snorting through his fixed lips, "You're done, asshole."

Across the back of my neck, there's the stark reality of sharp cold steel slicing. I turn to see Andre Gabriel with a straight razor, dripping with blood. Then the splattering birth of a new sun sets fire to the sky and the night closes in on me.

TUESDAY
4:56 A.M.

SOMEONE SHAKES MY SHOULDER. " Eh, you okay? You okay? He looks like he's coming around."

I feel something wet around my neck.

My feet have no ground beneath them. They are far from me. My vision teary, unclear, nothing seems to be out there. I feel like a sack of broken glass.

"He's okay, you okay, Detective?"

"Where..." My voice has disappeared. Dig for it D'laska. Find it. Terry Malloy! Wasn't that Marlon Brando's name in *On the Waterfront*? Dig. I need to feel. I touch my face, I can barely find it. I rub the towel filled with ice on my numbed neck.

Colored glass. Bottles. Liquor bottles on wooden shelves. I ache. I hurt. My neck is throbbing, and it stings. Somebody puts a drink in my hand. It drools down the sides of my mouth. The glass slips from my grasp and shatters.

"You were hit with a baseball bat across the back."

"Where am I?" Attempting to stand I slip into the center of a dark downward spiral. My chair saves me from splashing into hell. I ask again, "Where am I?"

"Basement of Marlowe's.

"Where's Cellini?"

"Long gone. D'laska, I'd be more concerned about yourself."

I stand, my feet are long ways down. My hair is matted, and my face is slimy with sweat. My neck is caked with blood. I stagger to a shelf of colored bottles. Liquor bottles. I gulp some vodka and spit it out because it's schnapps. Another bottle, green and shapely. Remy Martin, green and numbing. Nobody stops me from twisting the top. Not big biceps or the other cop. This stuff burns. The liquid whirls inside me spouting from the holes in my body.

"I gotta close." The unexpected loudness of the voice startles me. It comes from everywhere, pricking me with its sharpness.

Biceps takes hold of my arm. "Keep the bottle."

Outside doesn't help. The sticky air can't reach me. Bicepts dumps me at my car. "I thought it was better if we didn't take you to a hospital. I guess you fell on some glass. Don't come back to this neighborhood again. Something bad could happen to you."

TUESDAY
    5:23 A.M.

THE INNFIELD IS LONG CLOSED. Ainsworth is asleep in his car. I tap on the window. It rolls down slowly. His mouth opens. "Mike, what the..."

"Want a drink of Remy?"

CHAPTER 8

TUESDAY, JULY 8, 1975
6:00 P.M.

"Mike, it's late. Mike?"

There's a gentle hand on my shoulder, and a soft voice by my ear. "How ya feeling?"

My eyes open in tiny increments. The air is thick; it smells used, soiled.

Paul opens the shades and lifts the windows in my bedroom. His anger is thinly camouflaged. "How ya feeling?" he repeats. He looks at my reflection in the mirror as I struggle to sit up.

"These stitches burn."

He snaps, "You're lucky, I knew a doctor who would stitch you up without asking questions."

"Paul, how bad am I?"

His teeth clamp as he watches me pitifully roll on my side. "Mike, something ugly is gnawing at you, something very destructive."

"Later. Right now, I need sodium pentothal."

"Here's some Darvon."

"How many colors am I?"

"You're not in great shape from the crack of your ass to the Frankenstein stitches across the back of your neck. Your trapezius areas are black and blue." Paul shakes his head in anger. "Tell me what the purpose of last night was? You pride yourself on being intelligent. You call that a smart move? Getting beat up in a guinea joint?"

"I don't need a lecture."

"Maybe you do."

"Okay, but not at the moment."

"I brought you something to eat. There's nothing in your house except bananas and honey."

"I'm fortunate," I say. "I slept through the hangover. I'm only experiencing straight pain."

"You took a needless beating. Why?"

"To solve this case."

"Is Calabrese innocent now?"

"It tells me he's less guilty."

Paul swats the window blinds angrily. "Less guilty! What the fuck does that mean? I'm gonna confront the asshole."

"No!" I try to stand but can't.

"No?" His tone bites. "Why?"

"Give me a minute."

Paul comes over to the edge of the bed. "Do you want me to apply more ice to your back like last night?"

"I'm alright."

"Can you walk?"

I screech as I try to stand. I'm up. With every movement, heavy marbles seem to bank across my head. I have to make this pain radiate through me, to saturate me, so the aching becomes a part of my functioning.

I'm moving. The screams inside my head dissolve the marbles. I need to accept the pain.

I straighten up quickly and make it to the couch where Paul has some Chinese food containers on the coffee table. The won-ton soup tastes terrific.

Ainsworth plays with his beef and broccoli, then speaks, "They're gonna fuck us." He pauses. "On a radio talk show this morning,

Mulvaney said she was alarmed about an article in yesterday's paper. She's demanding answers to why this case wasn't handled through proper channels. Apparently, Ring wants the state's attorney general to file an official inquiry into the handling of the investigation. She actually guaranteed that by next Monday, a preliminary Internal Affairs probe will prove cover-ups and organized crime inroads into the Police Department."

"For once, she's asking the right questions."

"Her?"

"Paul, think about it. An incident involves a cop and mobster. With all the resources I.A. and Organized Crime have, why do they—and they must be high up the ladder—tell the Chief of Patrol they have a special assignment for him to head? He selects a Homicide detective and his partner who have no experience in a case like this."

"So, what are you saying?"

"What is the main advantage of choosing us?" I ask.

"Pass the soya sauce while you tell me."

"I have thought about this from every angle, and I always come up with the same conclusion which goes against what is happening all around us. Time."

"Time!"

"As police, we care if Calabrese is innocent or guilty. That is what Ring wants to resolve. My guess, Gage got to somebody, maybe Isserlyn. She's powerful, ambitious and her husband has deep political connections in New York and in D.C. They only care about reconnecting with Reno Piantini. I remember on meeting Gage he said to me about the Lafayette Hotel investigation, 'You thought it through.' A strange comment so I just dismissed it."

"With Mulvaney involved, nothing is going to be thought through."

"They didn't expect the publicity this case is getting."

"So, you actually took a beating for nothing?"

"Tell me about Filippo."

Paul wipes his mouth. "He's sleazy. Filippo is his last name, his first is long and unpronounceable. He passes himself off as Cuban, but he's from, get this, Trinidad. Picked up for drug offenses, robbery, pimping, and mugging. He did three years for throwing sulfuric acid in a prostitute's face. He's twenty-nine, never had a job in the twenty years he's been in this country. He's never been reliable enough for any crime family. Filippo's known to use his late grandmother's apartment on Prince, near Ivy, for prostitution, dope deals, and card games. I wouldn't count on finding him though; he's hiding in the Bronx. If he shows his face in Little Italy, he's a dead man. He's a loner, so the second guy is a mystery."

"The second guy helped set up Nickie," I say. "That means Filippo trusted him. You only trust someone you know."

Paul lets out a long sigh, "Finding Filippo in the Bronx is going to be impossible."

Outside noises creep into the apartment. I rub my face with my hands.

"Get that poster with all the names, write these three names on the backside."

Paul makes a face but does what I ask.

"Filippo, Diez, Vasquez. They're the last pieces to the puzzle."

"I have another scenario," Paul says. "Calabrese did a mobster a favor by killing Nickie and was promised protection."

"How could Calabrese have known Nickie Piantini would be at the corner of Vermont and Ivy the previous Friday when he requested an early out for Monday?"

Paul taps his fingers on the table. "Let Ring take over."

"If we're removed, Ring will not get this case. You can't control a bull in a china shop. It will get wrapped in some stall tactic, that buys more time. The focus will change from Calabrese to me. I will need to be investigated."

I move my plastic plate aside; my stomach is too knotted for food. I watch honey slowly leave the spoon and fold into a tall glass of cold milk. The liquid is both refreshing and satisfying as it makes its way down my throat.

Paul stands, brushes imaginary lint from his jacket. "I think I get what you're saying. Isserlyn pulls internal strings while Gage tries to reconnect with Piantini who now has leverage because a cop killed his kid."

My fortune cookie message reads, "Anger will soon fade, but regret lasts a lifetime."

Paul shakes his head. "Mike, you don't look so good."

"As a detective, I think of myself as methodical, preoccupied, and patient. None of those qualities would add up to finding a quick solution, would they?"

"I guess not."

"Calabrese is innocent of premeditated murder though he's probably not innocent of much else. He would have had a plan, Guzzetta would have been involved, and they would have zipped the murder up airtight."

I stand, taking a deep breath. Paul watches me struggle to move. He tidies up some, tells me there's more food in the refrigerator, then leaves.

My mind doesn't give me any peace as I practice walking. I can handle the constant dull pain; it's the sharp lightning bolts that humble me. I push myself, trying to deaden my body in preparation for what I have to do. I strap on a back brace. Time to pay Andre that second visit.

TUESDAY
9:45 P.M.

A DARK HAZE surrounds the skyline. I didn't miss much of a day. It's transition weather, between wet and dry. Tomorrow will start a new cycle; the rain will ebb for a while.

I gaze at the many windows in Andre Gabriel's worn, liver-colored building. Walking up to the landing, I check my pockets and gun.

Outside his door, I listen for a long while. Quietly, I manipulate the lock with a pick, and it clicks open. Lights are on throughout the apartment.

I tiptoe toward his bedroom. I have no fast heartbeat, no thoughts, just a goal.

Andre is in a deep sleep, lying on top of his bed nude.

I slip the oily cold barrel of a .45 into his brown mouth. He's startled to see me. I push it farther down his throat. "Suck on it, Gabriel."

He sees what the ugly, one-eyebrow Italian saw—eyes dead of expression, devoid of reason. The difference being the nasty Italian didn't slice my neck with a razor.

I push Andre into the kitchen, seating him on the chair we used the night before. It hasn't been moved. I give him instructions to put both his hands on his cock.

Taking the cocaine from my pocket, I put it on the table. When Andre tries to speak, I advise him to only answer when I ask questions. He thinks he's going to die, that I'm going to kill him. Trembling, he watches as I put a syringe on the table and handcuffs.

His sweaty naked flesh begins to imagine what he believes I'm going to do to him.

I take two pills from my pocket, one bright red and round, the other white and oblong. I examine each one before I place them on the table. I pull up a chair close to Andre. He has to spread his legs to make room. His face contorts as he tries to hold back tears. My gun is between his eyes. I advise him that if he opens his mouth to speak, I'm going to shoot.

Ten long minutes pass. Each minute heats the room more. I say nothing. Fifteen minutes. Andre strains to see the table, trying to guess what's going to happen. His perspiration is all about me.

Finally, I ask, "I want the names of men Filippo would trust. Do not tell me anything I don't want to know."

"Ah, ah, I, told you everything last night."

I reach into my pocket. I pull out two more pills, one yellow, the other a striped capsule.

I inform him of my dilemma. "I have drugs on me. One speeds up the heart rate drastically; it's not recommended for humans. A veterinarian friend of mine told me to be very careful with it, but I've forgotten which color pill it is."

I force a pill down his mouth, but his throat convulses. On the second try, he succeeds.

I ask, "I only want names."

He quickly repeats two names, but I don't believe him.

"Where can I find them?"

"I don't know exactly, around."

"Who would Filippo recruit to set up Nickie Piantini?"

When he starts a sentence, I give him another pill to swallow.

He's frantic. He wants sympathy, but it doesn't exist.

"Andre, I'm prepared to torture you all night. All night. Do you understand? You are giving me the information I want."

He marinates in his own sweat. I repeat the question.

He falls off the chair to his knees, pleading with me not to kill him. He sobs, imploring me to stop, calling to God. Appealing to saints. They're deaf. I am relentless in my pursuit and he is at the fringe of a terrifying abyss.

I take a straight razor from my inside pocket. Andre pleads, kissing my shoes. He offers me money, the world. I lift his head by his hair and cut too close to his scalp, beads of blood appear. I cut more.

I direct him to sit in his kitchen sink next to the stove. His face is streaked with lines of blood. He watches me put water in a tea kettle and set it on a lit burner.

"Is your mouth dry, Andre? I hope not."

He shakes, watching me take another capsule from my pocket. He begins to plead again.

"I know you're never supposed to take two of these pills together. Something to do with the respiratory system collapsing just before the heart begins to burst."

I place my hand on his forehead. "Bad sign, Andre, you're getting feverish. If you don't get to a hospital soon, your heart may explode." I force another capsule down his throat and make sure he swallows. I move away from him.

When the kettle starts whistling, his head dodges back and forth from the hot steam to me.

"I'm listening."

He screams, "I don't know."

"One more outburst and I am going to remove your nose with this razor, then your lips."

"Don't, please! No! I'm sorry what I did to you last night, please, I got money...jewelry...cash, I have ten grand cash. It's yours."

I squeeze his throat tight. "You're going to die very slowly and painfully if you don't give me an answer."

His face is the color of death.

"Please stop, you're crazy. I'm sorry."

The hot water kettle seems to be whistling louder.

"Dickie Green," he says, "could be Dickie. Please get me to a hospital—my heart is beating fast."

"Green doesn't sound Hispanic. I want a Cuban."

"Green's half black, half Cuban."

"Who else?"

"Ginger Ortez, Dogface Gomez, no he's dead. I can't think."

I let go of him, he's a small brown man who doesn't want to die. Andre's intestines growl as his eyes swell with filmy tears. He's just talking now, agreeing to what he thinks I want to know. The kettle keeps blowing steam toward him. I can almost hear his thoughts—he's praying for a miracle.

I scan the room. "Okay, Andre."

The kettle flies past my neck, the hot liquid spills wildly. A blurred movement barrels into me. My back catches the corner of the table, folding me easily. Andre's hands are around my throat. I grapple with his arm, my hand wraps around his wrist. His leg chops into my crotch. My back slides along the hot water on the floor as I try to shoulder away. I begin to lift him. We roll. I claw at his chin, pushing against him. I clamp harder, digging my fingers into his flesh. We've reversed, and my fist comes down hard on his face. I stagger off him, then come back and kick his belly once, then one more time.

I collapse on a chair and take aim with my gun. "Don't fuckin' move!" My voice bounces against every wall, then resounds in my head. My neck throbs. The hot water seeps into my stitches.

I walk over and try to kick him once more, but my foot slips and I fall. His nails immediately dig into my neck, attempting to pull at the stitches. I smash my gun hard into his forehead. His hands go to his bloodied face. I find the strait razor; his eyes fill with tears. I cut his nose just enough for him to remember and hate me for the rest of this life.

I walk him into his bedroom and force him into a small closet. I reward him with another pill.

He begs me to forgive him, but I'm oblivious. He pleads, praying like every man would because he thinks he's innocent. I tie his hands, give him another pill, some water and tell him to sit on the floor of the closet. I prop a chair under the handle, tell him not to yell or else I'll cut his neck this time, deeper than he cut mine. I gather what's mine along with Andre's address book. I wrap ice in a towel and place it around my neck.

Andre taps on the door. "My heart, I need to go to a hospital."

"Shut the fuck up." I holler.

I quietly slip out of his apartment.

I LOOK at myself in the car's rearview mirror. I recognize my face, lips, nose, teeth, and the flesh that surrounds them. These black eyeballs are unfamiliar though, without depth, without intelligence, and bordered in pain. I lean closer till they fill the mirror. They are painted eyes, painted dead. I put three Darvon in my mouth. I rest my head back. Tomorrow, Andre Gabriel will look at the world from a new perspective; he's ingested potent laxatives.

TUESDAY
 10:25 P.M.

THERE IS a faint scent of Suzanne in her empty office. I think about that night when that intractable blue horse made me aware of my fragility. That seems like years ago. I run my hand along her chair. There's an empty manila folder in the trash. Her appointment calendar notes a meeting for McConnell with Gage and Isserlyn at the commissioner's office earlier this afternoon.

Suzanne has carefully piled my incoming messages: Mulvaney, Roberts. The last one intrigues me, and I find it timely, Isserlyn.

I scan the ballistics report; it doesn't mention any bullets in Nickie Piantini's car. One round, a .45-caliber, was found embedded in the apartment building housing the laundromat. Piantini fired at Calabrese with a .45, then tossed it somewhere between Ivy and the hospital. After this much time, it's safe to say, it won't turn up. Maybe it was Garcia's gun Piantini used, figuring the black .38 looked too much like a toy.

TUESDAY
12:10 A.M.

Suzanne gives me a cautious smile as I enter her apartment. She's wearing a kimono. Classical music is playing in the background.

"Bacardi or Courvoisier?"

"The more expensive stuff will be fine," I say with a smirk.

She had been reading. There's an open book on the coffee table, the biography of Gustav Klimt. The inscription reads, "We're walking with the moon, aren't we, Suzanne? All my love." There's no date, but the book doesn't appear old. What am I doing here?

Suzanne hands me the snifter. We sit in awkward silence swirling the amber liquid, unlocking its distinctive aroma. After taking a sip, her large green eyes lock on me.

"Why are you here?"

I place the glass on the table and walk over to her. "I've wanted to do this." I kneel and take her smooth white chin and bring her thin lips to mine. It's a gentle, careful kiss. A tolerant kiss, accommodating my immediate wishes. The music ends, and she excuses herself.

I take a healthy gulp of cognac but remain on the floor. The music returns again. This time it's familiar; I remember my mother playing this piano piece. Suzanne steps from the bedroom, her robe opened, wearing white panties. She crosses the room in long strides to the couch where she sits with legs spread. "Is this what you came for?"

It's impossible to keep my eyes from the white fabric between her legs. I inevitably edge closer and only see what is there. My imagination is not skilled enough to understand how a fleshy slit controls every move I'm making. A candle flickers. She must be smiling, a wicked, broad, narcissistic smile. On my knees in a praying position, I remove the panties. The beautiful drama of legs widening draws me closer. I part her lips with my tongue, her sweet womanly fragrance guides my face as I crawl into the velvet darkness, pretending to be a part of something.

CHAPTER 9

WEDNESDAY, JULY 9 1975
6:25 A.M.

SUZANNE SLEEPS ON HER SIDE, facing the screened window. Her pale complexion absorbs the morning sunshine. Her composed features do not soften. Instead, tiny lines look like fine cuts in smooth marble.

My arm snakes its way beneath her torso to her large tender breasts. Suzanne's eyes are fully open as she turns and folds into me. She's musty-warm and faded-perfume sweet, the seductive odor of a woman's power. I lower my lips to her and play with her nipples till they pout in my mouth. She purrs, pulling my head back by my hair. She covers my mouth with hers. Her legs open and she arches herself for me. Her muscles contract and inch me in deeper. I lift her round white ass higher, staring into those unforgiving eyes. There is a hunger for completeness. A dance begins, slow and playful. Finely ground glass flows through my bloodstream, sharp, pointed edges from ankles to my brain. Her legs raise, Suzanne's opened eyes insist on something more, something that will add meaning.

I defy the blue horse, pinching her proud pink nipples till her body winces. Suzanne ripples in anticipation, loud moans crackle from emotions deep within her.

We gain momentum and speed. Two lovers contending, challenging, daring a burst of perfection, a soul's unmasking. Harder with more intensity we pursue each other. Her teeth bite into me. We're skin against slippery skin. I grab and pull her breasts and watch the whiteness appear within the pink. Her nails scrape across my back. A rainbow of pain surfaces under the numbing pleasure. I imagine myself opening her flesh and enfolding her around me. We thrust and gyrate, resurrecting ourselves. Her fingers grip my neck tightly while her body begins to stiffen. I plunge myself deeper. Suzanne's eyelids scroll, fluttering with her internal tempest. She convulses with a shriek as her fingernails dig deeper into my stitches ripping them from my neck. I screech in anguish, chomping down hard into my lower lip, feeling myself emptying. Painlessly this un-magic fluid leaves me.

Inert, the seconds pass. My eyes move from the white ceiling to the horse, they creep down the white wall to the white bed. On the white sheets is a beautiful white woman with my bright red blood running down her lily-white arms.

―――

WEDNESDAY
8:48 A.M.

ROBERTS INTERCEPTS me entering my apartment.

Once inside, he hands me a business envelope. I crumple the letter it contains. "I'm not requesting to be removed from this case."

Roberts moves to the door, formless in a cheap tan suit. He scowls. "Is it a doctorate in skycology you want?"

"Psychology."

"Toilet police work that the department ain't gonna be payin' for anymore."

I run my hands through my hair and realize nothing I say will change matters, so I confront Roberts. "The point is, you and Ring see Nickie Piantini's death as a means of furthering your careers, but you've hit a stumbling block, and you're too fucking stupid to see a bigger picture."

"D'laska, just seeing you makes other cops puke."

"Here's the point, even if I was removed, neither you nor Ring will even be thought of to take over. You are incapable of logic and deductive reasoning." Once I say it, I can't stop laughing. Which makes Roberts furious.

He drills his finger into my chest. "Here's the point: you demanded shakedown money from Claudio Cellini. When he refused, you beat him in front of a bar full of people. He has at least two officers as witnesses. Cellini's suing the city. He and his prominent uptown attorney have an appointment with the mayor's office. Here's the point: Andre Gabriel was admitted to Mother of Mary Hospital for extreme dehydration and other complications from forced ingestion of laxatives. You cut his face. His lawyer phoned the commissioner. Here's the fuckin' point: insubordination is just one of the many charges Captain Connors has lodged against you. Lastly, the attorney general of this state is going to take a personal interest in prosecuting you for obstruction of justice."

"I haven't figured out if it's your ugliness or your stupidity that's your most nauseous quality."

He scowls. "Both McConnell and you are going down. I'm seeing to that."

Unamused, I walk past him and open the refrigerator, take out the milk, pour some into a glass, spot the honey on the counter, and drop a spoonful into the glass, stir, sit down and take a long drink. "Let's stop pretending. Cellini is a known criminal who isn't going to do a thing, and neither is his stooge, Gabriel. Connors, much like yourself, is a repugnant relic whom I doubt anyone takes seriously anymore."

"For the short time you have left on the force, you better watch your back."

WEDNESDAY
9:50 A.M.

Quincy smirks as I pass his desk. "The Piantini shooting isn't going well for you, is it?"

"What do your sources say about why the district attorney's office hasn't scheduled an arraignment for Calabrese yet?"

Quincy covers a yawn. "Mulvaney and a lieutenant from Internal Affairs were with Chief McConnell earlier. Rumor has it there's a lot of ammunition against you. Guys are very pissed because when you go down you'll take McConnell with you. Only a real asshole would do that."

"What if I don't go down?"

A big smile appears on Quincy's face.

I ask again. "Why no arraignment yet?"

"There's only one question everybody has: is Calabrese innocent or guilty? Odds are now that he is."

"He's innocent of premeditated murder."

Quincy shrugs. "You have proof?"

"I'll tell you why an arraignment hasn't been scheduled because there is a bigger picture here and that is something your limited intellect could never comprehend."

"They say the commissioner met with Gambacorda. They must have come to an agreement because no violence has broken out and your buddy Calabrese is still alive."

"Is that what Roerts told you?"

Quincy picks at his teeth. "I guess your record with the crazies was pretty impressive before now. Maybe you'll get a job at Bellevue."

"So, you don't think I have a future in law enforcement either."

His laugh fills the area and every officer in the vicinity looks to us. "Absolutely fuck' en not. Nobody is gonna miss you either."

I twist my mouth before speaking. "Agreed, but, there are surprises yet to come."

WEDNESDAY
 10:14 A.M.

Suzanne wears little makeup. Her green eyes are slightly lined.

"How's your neck?" she asks.

I give her a naughty look before speaking, "The Doctor restitched it."

"Mulvaney was here earlier."

"Who's with McConnell now?"

"He's alone. He's been expecting you."

She follows me into my office, closing the door behind.

"They've been following you. Mulvaney insists she can prove that Calabrese is guilty and there's evidence to show you're also involved with police corruption in Little Italy."

"Suzanne has Gage been here in the last week?"

"No, he usually calls."

"And Isserlyn?"

"When she calls, he goes to her office."

"What do the papers McConnell receives from Gage refer to?"

She doesn't hesitate. "I don't know."

WEDNESDAY
 10:22 A.M.

McConnell stares at the center of a vast cloud, watching it turn silver, then fatal gray, like a dying lily in a polluted pond. He glances over his shoulder at me. "D'laska, do you have the proof that Calabrese is innocent?"

I join him at the window. He says, "There are a dozen reasons on my desk why you should be suspended, may be dismissed from the force or jailed. I asked you a simple question after you met with Calabrese. I thought you would be able to give me an answer. If you had, this mess would be out of my hands. I asked you one question—not is he guilty, but what do you think, your professional opinion, innocent or guilty? You couldn't answer. Now, you contend that Calabrese is innocent."

His face is red and ugly. "It's your indecision that's to blame. Now, there's too much to prove him innocent of and too little time left."

McConnell walks around me; his anger being displaced by a brooding seriousness. "Is there anything you want to tell me?"

"I believe Calabrese is innocent of premeditated murder."

"What proof do you have?"

"I'm gathering."

"How many laws have you broken?"

There's an edge to my voice. "Nothing that can't be explained away."

He walks back to his desk and signals me to take a chair. Beneath the irritation, McConnell is an exhausted man. He grabs his paperweight. "Yesterday, I met with the commissioner and Isserlyn. We discussed this case; it will continue to be handled through this office. Mulvaney and I.A. could make my life very difficult, but you're going to prevent that." He pauses. "You say Calabrese is innocent. I'll give you until Friday morning to prove it. If not, you will be removed, and a thorough investigation initiated into your failure. Calabrese will also be held accountable. This case will be handed over to a special investigative team not associated with the department."

"Nobody expected Mulvaney to be so involved with this case, going to the media, making waves, did they?"

"She can be a nuisance."

McConnell goes to his bureau and pours whiskey into two small glasses. He hands me one. My memory focuses on that morning drive to meet Gage and Isserlyn—and McConnell's loathing for the feds. Gage's bitter pill was fresh in his mouth during that trip.

"Chief," I say, "Gage is in control, isn't he?"

There's a long silence with only inhales and exhales of breath. "I told you, I'll handle that end."

WEDNESDAY
11:10 A.M.

FROM MY OFFICE WINDOW, I look down on the trash heap below. How orderly garbage seems from a distance, yet I know it's convoluted and filthy down there. Artists use perspective to give their work depth. People use assurances to accomplish the same illusion. McConnell figured on me to make a quick, subtle splash of this case. He wanted to stand on the sidelines and gloat that the "kid" he helped get an education wasn't frightened of a sticky situation.

The phone pulls me from my thoughts.

"Mike, it's Paul."

"Shoot."

"Calabrese was waiting for Guzzetta to pick him up on the street behind his house. They drove to the Trenton Avenue Social Club. They must have attended a meeting of some sort because there were Cadillacs and Lincolns everywhere. It was all mobbed up probably from the Alessi family. Calabrese and Guzzetta were there for nearly three hours, and they left with Floriano and Stone. They're all at the Blue Chateau now."

"I'm on my way."

Suzanne walks into the office and closes the door behind her.

"I have to meet Paul," I say.

She picks up the letter opener from my desk, then throws it down. I approach her. "I have to leave."

I attempt to hold her, but she recoils. "Suzanne, what brought this on?"

"I hate what I'm feeling again," she says. "I'm frightened."

"Caring about someone does that sometimes."

Her voice cracks with emotion. "I owe you nothing."

"No, no you don't, but you can't deny your feelings."

She wrings her hands while the rest of her body seems to be weighted with hostility.

I say, "We'll talk about 'us' later."

"Later!" Those cold green eyes show no emotion. "Later! What makes you decide when?"

I walk out the door. Then out another door. I can't understand why the whole precinct can't hear the echoes of her voice in my head.

WEDNESDAY
12:35 P.M.

I PASS an old tavern on the corner a few blocks from the Blue Chateau. I watch it slide by with a young man's envy. A snapshot of the way it was. Simple. Shuffleboard simple. Two teams get four shots to knock their opponent off the dusted board. Then beer and another challenge while the losers move to the bowling machine.

Paul is waiting a few shops from The Blue Chateau.

"What happened with McConnell?" he asks.

"Friday is the deadline for whatever is going to happen to Calabrese. Gage must be close to a deal with Reno Piantini."

"You've been used."

A scornful smile emerges from the corners of my mouth. "It's not over yet. Calabrese must have found out from his mob sources that Reno Piantini will be deciding what his next move is going to be. Alessi being at the Trenton Avenue Social Club tells me Calabrese, through Guzzetta's uncle, is trying to arrange something. I bet Floriano and Stone prompted the request that ultimately brought Alessi around."

Paul pretends to watch the cars pass.

I fix my jaw. "We still have time to prove Calabrese innocent."

Paul jerks his head back as if he were just hit in the forehead. "You're so goddamn obsessed you don't understand what's happening. They're going to fuck us."

"I'm walking in there." I point toward the Blue Chateau. "Are you coming?"

I don't hear footsteps behind me as I walk toward the entrance. I swing the door open.

There's no daylight penetrating the interior of the bar. This isn't a favorite lunch spot. A few salesmen are at the bar along with a couple in shorts. All the booths are empty except the one closest to the back room.

Guzzetta is the first to notice me, but he's unsure of who I am. He leans across the booth, his gold chains swinging forward. Calabrese's head turns around; he watches me as I move toward them.

I can feel Ainsworth behind me. I turn my head to the bar. He's ordering something.

In the booth, the exaggerated mannerisms typical of Italians cease. The four of them are dressed in their expensive suits with unbuttoned shirts. They watch me. Calabrese grimaces; Floriano and Stone project an inflated attitude of importance.

Guzzetta swishes a smoky liquid in his glass. "I thought you never came to Brooklyn?"

"Calabrese, I want to talk with you."

He snorts. "Go ahead."

"In the back. I'll give you a minute to finish up."

Paul hands me a glass of vodka and ice. I squeeze lime into the drink and take a sip. It's watery and bitter.

Paul whispers, "Stone is the swarthier of the two."

Stone also has the more hardened, nastier features, blunter and more physical than the rest. I could picture him putting out a cigarette in a puppy's eye. Floriano's features are wrong, off-center and oblique. He has big ugly ears, sad eyes, and a small crooked nose. I can see him holding the dog steady for Stone.

All four stand shake hands and hug like good Italians. The two punks swagger past us, cigarette smoke billowing from their lips. We exchange long glances. We know we'll cross paths again.

Calabrese waves us into the dark back room. Guzzetta slips into a booth, Calabrese follows. He sighs and clears his throat. "What do you want?"

We're an uncomfortable foursome. I inhale before beginning, "I know Nickie Piantini's death wasn't premeditated." Heads nod in agreement. "And I don't want a cop set up, any cop." I gulp my drink then continue. "I've put one foot into your life, and it's like quicksand. I know about your gold blunder, your real estate deals, and your apartment buildings in Brooklyn. Your pizzeria joints, everything, even your plans to open a bar. It's not much of a secret about your affair with Kitty Jacovino. I can't believe how careless you are for a seasoned cop. I also know that when you worked at Internal Affairs, you rifled the files for information."

Calabrese never flinches. Guzzetta grins.

I go on, "And you never bought uniform accessories the day you busted that movie set. You lied then, and you continue to lie. You being at Barone's gas station involves your courier service. It had nothing to do with meeting your father and brother."

I tip an ice cube in my mouth and crush it. "The second phone line into your house is for that courier business. A third line is an emergency number you give your apartment house tenants."

There is no noise, no movement, only the wispy black smoke from the candle.

I continue, "I realize once you'd made up your alibi, you had to stick to it or else everything you said afterward could be taken as a lie also. You knew you were in trouble at the hospital when you were informed who you shot. With Connors down your throat and the ramifications of the shooting becoming clearer, you gambled. Somehow in the confusion, you found a phone and called your best friend, Gino. You instructed him to phone the P.B.A. lawyer who helped you both out years before. That's why he arrived so quickly."

Calabrese shakes his head. "You came all this way just to tell me how important you feel about digging into my past?"

I begin again, "I only care about this case. I don't care about your connections to the Alessi family or anything else. Some other cop can investigate the toilet you live in. You're a reckless hypocrite without pride for your badge or your family."

Guzzetta grips my wrist as I try to rise. His voice booms, "What else do you think you know? Asshole!"

His grip tightens, squeezing my wrist. I scrutinize both men before answering, "It doesn't matter. Does it, Calabrese?"

Calabrese places a toothpick above the candle's flame. When it's about to ignite, he pulls it away. His stretched facial features are thinly lit as the flame flickers. His hand comes up to his chin, and his first finger takes aim at Paul. "I bet you never feel safe being this guy's partner."

Paul begins to move forward, but I stop him with my free arm.

Calabrese gives me a sinister grin. "I know what you don't have, that's why you're here. What you'll never find. Because what you need to prove me innocent doesn't exist. I'm supposed to be guilty. I've known that since the hospital. To a real cop, it's obvious. You're a messenger boy with a badge. On the streets, you'd be killed in a minute, and no other cop, except maybe your partner, would give a shit. You've been used, schoolboy."

"I could say the same thing about you."

"So, you said your piece, are you done?"

Paul and I leave the darkness for the struggling sunlight of the day. He would have handled Calabrese differently—more directly. Both would have screamed and bellowed until the truth emerged as an offspring of the hatred.

Ainsworth rests his arms on the roof of his car. Traffic sweeps by. "What's next?"

"Go back to the Trenton Avenue Social Club. Floriano and Stone should be delivering a message from Calabrese. When they leave, stick with Stone. He's the more dangerous of the two."

"You think Calabrese has a deal with Reno Piantini?"

"I think it's going to get ugly."

Fumes from cars and the stench of garbage surround us. "Why should we care what happens to Calabrese?" Paul asks.

The question strikes a chord. "Calabrese knows there's no out for him."

Paul ignores the comment. "What's your next step?"

"I'm going to watch a film again."

He smiles. *"The Godfather?"*

WEDNESDAY
2:00 P.M.

Ring isn't at his office, so I have a young officer set up the film of Nickie Piantini's funeral in a meeting room. I settle back to watch the jumpy faces move across the screen.

Twenty minutes later, I stop the reel and run it back slowly. My instincts were right. I knew the two of them couldn't pass up an event to rub elbows and be seen. Floriano and Stone are mingling with those they admire. They're backgrounded to a clutch of men led by the leader of the Alessi family.

The next reel is from the second day. I recognize faces from the bars. Floriano and Stone are back, filtering through the crowd. My eyes widen as I watch the screen. I rush forward, but the scene advances from sight. Hurrying to replay it, my thoughts race.

The camera momentarily catches four men near a side entrance of the funeral home. It's hard to make out how familiar the group is as another figure is passing before the lens, but there they are, Floriano and Stone, talking with Vasquez and Diez, the two from the morgue. I rerun it, trying to read a gesture, an expression, anything to make this equal to what I can imagine may be going on. Are they being socially polite or becoming acquainted?

I can't locate Floriano and Stone outside the church. At the cemetery, the camera passes quickly by Vasquez, who's standing next to Stone. I stop the projector again, a gritty still remains on the screen, both of them on the fringe of a large group of people packed tightly together. I study the grainy portrait for a long while, then shut down the machine.

I enter Ring's office without knocking. "I need a twenty-four-hour tail on Vasquez."

Ring looks at me as if he can't believe his eyes. His chair pushes back as he quickly moves around his desk, his forearm immediately goes into my neck, he pushes me backward and pins me against his office wall. Picture frames drop to the floor with glass breaking.

"Tell me why you're the best guy to investigate this case? Something is not right about this whole investigation, not since the beginning and I want to know right now, who is involved and why."

I try logic. "If I was as informed as you say, would I be here asking you for help?"

He just scowls at me, his face red and his dark eyes wide. Moments pass; my breathing is labored. Finally, he removes his arm, I fall to my knees, gasping as he makes it back to his desk.

I find my way to the men's room. I feel like a truck hit me in the chest and my back is aflame from the beating I took at Marlowe's. I just sit on the toilet seat trying to regain my composure, wondering the same things that Ring has asked.

I walk back into Ring's office. My voice is shaky but loud. "This case is mine, and your office is obliged to cooperate."

The veins on his arms and neck budge. "I outrank you. Get out, press me, and the beating I'll give you will be worse than the one you took a few nights ago. When I assigned a man to follow you, he told me you went down easy. I had to laugh. What the fuck is a college guy doing playing with serious gangsters? This ain't no game. I don't understand any of this, D'laska, but I will, and when I do, the people involved will be in serious trouble. I'll see to that."

It falls silent. A numbness settles within me. My colleagues watched a baseball bat smash against me, and they did nothing.

My voice comes from far away. "I want Vasquez followed."

"Doubtful, but I'll take it into consideration. Get out."

WEDNESDAY
3:57 P.M.

As I sit in my car, I keep telling myself it doesn't matter. They watched me get sliced and hit with a bat and did nothing.

Through this whole ordeal, the only one who has remained consistent is Calabrese. The accusations come and go, the danger, the threats from all sides, the investigation—nothing matters, he lives in an unflinching present. Forward motion, that's all there is. One-minute leads to the next. Once one disappears, so does the chance to retrieve it. A straight line forward, the past is for mourners. That's why Calabrese needs to clear the slate to breathe freely. One obstacle stands in his way: Reno Piantini. Calabrese must arrange a meeting to face Reno Piantini.

I ease into the street, and my tire hits a pothole. I'll call Suzanne from Phyllis Bales-Isserlyn's office.

WEDNESDAY
4:20 P.M.

Ms. Isserlyn's secretary has a high, strained voice. She moves away from her desk when I ask to use the phone. After repeating I'm sorry numerous times, Suzanne agrees to wait for me at the office.

Isserlyn's secretary directs me to a straight-backed, uncomfortable sofa. The magazines on a contemporary round table reflect the tastes of modern, aggressive women, unashamed of having beautiful breasts and using whatever is necessary for achievement in what they believe is a man's world. The women are all tall and shapely with fresh complexions. Though the ads infer body odors, blemishes, menstrual cramps, embarrassing facial hair, and other flaws, none of the featured corporate movers seem to be suffering from anything except a nostalgic loss of harmony in their hectic lives.

Ms. Isserlyn gives me a pleasant, professional smile, gesturing for me to enter her office. She's wearing gold wire-rim glasses, a navy blue blouse, and a straight charcoal skirt. We shake hands diplomatically, and she instructs her secretary to screen her calls. She sits behind a meticulously arranged desk. Her eyes sparkle darkly as she places a thin black pen to the side of her art nouveau daily planner.

"Coffee, Detective D'laska?"

"Nothing, thank you."

She folds her manicured hands. "I'm getting conflicting reports.

That's why I've tried to contact you. I appreciate you coming by. I'll be frank. I would feel much better knowing the city is spending its money protecting an innocent police officer and not a criminal."

I tap my finger to my chin and begin to pace.

She delights in letting me believe the ground between us is balanced. The thrill of being in control oozes from every one of her honeyed pores. She watches me place my foot in the trap she's created.

"It's impossible for Louis Calabrese to have planned Nickie Piantini's death," I say.

"I'm listening."

Pressing my index finger into her desk, I lean forward enough to catch the delicate lines beneath her scant blue eye makeup. "There's no link between Calabrese and premeditated murder."

She also comes forward. Uncomfortably close, her perfume and breath mingling, wafting a warm, minty-sweet flavor that distends my nostrils. "You're a majority of one."

I straighten and backpedal. "All the evidence points to Calabrese's innocence."

She removes her glasses. "You have witnesses?"

"One."

She walks to a small fridge and turns to me. "Soda?"

I nod.

She returns with my drink. I feel myself under the microscope, on the slide etched with a question mark.

"We've been lucky so far," she says. "The press has been favorable to Calabrese, but that might turn around after Friday. And that would make us look like fools. A bankrupt city protecting an allegedly crooked cop. I personally would rather have an innocent Louis Calabrese."

"He is."

She lets her arms fall to her sides, forcing her chest to puff out. "Are you innocent?"

I make a sour expression. "Sometimes I get the impression nothing is what it seems."

"Whatever do you mean?"

"Are you planning to run for office?"

She runs her fingers on the pearls she is wearing around her neck. "A handsome detective with roaming eyes, I thought you would have come around sooner."

"I'm flattered."

"Ms. Baxter is quite stunning. I'm sure you wouldn't do anything to put her in jeopardy."

My mouth remains open longer than I expected. "They say politics is ruthless."

"We're both interested in the truth, but I'm more interested in it when it can be used to my advantage."

I don't react.

She pouts. "Stop acting the moody pessimist. It's old, used and unbecoming."

"A man's life is at stake."

"Aren't there always lives at stake?"

"Tell me about you, Gage, and how you got McConnell to bend to your wishes?"

Isserlyn comes around and leans against her desk, widening her legs till her skirt travels upward to where danger awaits. She runs her eyes down her exposed legs. "You're not any less ambitious than me. The difference being, I make sure the system works in my favor."

"Calabrese is being set up, isn't he?"

Isserlyn laughs. "You're not as bright as you are handsome, do you know that?"

"And McConnell?"

She casually looks one way, then the other before she adjusts her skit and returns to her chair. "Sometimes, circumstances determine outcomes."

"I think you mean ambition, not circumstances."

"I thank you for coming by. We should chat again."

WEDNESDAY
5:40 P.M.

. . .

PRINCE, like Vermont, is another interchangeable street for crosstown traffic with abused apartment buildings and small storefront businesses. Vehicles roll, build up, and screech. Kids play, and blank faces line the dulled windows. Tired women sit on stoops in inexpensive shifts and watch babies in tattered playpens.

I find a parking space and start my walk. Step by step, I nod to the curious and give a smiling hello to some children after retrieving their beat-up softball.

I pass the laundromat on the corner, and the squalid buildings the powerful use as toilets. Lining the curbs are trash cans buried under heaps of garbage. An occasional rat runs from the infested smorgasbord with a cat or dog chasing after its tail. It's a productive time for animals.

Old Italian and Hispanic women sit on hard wooden chairs along the street. Everything is permeated by exhaust-ridden humidity. I see little of interest, though I'm not sure I know what I'm looking for. It's more a sense of something out of place, odd, tipped, and different. I complete the first walk around. Now, I have to approach those who lead miserable mistrusting lives. They'd rather piss on me than help —that's how bottomless the roots of hatred descend, but someone may help, someone fed up enough.

From stoop to stoop, no matter how simple the questions, English becomes a troublesome language to understand. Nobody has seen anybody, nobody knows anything—and they don't expect to either.

I enter the musty candy store, the confining acrid air stings my nose. The old man recognizes me and smirks in disgust as we watch a man wearing fatigues and an oily Army jersey linger on the steps outside the store.

I ask the old man, "Is he from the neighborhood?"

"He was too long in Vietnam."

I hand him five dollars and take a sticky string of black licorice from a plastic container.

He grunts. "He's *pazzo*, crazy. Too much drugs."

I leave to follow the vet as he aimlessly moves down the street. Hearing my approach, he stops.

I show him my badge. "Are you from around here?"

He stares at me, but his eyes are vacant. "War climbs into your head."

"How long have you been home?"

"What you need, man?" Sweat beads form on his brown forehead. He grinds his teeth before speaking, "I was a cop once, an electrical cop into cosmic criminals. Gotta smoke, twenty bucks, shit like that?"

The words leave his mouth gnarled. Life for him is a coalesced nightmare of deformed thoughts with occasional flickers of reality.

"I've got the twenty. Which apartment building can I find Filippo and Dickie Green?"

"Want me to kill somebody like I killed gooks in Nam?"

"What's your name?"

He moves away. "Names are bullshit."

I have to remind myself why I'm having this conversation. "Filippo."

"Gots the money?"

"Which apartment?"

"Behind the other building. Let me feel the money."

"Let's walk that way."

"Fuck with me, and I'll kill you."

The people on the stoops watch as we walk toward Prince. Their whispers fall short of reaching us, but their expressions tell me my companion is local.

Young kids begin taking notice, following at a distance. The vet whistles monotonously, swinging his head side to side like a dazed animal. The smell of gasoline trails him. We stop shortly after turning on Prince.

"Through that alley, man. 'tween those buildings."

I rotate him. "Lead the way, soldier."

"Got your weapon? Com'on." He laughs, but I'll bet he doesn't know why.

The alleyway between the tenement buildings is lined with one long, generous mound of garbage and stinks strongly of urine. Plump rats pay little attention to us as they hustle through the filth. Pockets of annoyed pigeons barely dodge our steps. Above us are fire escapes and shadows. There is no sky, just shades of darkness. Faces press against windows—frightened faces older than their age.

He leers at me. "It's Nam, man, the rats, and shit. I ate rats over there. Spiders too."

We come to a small concrete square bordered by red brick. Cheap clothes hang on laundry lines. Behind me are the rustling and fidgeting sounds of little creatures scurrying in the putrefying refuse.

He stops, wipes his saliva-wet mouth. "The money, man!"

His foul breath wrenches in my stomach.

He says, "You know Dickie Green's a spook."

From somewhere under his coat a bayonet appears. He waves it at me. "Give me your money and your shoes."

"Really!" I slap his arm, the weapon flies from his hand. I push him against the building. He crumbles, blending into the garbage.

"Get up!" I shout.

The vet grins, another thread of sanity unraveling. "Man don't get excited, I'm a hunter, I'm a sky pilot. You dig?"

He pops some pills into his mouth then pours some liquid from a canteen onto a dirty rag and brings it to his nose to inhale. The pungent smell of gasoline hits me. It takes me a moment to realize he's sniffing paint thinner."

I lift him by his lapels.

He comes alive. "Man, got a smoke? Filippo was cool, smoked Kools. Cool, Filippo, across the street. I been there. His grandmother is a spirit now. Spirit in the sky. Ghost riders in the sky. Got my money, man?"

He grins; drool hangs from his lower lip. "Up, see where I'm aiming. I hate the sun, it ain't got no time. Thirty bucks, man. Number five floor, there's the door. Then one and two buckle my shoe, ah."

I push past him. "You'll get your money when I'm back."

"I'll wait, man. I tell fortunes." He sits on the stoop then brings the rag to his face.

The building smells of mildewing lives, urine, and pine-scented cleaning fluid. The odors cling over layers of continual hopelessness.

On the fifth floor, I tap at the metal door. The echo ripples through the small rectangular hallway. Putting my ear to the door, I fumble through my pocket for my lockpick. Below me, I can hear men's voices whispering to each other to be quiet. I grip the handle of my gun. I listen to footsteps trying to be light coming up the metal stairs. My fingers seem thick and not nimble at all. Finally, a click and the door creaks open, revealing a musty living room. I lock the door behind me.

Everything inside is old. A portrait of Jesus with big blue eyes, plastic flowers in carnival vases, and all kinds of bric-a-brac on cheap end tables. A frayed blanket is thrown over a scruffy brown couch, plaster Christmas figures kneel below rabbit ears on the TV. Joseph is smiling, Mary's face is chipped away, and a camel's head is missing.

A table with scattered poker chips is pushed against a radiator. The kitchen stinks of rusty water and rotting linoleum. Empty beer and liquor bottles are strewn about the floor.

I grip my gun tighter when I hear a sound. I become flush with the wall. There are muffled voices. I follow the wall to a closed door. I push the door open, gun in hand.

A startled couple in a rumpled bed grasps each other. A young girl begins to tremble. "My god, please..."

I take aim at the guy. "What's your name?"

"Dickie!" He swallows hard. "Don't shoot us, please, man."

Everything is still. Long, hot moments pass. We all remain in place.

"Are you Dickie Green?"

She clings tighter. His voice quivers. "Yeah, why?"

I lower my gun. "I'm a police officer."

The pretty girl makes the sign of the cross.

"Get your pants, Green."

He kisses her forehead. "He ain't gonna hurt us."

"Out here."

Green is wiry and naturally muscular. Tawny smooth, each race is represented in his features, basic black carefully rounded to handsome Hispanic with lemon-brown eyes. "Man, you scared the shit outta that woman, she 'bout lost it." He giggles to himself. "She thought her boyfriend sent you to kill us. Shit, man, mind if I get a shot of gin?"

"Stay in sight."

"I done nothing wrong. I ain't never spent a night in jail. You like gin?"

Green opens a cupboard, cockroaches scurry out. I aim my gun at him. "Real slow."

He removes the bottle.

I lower my gun. "You're looking at an accomplice to murder charge."

"I ain't done nothing!"

"You helped set up Nickie Piantini."

He downs the liquor. "Murder, 'cordin' to the papers. That cop's a hero."

"You're in trouble Green."

He laughs. "We didn't have shit to do with that shooting." He reflects. "Man, that is bull fuckin' shit. Filippo and I shit our pants when Nickie appeared with his gun. I thank that motherfuckin' cop."

He leans forward, looking back to the closed bedroom door. "You want some of that? Very tasty, I'll fix it."

I grab his arm. "Sit down. How long had you been cheating Piantini?"

He scratches his armpit and runs his hand over his head. "We scammed him twice. Once for a grand, the other time for 'bout twelve hundred. Filippo did him a few times alone for a couple thou. Nickie was easy when he drank."

"He was sober enough to catch you."

"Yeah, but we didn't have nothing to do with killing him."

I take a black gun from my jacket pocket. "Ever see this gun before?"

"Why?"

"Is this the gun Nickie Piantini pulled on Filippo?"

"Na! It wasn't black. It was bigger, silver."

"What happened that afternoon?"

"It was really quick. This car cut us off on Ivy. Then Nickie appeared with a gun in his hand. Filippo looked at me, we both froze. Nickie slapped Filippo, then grabbed him by the shirt. He was boilin', pissed. Nickie stuck his gun in Filippo's face. He wanted the eighteen hundred we took from him that day plus a fuckin' grand more. Then this crazy cop appeared, guns went off, Filippo backed that motherfuckin' car halfway down the block.

"Then we watched Piantini's car take off, so did we—straight to a liquor store. We were scared." Green pauses, running his sweaty finger inside his glass. "In a way, that cop saved my ass. Nickie was gonna kill us, sure. He knew we couldn't get that much money."

"Was Nickie alone?"

"Shit no! Gorilla Garcia was with him."

"How come Garcia didn't hassle you guys?"

Green shrugs. "I guess 'cause he never played with us."

"Where is he now?"

"Florida, Puerto Rico, somewhere south is the word."

"What else do you have besides gin?"

He smiles and hums. "Kessler, ah and...pussy."

A big self-satisfying grin appears on my face. "Whiskey."

He pours the liquor into two dirty glasses.

I toast him. "You're a real hero, Dickie." The liquid runs smoothly down my throat.

Green gives me a sneaky smile, looks back to the bedroom. "I don't have to go with you to make no statement, do I?"

"Give me your wallet."

After checking the meager contents, I hand it back. "Don't get lost. I know where to find you, and I'll be in touch."

With my gun ready, I open the door. The stairwell still stinks of decaying lives, but I smile to myself: Calabrese has been vindicated.

The vet is still sitting on the stone steps with the paint-thinner-soaked rag in his hand. I drop two twenties in his lap.

I turn the rearview mirror toward me. There it is, a legitimate smile set in a smug expression. I can still taste the cheap liquor on my gums.

I look into the mirror. "You were right, D'laska."

WEDNESDAY
  7:35 P.M.

Suzanne is at the window staring at the darkening sky. I join her in silence.

I stroke Suzanne's arm; she stiffens. My hand slides to her shoulder. Her imperfection appears, the crooked tooth among a row of white. She removes my hand. "What do you want?"

"Answers, you."

"Why?"

"I want you, but first I want the correspondence between Gage and McConnell."

Suzanne steps away, crossing one arm over the other. "Fucking me doesn't give you the right to ask for either."

"I need that correspondence."

She puts my face between her hands. "You want me? I want to know what you really want."

Suzanne and I stare at, in, and through each other. I gently bring her to me.

She asks, "If I let you see those papers, what will happen?"

I kiss her cheek. "I have to see them first."

She sighs. "You know what I mean."

"I need to find out the connection among McConnell, Gage, and Isserlyn."

She walks to the window to watch the steel-clouded sky, sudden gusts of wind thread through the skyline. Though she believes in art, it's the perfection, not the effort, she admires.

"I feel you're using me again," she says.

The moment's pass. "A man's life is at stake."

She wraps her arms around herself as if a chill has crept through her. "You want answers, you want me, you want files. That's plenty of wanting, plenty of selfishness. What about me?"

"When this case is over, we'll sort us out, our needs, our expectations."

Suzanne's eyes become moist. She is perhaps recalling, unfolding an old relationship and remembering what destroyed it. A vulnerable part of her has surfaced, a slight tear in the cold veneer.

My arms close around her.

She says, "No matter how you might try, you can never understand what's going on inside of someone. Inside of me."

"I will try, but first I need to free myself of this case."

Suzanne opens McConnell's door. "Once you touch those files, you're as guilty as all those you're accusing."

I open the metal drawer and find the correspondence. My fingers trace the sentences. The governmental tone is firm, though the language is purposely vague. However, the underlying meaning is implicit. They want the information Reno Piantini was to provide. Efforts have increased to reestablish contact with him. The killing of Nickie Piantini is seen as an unfortunate delay in which the government must indirectly acknowledge guilt. However, they would be willing to restructure a new deal to compensate for the loss of his son at the hands of a police officer. The chain of command is evident throughout. The power rests with Gage and the Justice Department. The NYPD is handled like a kid who has wandered into trouble and is being treated indifferently. The punishment is paralysis—a complete turnover of authority to the Justice Department. McConnell, under orders from the commissioner, works directly with Gage. Roberts and the others are politely in the dark on the fringe. Isserlyn is Gage's confidant.

McConnell had faith in me. He trusted me, thinking by assigning me I'd quickly establish whether Calabrese was innocent or guilty. If Calabrese were innocent, McConnell would have protected him and cut any attempt to use Calabrese as a bargaining chip in negotiating with Reno Piantini. He wanted to bypass all the politics that he thought might accompany Justice Department involvement. If Calabrese were guilty, it would have become ugly, but at least the city would have kept some control over the case. Now, I've boxed McConnell into a corner.

Suzanne asks quietly, "Did you find what you wanted?"

"It confirms what I thought but not what I am frightened of."

"What is that?"

I unbutton her blouse, clumsily, at first, like an outcast child looking for a secure place to hide. The white bra warns me with its two buoyant cups of silky milk that to remove the contents might leave scars. I snap something in the center and flesh falls. Sweet, white caramel finding its shape. Ravenously, I suck hard on her nipples, craving more, what's beneath. Desiring her, all of her. Wanting answers. This is my feast. She wanders away from herself, embarrassed by all men who need to suck on women. My hand fights her skirt, lifting it, pulling down her panties. My fingers find access, quick candied access. I probe, it's what I want, need. I fumble with myself, I'm hard, ready. She doesn't accept me readily. I press, poke, shove, thrust, and force. She moves mechanically. Finally, I'm swallowed.

I need more, to fill the emptiness. I stab more forcefully and suck intensely. I can feel the marks I'm making on her breast, the stains of red beneath the white. Her nails dig into my ass. Two tattoo artists at work leaving their permanent marks. I lift her and plunge. Spasms occur, weakness occurs, she catches herself saying "Why!" out loud. I can feel her heart pumping through my body. We rest, holding each other. Breathing hard.

We unlock. Those breasts go back into their separate nylon caskets. When she leaves the room, I become aware of how alone I am.

Suzanne returns to her office. She comes close, kisses me tenderly. I want to take her breasts out again, strip her, subdue her. There is something about her smooth whiteness, the cleanliness I wish to possess. I lead her by the waist. "I have some loose ends to tie. I'll walk you to your car."

WEDNESDAY
9:45 P.M.

THE EXHAUST FUMES from Suzanne's car combine with the other foul odors of the clammy city. McConnell wanted it clean. Maybe not white but a passible gray. He wanted it done correctly, but the self-serving fingers of power dictate without regard for anything but their demands. McConnell made a deal with the devil.

I was off guard from the beginning because I didn't understand the depth when federal influence is exerted. Would they murder someone to convince a murderer they're serious about doing business with him?

I enter a grocery store around the corner from the station. I need to make some small white packages for my next stop. The tired lady behind the store counter lifts the box of sandwich baggies I've placed in front of her. "This it?" she asks.

I point behind her, "Bit-O-Honey."

WEDNESDAY
11:48 P.M.

THERE'S a column of neon signs in the large windows of Juan's Caribbean Club. At the entrance, there's a large placard with something written in Spanish. I take a deep breath and walk into the booming music.

Colored lights flash, and the DJ crackles through a tinny sound system. The amused muscular doorman looks me over before saying, "Five-dollar cover."

The beat-up walls are lacquered in orange and yellow with waves of blue.

I stroll forward, the crowded corridor taps into a packed rectangular room. I make my way to the bar. Liquid colors fan across the room, splashing against the liquor bottles and back mirror. I feel like I've dropped into a cheap velvet painting.

There are mirrors, plastic-covered lights, and woven through the smoky atmosphere, loud Latin music. Males in tight, showy clothes bristle about overly made-up women.

I'm pushed to the wall at the end of the bar.

Two gossiping women have pushed to the bar next to me. One shows ample cleavage and has a generous slit up her dress. The other has burnt-orange hair and large dark nipples crushed against pink nylon. With their intrusion, I'm flattened against the wall. The smell of cheap perfume blends with body odors. The bartender, a short, sweaty man, speaks to me in Spanish. I may be the only "Anglo" in the joint.

Every time I look at the center of the bar, three guys give me nasty looks. It's only a matter of time and alcohol before things turn hostile. The bartender overcharges me as if it's understood I'm here to be screwed, and he's just playing by the established rules.

I catch a flash of someone on the dance floor I know is familiar, but I can't identify. I begin to shut off the noise, place the quick-glimpsed face at center stage in my thoughts. I have no recollection, no connecting link. The dancers swell, crowding out any view. I search as one song ends and another begins. It's time to wander. Behind the dance floor, along the back wall, a vibrating lacework of people has gathered in a colorful chain.

I see him again. He's filing his nails like he did that first time at Three Deuces. He works for Cellini. When I tilt my head for a sharper view, another person comes into focus. Directly behind the Cuban, back a few feet sitting on a chair and talking to a woman, is one of the men I hoped to see—Diez, one of the two men parked in front of the morgue that morning.

A stunning black waitress touches my elbow. "Another beer?"

"Please."

The seams of her red stockings run straight and smooth from high heels into a red Danskin. I keep Diez and the other Cuban in view. It's impossible to determine if the two are friendly. Diez is an animated man, full of gestures, and an exaggerated sense of confidence. By contrast, the filing Cuban appears introverted and scheming. I press my hand into my jacket pocket; the tiny wadded plastic packets are still there—the fool's Shangri-La. The cocaine I confiscated from Gabriel, sorted in generous helpings.

The waitress taps my shoulder. "Your beer."

"What's your name?"

"Why?"

"I need a favor." I drop a ten on her tray.

She looks at me, her large brown eyes growing fuller and more distant. "What?"

"You see that man filing his nails across the room. Do you know his name?"

She shrugs. "No. You want change?"

"Find out?"

"Listen, mister, you don't even belong here. You people come here on Friday Fiesta night, not Latin dance night. You want change or what?"

"I only need a name."

"Screw off!"

The dancers form a textured stream of colors. Diez continues to tease a woman sitting on his lap. The filer's gaze shifts through the thickening crowd.

I'm biting time, chewing it, and spitting out the minutes. The girl rises, Diez gulps the last of his drink, and I follow him into the men's room.

No attendant. Shuffling feet, urinals swishing, smoke and faces in mirrors. There is the smell of piss, body odor, and running water. Diez enters the last of four stalls. I wait till the one next to his empties. There's no sound of piss hitting the water. I make noticeable noises, clearing my throat, inhaling, exhaling. I blow my nose. Jingling my keys, I select one and untie the yellow twist, opening the small plastic bag. He flushes the toilet and inhales. I'm aware of Spanish accents, swearing in English, toilet talk, tits and ass.

I hear piss hitting the water. I notice Diez's shoe at the imaginary line between the partitions. I hold the cocaine and key ring. One, two, three, they drop from my hand. The flowing urine in Diez stall stops. The keys hit the wet tile, and the white powder spills over the side of his shoe. I curse. His diamond-ringed fingers lift the bag and disappear behind the partition

"Hey!"

"Whaa?" The voice comes from above. Diez must be standing on the toilet. A tiny gold spoon worn around his neck is inside what remains in the bag I dropped. "Unfortunate accident. You got more?" He lets the empty bag float down into the toilet bowl in my stall.

I pat my pocket.

His voice is greasy slick. "What are you doing here? More accidents could happen ya know."

I begin to unlatch the door.

His arm touches my shoulder. "Wait!" He tries to hand me a bullet-shaped silver cylinder filled with white powder. "Take a hit."

I dangle a handful of white bags under his nose and walk hurriedly out the door.

Now I know how the worm on the end of a hook must feel. Trapped, frantic, waiting to be swallowed. The quickest way to a drink is the bar. I bypass the nasty eyes and order a double Smirnoff. I ask for ice. The bartender will get around to that by the time Puerto Rico becomes a state. I gulp the vodka.

I look over the people at the bar and see a woman staring back. She has dark, deep-set eyes with a long, pinched nose. I look away but come back. She's still looking. I finish my drink and walk toward her.

Her lips are thick and painted with a white film over pink. Her eyes are lined to match. She's unattractive and attractive at the same time. All the parts are bold, but the whole is beautifully balanced. She wears hot pants and a sleeveless pullover. We semi-embarrass ourselves for a few awkward minutes, then settle into our conversation. She's a dental assistant named Jean, and I sell cars.

Jean sits on a hard bar stool with her long, shapely legs crossed. The sweaty bartender interrupts to ask if we'd like to have a drink with Mr. Diez at the end of the bar. I wave him over.

The art of deception calls for coolness while showing calm and warmth. I place my hand on Jean's thigh. She smiles.

"May we join you?" Diez has a wide grin, and his girlfriend's eyes are large saucers. He tells me to call him Landy. I shake his hand and introduce myself. "I'm Mike, an associate of Richie Stone."

We talk about nothing, laughing, tentative looks, while we size each other up. Diez is the ringmaster, the women, visual trivia, and I'm the ambiguity, the unmade form inside the marble. Diez jibs at my lack of discretion to come to "the Caribbean" on dance night. He's not dumb, but he's no seasoned pro either, as he measures my resilience to his tenacity. He puts his arm around my waist. When he finds no trace of a gun, his arm comes up and rests on my shoulder.

I lean toward him. "I'm looking for Vasquez. I met him at Nickie Piantini's funeral. I was in the neighborhood, so I thought I'd say hello."

"You got business with him?"

"Nothing definite."

"Let's take a walk?" He holds my elbow. "My car. I'll give the girls a bag for the powder room."

I follow his compact, round frame to an Oldsmobile parked on the nearest side street. He opens the door for me. Diez jumps in the back seat, directly behind me. When I turn to look at him, there's a gun pointed at me.

Diez is lost in the darkness. I find a bag in my pocket and untwist the tie.

"Your hand is busy Landy; we'll snort mine."

His voice comes from the void, "Give me your wallet!"

Light from a passing car sprays the interior, exaggerating his set jaw and flared nostrils.

I say, "They told me this was flake, but I think it's compressed shake."

One of my hands grasps the bag, the other holds an overflowing key between us. Sweat glistens on the outline of Diez's shadowed face.

He inhales the cocaine, but the gun remains.

"The wallet."

The barrel pokes me in the head.

"You want more?" His gun doesn't move. Another car passes, bursting the darkness with silver light.

"I want to get back to that set of legs in there," I say.

"The wallet."

I turn and put my finger on the barrel of his gun. "How come you weren't at Nickie Piantini's funeral?"

"I was."

"Vasquez and I bullshitted briefly."

I ask him to lean forward to pack his other nostril. The gun disappears.

Diez sticks the silver bullet to my nose. Something strong with a burning trail shoots up my nostril. I stop myself from a dry cough and swallow. The silver bullet is pushed up my other nostril, and I take a deep breath.

His gun is somewhere in the darkness, so I deftly remove my weapon from its ankle holster and turn, aiming it at his face.

"Surprise, Landy!"

I hold the gun there. His breathing is like oars slapping hard against waves. Short, drugged breaths.

"Listen, Landy, no more gun games. My name is Mike from Brooklyn. Alessi family. There's a price on the head of the cop who killed Nickie. All I want is fuckin' information and maybe make a drug deal. I'll snort your stuff. You answer some questions."

I grab the cylinder from his hand, turn slightly away into the dimness, tip it, rub my thumb across the top, push it up one nostril, and breathe through the other. Once. Twice. Three times. I rim my nose with the white dust from my thumb for effect and toss it back to him.

My gun disappears. "Happy?"

"Your wallet."

I give a loud sigh. "Can't you answer my question?"

"What's the question?"

"You know anything about the contract on the cop?"

"Yeah, why?"

"I could make a name for myself. Supposedly, this cop comes from my neighborhood."

"Just kill Calabrese. You'll get paid."

"If it was that easy, I figure he'd be dead already."

"So?" He says with an edge.

"Calabrese ain't dead. Why? Is there a contract or not?"

"Word's on the street, how come you don't know?"

"You Cubans are impossible. I'm outta here."

We walk back into the wall of tinseled color and noise. Jean kisses my cheek and whispers "thank you" in my ear. She has cocaine breath, dry and harsh.

Diez concentrates on my reflection in the mirror behind the bar. The situation doesn't feel right. Diez's original animated veneer has changed to watchfulness. Shortly, he should make inquiries. I would in his shoes. If Vasquez or Gabriel walk into this place, everything will get evened out. I'll be traded instead of Calabrese. I'll be hung upside down and skinned. Amateurs would do that. No respect. No quick kill. I once found a faceless skull, the lunatic traced around his wife's face with a scalpel, then ripped it off and pissed on her. Another picked out a brain through an eye while the victim screamed.

The Smirnoff goes down smooth and fast. I run my hand from Jean's knee up to under the hem of her hot pants. She edges back on her stool, holding away my hand and whispering "don't" under her breath. I place my hand between her thighs. Diez's friendliness has peeled away, leaving a suspicious air and sparse conversation.

He says, "What did you and Vasquez discuss?"

"Business. He said he'd like to collect that contract money."

"I thought you weren't sure if there was a contract?"

"Favor, job, contract. You know how Italians are."

The filing Cuban appears at the end of the bar near the kitchen door. Jean's scent is rising through her clothes. Cocaine is at work, pushing out from every pore.

The disc jockey chatters away in Spanish. Cigarette smoke curls, stalls, and travels between us. Jean kisses me. My heart begins to trot, and my mind gags because moving toward us is Dickie Green.

Anxiety ripples through me. How do I dissolve in a dense, homogeneous crowd? Green is coming our way. I rest my shoe on the bottom bar rail to give me faster access to my gun.

Green is stalled among customers.

I lift my leg, maneuvering my belly to the bar, slipping my gun into my belt. I free my hand and lift Jean off her chair. "Just move with me!" She's wide-eyed and quizzical. I'm pressed against her backside leading her into a crowd that seems to be pushing against us.

Faces, bodies, colored light, noise, and foreign words all converge on me. The filer is now talking with Diez. I push harder into Jean.

"My purse!"

"Just move."

Over her shoulder, she speaks, "What! What are you doing?"

I give her a fake laugh and a quick hump.

"Move, or ya gonna get poked."

When Green slides into our path, I turn my head toward the bar. Green's expression widens. "The cop? Right?"

The masquerade is over. Green wears a big smile as he moves closer toward us. Diez shouts in Spanish and forces himself into the crowd. I encircle Jean with my arm and push her forcefully toward the kitchen door. Green is sucked into the sweep of the crowd.

Once my gun becomes visible, women scream, and the men freeze. A sinkhole opens inside a wave of commotion. There's a wall of hate before me as I push forward. A glass flies past hitting a bystander and crashing on the floor.

Several guns appear in the hands of angry, drunk, and stoned men, with no knowledge of what's transpiring. They're reacting, and that's dangerous. Diez pushes people aside to get to me. I fight to pull open the kitchen door. I push Green forward into the white kitchen light. Metallic silver reflects from every side. There are all kinds of smashing noises, metal bouncing and kitchenware ricocheting all around us. Another door, this one opens into sudden darkness. I realize Jean's hand is glued inside mine and the three of us are running for our lives.

At the first side street, I slide Jean into Green's arms. "Stay here! Don't move. Green—you hear me?"

He stares at the gun in my hand. "Yeah, but those motherfuckers come, I'm gone."

"Don't leave her alone or I'll find you. Understand? I'll be back."

"Hey, you got another gun? I don't even have a knife."

"Just stay here. You'll be safe."

I dodge the light, creep low, following the parked cars till I'm underneath the car behind Diez's Oldsmobile. It's only a matter of time—drugged ego and alcohol-fueled time.

Footsteps and voices get closer.

There's no crowd, only two voices heard between panting breaths. Keys are being separated. I see Diez's shoes at the Oldsmobile's door. I quietly roll from under the car and smash my gun against Diez's face. My gun then cuts across to the Cuban. "Lock your fingers on the back of your head! Come here!"

He comes around the car.

I kick him hard twice. His ID says his name is Emilio Reyes. I push them into the car and handcuff them through the steering wheel. My gun is square in Diez's bloody face. "I've got five kilos of cocaine, plus heroin. How much of that you get charged with depends on the answers you give me. You were sent to the morgue last Wednesday. Why? By who?"

"Fuck off!"

I twist the cuffs tighter and they dig deeper. Both their faces cramp with pain.

Emilio spits at me. I smack him hard against his forehead with the gun butt. Then Diez gets it across the ear.

"I need answers" I tug at the cuffs. They both wince in pain.

Both are bleeding. I push the gun into Diez's ear. "Beethoven continued to work deaf. I don't think you'll fare so well." I push in deeper.

He screams, "Okay, okay! Stop."

"Talk, fuck!"

"We were supposed to get Calabrese."

"And?"

"He didn't have his uniform on with a name tag."

"Get or kill Calabrese?"

"Whatever, kill, deliver, what's the difference?"

"Why isn't Calabrese dead?"

"The Italians want everything cool for a while, but if Calabrese has an accident, that's another story."

"Calabrese being watched?"

Diez pulls his face down by tightening his lips. I rattle my gun in his ear. He yells and tries to bring his free arm across to grab my face. I backhand him hard and whack Reyes again.

He yells, "What the hell you think?"

"How closely?"

"You think you could stop Reno Piantini from killing that prick if he wanted him dead?"

Reyes says to Diez, "I think you just committed suicide by talking." Then he looks at me. "You got nothing on me?"

"Cocaine's illegal. You shouldn't be dealing it."

Emilio stares hard at me. "You're the pig who fucked with my partner Andre. Aren't you, pig? You cost me money. No matter what you got on us, we'll be out in hours. You and Calabrese will be buried in the same stinking hole. Andre and I will make you suffer. We're gonna fuck your wife in the ass while you watch."

I punch Emilio's face hard, blood splatters. I yank back his head by the hair. "This should halt your hysteria." His mouth opens, and I pour a bag of cocaine down his throat. Pinching his nose, I cover his mouth long enough for him to remember me forever. He hacks and coughs into Diez's bloodied face.

The patrol cars from Precinct Five have arrived. For a few minutes, the world is livable again. Two fewer rats pissing on anything decent.

Green holds Jean close to him. "Everything cool, man?"

"Yeah. Here's your purse, Jean."

Green's face lights up. "You went back in that joint?"

"They were very courteous this time."

"This got to do with what you were asking me about today? That cop who killed Nickie?"

"Losing your nerve, Dickie?"

He grins in Jean's direction. "Diez and Reyes ain't any tougher than Nickie, and Filippo and I weren't scared of him." He starts strutting like a peacock. "What now, Lone Ranger?"

"You know Manuel Vasquez?"

He shakes his head. "I see him around. He knows me."

Jean watches me as a smile creeps across my face. "You're priceless, Green."

Jean smiles. "What's your name anyway?"

I grin. "D'laska. Jean Louise Moderna. When things get settled, we'll go out dancing."

She runs her tongue over her full lips before speaking. "That's it? You almost get me killed, go through my purse, and it's catch me later? Listen, Ala...aska...I need a drink. Now!"

I force three twenties in Green's hand. "D'laska, not Alaska. Dickie go somewhere nice and buy this lady two doubles. She deserves it."

THURSDAY
4:07 A.M.

AFTER BOOKING Diez and Reyes and filing the paperwork, I stare at the phone. Do I wake Suzanne to say good night? Or do I let her sleep, knowing when she wakes, she'll be thinking I've broken my promise to call her? Reluctantly, I dial.

"Hello!"

"Suzanne, ah, good night."

"Night!" Click.

CHAPTER 10

THURSDAY, JULY 10, 1975
8:30 A.M.

THE RED DOTS between the numbers on the clock keep flashing off and on. Whoever is on the other end of the phone annoying me is late. I've almost had four hours of sleep. Sharp pains ripple up my back as I reach to grab the receiver.

"Yeah, this is D'laska."

"Good, I wanted to catch you before you left. This is John Gage, Justice Department."

"Gage!"

"I've made reservations for us at twelve-thirty at the Prometheus Club on West 14th for lunch. Any problem?"

"Wha...no, why?"

"See you then. Goodbye and congratulations."

Replacing the receiver, my head hits the pillow, and my eyes close.

THURSDAY

10:55 A.M.

I ALMOST FEEL ALIVE. From my bedroom window, it looks like a dirty watercolor day with that gray metallic haze that protects us from any direct sunlight.

Ainsworth was right: my refrigerator is a disgrace, and I'm out of bananas. I place a Bit-O-Honey in a spoon and add honey.

I dial Ainsworth's number, the desk phone rings, then a computer click transfers the call.

"Chief McConnell's Office."

"Suzanne? Where's Ainsworth?"

"Michael"

"Why is his phone ringing in your office?"

There's a long pause before she answers, "Last night on the Lower West Side, some maniac cut up two college kids. Detective Ainsworth is needed."

"Why are you answering Ainsworth's phone? And it sounds like you are reading from a script."

"Didn't Chief McConnell talk to you? You better get here right away."

I listen to the tiny crackling becoming more distant until I hang up.

THURSDAY
12:22 P.M.

THE VALET WEARS a pair of snakeskin boots worth more than my entire closet. Approaching the maître d', I suck in my stomach. I'm a few pounds heavier since the last time I wore this funeral suit.

The Prometheus Club is a private inner sanctum known for its business atmosphere, excellent food, influential crust, and rumored back room where the women and gambling are said to rival Las Vegas.

I'm ushered into a chandelier packed, sophisticated dining room to a single corner table where John Gage is occupied with a large, beige folder. We exchange courteous necessities. He thanks me for coming, and I thank him for inviting me. It's sickeningly contrived. He raises his finger, and a waiter appears. I order beer instead of wine.

"Okay Gage, what's up?"

"Call me John."

"Sure! John!"

"Thank you. I want to congratulate you on your handling of this Calabrese affair. You performed admirably." He fluffs his thin eyebrows. "When I read your qualifications after the shooting, I knew you were the perfect person for the case. Any other cop would have been disastrous. You acted exactly the way I thought you would, with intelligence and not emotion. You actually investigated the incident. Thought about it before making any rash decisions or moves. You understand that all crimes have a why, when, where, and how. The other Neanderthals would have had me doing paperwork for the rest of my career. I'm impressed, D'laska. You're bright. You graduated near the top of your class. You're overqualified to be involved in local law enforcement. Leave the dirty shit to the pawns.

"I've made a few calls on your behalf. There's a Justice Department internship in Seattle, where you can also finish your Ph.D. at the university. We reward, not look down on, intelligence."

I sip the beer from the pilsner glass. "You chose me?"

"The department had influence over who was selected. McConnell recommended you, and after reviewing your file, I agreed. I couldn't afford to have Roberts in control, he couldn't pass a grade eight IQ test, but his wife's father was once an assistant commissioner with a lot of local influence, so he had to be tolerated. And with Ring, the whole investigation would have been about him, not the shooting. I needed someone level-headed and respected, like McConnell, and an intelligent, methodical operator. Michael D'laska, you were made to order."

"You used me!"

He looks around and returns to me. "Let's say you've auditioned for a part and you've won the role."

"Why are you telling me now? Have you sold Calabrese out?"

Gage's long face turns serious. "Listen, if you're too childish to see what I'm offering, try walking out of here. You have nowhere to go. You're marked, tainted. Not only have you been tied to Internal Affairs, but soon you'll be linked with us. You try to explain the truth to those ignorant bastards out there. Do you think your cop buddies will ever trust you again? You've pissed off Ring, Roberts, Connors, the Desk Sergeant at the Two-two and even Peter Wrobel thinks you're an arrogant asshole."

The beer isn't as refreshing as I first thought.

He taps the table. "Don't blame me for your proper handling of this case."

A giant scoop digs deep, scrapes against my insides and deposits me outside myself. I'm being emptied.

I catch Gage's voice calling my name, while the waiter patiently lingers for me to order.

"Another beer," I say without thinking. "Cold, coldest you have."

A faint pinkness returns to Gage's hollow cheeks. "Yes, you were played, sometimes the ends justify the means. None of that matters anymore."

"What about Calabrese?"

"Calabrese, Guzzetta, and their families were asked if they wanted to leave New York for a while till things cooled. They chose Toms River, near Atlantic City. We're picking up the tab."

"Who's watching them?"

"Calabrese insisted that he only trusted Guzzetta."

"What about Reno Piantini and the contract?"

"Things will take their course."

"What does that mean?"

"I am curious to see if you did any research. Do you know who, Giuseppe Petrosino is?"

I rub my temples. "Should I know?"

"He was a detective sergeant investigating Mafia activities. He was the only other cop we know about that had a contract on his life. Petrosino was murdered in 1909."

"Gee, I'm sorry I missed the funeral."

"Times change. We better order lunch."

"I'm not hungry."

"Well, I am."

The waiter reappears with my beer.

Gage looks over at me. "Mike."

I snap, "Smirnoff, rocks, a double. I've lost my appetite."

He gives the waiter a proud grin and orders the wild salmon for both of us.

When the help scurries away, Gage says, "I would have chosen Isserlyn over Baxter. But you're a psychologist, and from that perspective, Baxter is a better study. Lovely breasts. Did you know that her fiancé was a classical musician and war protester who committed suicide days before their wedding? Her depression was so bad she spent time at a clinic."

"Leave her out of this."

"Phyllis Isserlyn, on the other hand, comes from power and money, much more to gain but with much smaller tits."

I swallow hard. "What's your fucking point?"

"No point, just conversation." Gage's eyes brighten. "I also thought it was very clever the way you happened upon Barone's ledger."

"How long have you been following me?"

"Don't get emotional. It wasn't personal. We thought it amusing that Ring also had a man following you. How are the re-stitches holding up?"

My hand tips the beer glass almost spilling the contents. "You are the lowest form of life."

A perverse grin overcomes him. "I am always protecting the government's interests. Exactly what you swore to do when you took an oath."

"Fuck you."

He glares and sighs. "You're not from New York so I thought you'd be capable of an intelligent conversation. Don't prove me wrong."

"Calabrese didn't commit premeditated murder."

"We know that. We knew that shortly after the shooting. But it's not your fault he stuck to that ridiculous story. Makes you wonder."

"If Calabrese changed a word of it, everything he's ever said will be disputed."

Gage gloats. "That's not my fault."

"No, but it works in your favor."

"No! It's worked in your favor. You solved the case."

"When was that? Is the contract rescinded or whatever the fuck they do to have it go away? And does it really go away?"

He sips his white wine. "Excellent question. Just because the money is no longer there, there could be other motives to kill Calabrese, and none of those would be your fault. You found the man innocent."

I say again, "Yes, he is."

Gage sets his glass down on a small white napkin and laughs. "Calabrese's courier clients have close connections to Henry. He's under investigation right now. When he's indicted, I'm sure Calabrese's name will be mentioned."

"Calabrese's business affairs have nothing to do with the shooting?"

"We're looking into that."

"What deal did you make with Reno Piantini?"

Gage lifts his stemware to the diffused sunlight that pushes through the rows of beveled windows. He shakes his head. "That was nasty of you to leave Andre Gabriel in such a state. We weren't as subtle. He thinks you sent us. You'd better hope those punks, like Gabriel, Reyes, and Diez, don't gain any power, or else you're in a real precarious position if you stay in New York. You'll be hated equally by both sides. Poor Ainsworth, he seems to be caught in the crossfire. He's going to need to keep his job, with him getting married soon. The salmon here is superb."

Every door is a wall. Every exit a toilet. McConnell was right. God, he was right. I've been gutted, skinned, and fucked. I gulp my drink.

My voice is sharp, "Have you stopped following me?"

"This Calabrese thing is just about over. Don't worry about Mulvaney, our state senator needed her to go on a two-week fact-finding tour of Western New York. Anyway, you should be thinking about your future. Seattle is the most interesting city, and our office there is first rate."

"What did you mean just about over?"

Gage's surgical technique is flawless, emotionless, and harmonious. He opens the cavity, and while gangrene is setting in, he comes to lunch.

Gage raises his thin eyebrows. "Things will fall into place."

"Has Calabrese been set up?"

"Whatever happens to Calabrese, he brought on himself."

I lean toward him. "Fuck you!"

Gage clenches his jaw to hold back his anger. "Know what I hate most? Bright men who act ignorant and stupid."

I lift Gage by his jacket. Glass and dishes crash from the overturned table. I toss him to the wall. He crumbles easily as the frantic staff runs to his aid.

"I hope you all choke to death," I yell.

The heat of the afternoon slams into me at the valet station. A patrol car arrives with lights flashing and sirens blaring. I show them my badge. "The thin-faced prick with wine all over his blue suit says he's from the Justice Department. I wouldn't believe a thing he says. Let him stew for a while without making any calls."

THURSDAY
1:40 P.M.

Suzanne isn't at her desk, I flip through the copies of her messages. Ainsworth left a number for me to call him at eleven-forty-five a.m. It's a New Jersey area code. She was reading from a script, word for word that Ainsworth was needed in the Lower East Side.

"Michael, what are you looking for?" It's Suzanne. I replace the message book.

"Nothing. Can I see McConnell?" She stands erect, feet together, chest out, all wrapped in a lime-colored suit. Her pale face has traces of green eyeshadow.

Suzanne comes forward, her movements definite. She takes my arm. "What are you looking for?"

"What time did Gage call McConnell today?"

She comes closer. "Gage hasn't, but Ainsworth called around noon."

"Why are Ainsworth's call being routed to this office?"

"That came from Chief Roberts."

"Roberts!"

"Did the commissioner call this morning?"

"No. Chief McConnell met with him and Phyllis Isserlyn last night."

"Was John Gage there?"

An angry McConnell erupts into the room, pointing his finger at me. "Get into my office."

He slams the door behind him. "You booked two men last night. They're screaming police brutality. According to Connors, you pistol-whipped them and almost sawed their wrists off. What's wrong with you?"

He falls into his desk chair. His face is weary, but his voice is loud and bitter. "One was taken to St. Vincent's to have his eyebrow stitched. They contend...you listening, D'laska? The drug charges are trumped up."

Suzanne intrudes. "Michael!" McConnell and I both stare at her. "Paul Ainsworth wants to see you. He said it was urgent."

I say, "Chief, you have to trust me. It's essential I speak with Paul."

"Chief Roberts needs him. There has been stabbings on the Lower East Side."

"Calabrese will be murdered in New Jersey."

McConnell's face becomes rigid. "Not your case anymore."

"Murdered!"

"It's out of my hands."

"You told me I had until Friday."

He groans. "You've made too many mistakes."

"Isn't that funny, Gage told me about an hour ago I did everything perfectly."

"What! Who?"

I appeal to McConnell. "Think about the consequences of Calabrese's death for a moment, while I talk with Paul."

I turn to walk away, but he shouts, "Come here!"

"Calabrese won't make it through the weekend."

He presses his knuckles into the desk. "All of a sudden you're clairvoyant."

"Trust me. I know I'm right on this."

The phone rings, and he picks up the receiver. "Hello, Agent Gage...what?"

I head for the door; he interrupts his conversation, shouting, "We're not through."

"I'll be in my office."

THURSDAY
2:10 P.M.

PAUL and I trot down the hall to the nearest men's room. I lock the door.

"You look beat," I say. "Where have you been all night?"

"New Jersey?"

"We haven't much time. Spill everything."

"What's going on here?"

"You first."

Paul says, "You were right. After Floriano and Stone left the Blue Chateau, they went to the Trenton Avenue Club. After that, they headed straight for a mob-run joint in Long Branch. From there they went to the Italian-American Club. Then they picked up two high-class hookers. Next, back up to Long Branch. After that, Point Pleasant had a few drinks in a couple of places. Continued down to

South Toms River, had a drink in a rundown fishing joint. Then they turned around and headed north again to Asbury Park."

Ainsworth runs the cold water, fills his hands and splashes some on his face. "They drove through Asbury Park, then they went to the amusement park till it closed at midnight."

"The amusement park? Did they go on the rides?"

"Sure. Then to a motel, and I figured they'd shack up till noon. I was wrong. They were up at eight, driving like sightseers through the countryside down to South Toms River, stopped for breakfast at some out of the way dump, then they drove north again to Asbury Park." Paul yawns. "I called you from the amusement park. Next thing I know, Roberts is reaming me out to get back, and here I am."

"Did they drive down any side roads or dead-ends?"

"Sorta," he says. "I couldn't get that close."

"Did they stop in Toms River?"

"South Toms River, on the other side of the water."

"Calabrese, Guzzetta, and their families are staying in Toms River."

Ainsworth stretches, twisting his bony frame from side to side. He rests his hand on my shoulder. "Floriano and Stone never met with Calabrese and Guzzetta."

I sigh. "Hookers and wives don't get along in Italian circles."

"What's going on here?"

"I don't know exactly."

"I thought they said Friday?"

I continue, "Do you trust me?"

"We're partners."

"I want you to forget about Roberts."

"Mike, supposedly two kids have been cut up pretty bad."

"I don't believe them."

"Who is they? Other cops?" Ainsworth splashes more cold water on his face. Pulls a few towels from the machine and looks at me. "Okay."

"Floriano and Stone are going to murder Calabrese at the amusement park in Asbury Park. Unless the feds have something planned to get Calabrese first."

"Oh really...you know this how?"

I pace in the confined space. "Floriano and Stone went to Long Branch first to pay respect to the Mafia chiefs in New Jersey and to assure them that the murder will go smoothly. This is going to be an orchestrated accident in the perfect setting—the New Jersey shore."

Paul shrugs. "Floriano is Guzzetta's blood."

"But not Calabrese's. This is their ticket to the big time."

"How do you know?"

"We're at the end. There are no more empty spaces. The last piece of the puzzle fell into place when you told me Stone and Floriano went to the amusement park. It's the one spot Calabrese would feel safe meeting Reno Piantini. His family had rides at Coney Island. He'd be relatively comfortable, especially with Guzzetta being there. He would believe he had the advantage. It is the perfect set up."

Ainsworth watches me as I put all the past week's pieces before us to produce a clear picture of what the next twenty-four hours hold.

I continue, "The meeting was set up by someone at the Trenton Avenue Club, probably Alessi, with the idea that it would be a legitimate appointment for Calabrese to plead his case. Both men would meet to see if a settlement could be negotiated." I pause for a moment, gathering my thoughts. "Parallel to that, Gage has been trying to restructure his deal with Piantini. Gage may be turning his head while those two pricks fulfill Reno Piantini's contract by killing Calabrese. Guzzetta is the scapegoat. It's so rotten, it's perfect—a traitor from the perspective of the mob, the fall guy for the department. Just like Garcia didn't protect Nickie, Guzzetta won't be able to protect Calabrese. It all fits."

I can feel my blood pumping. "We need to work fast. Catch up with Stone and Floriano. I'll be in Toms River later. Check the local Toms River phone book. I'll be in one of the first three bars under the B's. If I can't be reached, I'll leave a message with Britt at the Innfield."

"Let's switch cars. I don't want Stone and Floriano suspicious."

"Paul, thanks, I know I'm right."

Ainsworth shrugs. "I guess after I marry Clare, I'll be eligible for the Mounties."

THURSDAY
2:32 P.M.

When I walk back into the office, Suzanne approaches, her face more uncertain with every step I take toward her. She finds my eyes with hers. "What's going on?"

"I need you to be a sponge once I leave here."

I hug her then push her to arm's length. "I need you to find out for me where Calabrese is staying. Call me at the Innfield Bar, on St. Anne. If I'm not there, leave a message with a bartender named Britt, no one else."

She moves away from me into the weak sunlight. "Chief McConnell wants you back in his office, ASAP."

"I think Calabrese is going to be murdered."

"You think? Chief McConnell wouldn't stand for that."

"It's not a perfect system."

She fights my advance. I forcefully fold her into my arms. My lips circle hers.

She breaks away. "Your needs again. Why is it always somebody else's needs?"

I have no logical answer for her. So, I tell her what I'd like to hear. "Because I care."

"What do you want me to tell Chief McConnell?"

"Give him the same answer."

THURSDAY
3:05 P.M.

Once outside, I hurry to a phone booth.

"Flip Olearczyk, please."

"Who's calling?"

"Mike D'laska."

The phone is cupped, but I hear voices in the background.

"Flip, that prick Sergeant Connors is—"

"This is Olearczyk."

"Flip, I need to speak with you."

Polite, professional silence.

"Listen." His voice is low. "You ain't real popular in this precinct."

"Flip, Calabrese needs your help."

"Rumor has it he's dirty anyway."

I take a deep breath before speaking. "He's a good cop. I can prove it."

"So, what does that have to do with me?"

"I need a few questions answered."

A contemplative sigh makes its way through the wires before I hear his voice. "Meet me at a joint called Patterson's in thirty minutes."

THURSDAY
3:35 P.M.

PATTERSON'S IS a cheerful little tavern with nostalgic photos lining the newly papered walls. The slim blonde barmaid walks away after setting down my beer. I stare out the window to the empty picnic tables on the patio. The sunlight heats empty glasses and makes caskets out of abandoned beer bottles. By now, McConnell has little choice but to suspend me, dismiss me, or worse. They're probably expecting me to cower, apologize to the world, lick their collective asses, and admit I'm a piece of shit like the rest of them.

Olearczyk taps me on the shoulder and walks to the back booth without saying a word. I follow. His forehead glistens with sweat. He doesn't waste any time. "D'laska, the only people you haven't pissed off in this neighborhood are the Chinese, but I have faith in you."

His manner is rude and abrupt; the sparks of friendliness have diminished. He hunches over the table. "Connors is gonna put up a wanted poster for you, and I can't say I blame him. What the hell business you got in Little Italy?" He places his hands on the sticky tabletop. "Some Justice Department fuck came to talk with me about this Calabrese shit. Then I get a call from a real asshole from Internal Affairs who is working with Mulvaney. I don't know what's going on with you, and I don't give a shit. I'm telling you for the last time, I got a pension to protect, ya hear? I don't know anything that doesn't concern me. Don't come around anymore."

The barmaid approaches the booth. Olearczyk growls at her for a draft and a shot of Black Velvet. I nod the same.

I try logic. I don't know why it never worked before. "Listen, Flip, you came here for a reason, and it's not to vent."

He wipes his nose and looks away. "Don't call me again."

"Calabrese is innocent. I can prove it."

"Ring says he's dirty. Mixed up with Mafia slumlords who are ripping off the city."

"Ring's wrong."

"Who the fuck are you? God? You can't be—you're not Irish."

I move on. "Have you heard anything about Reno Piantini turning himself in?"

He shrugs.

I ask, "Would Reno Piantini risk going into New Jersey?"

"How do you know he doesn't live in New Jersey?"

It clicks at that moment. "Because he's safe in New York."

"What are you getting at?"

I push my hair back. "Anywhere else but New York, he jeopardizes his security. Anywhere else, he could be picked up, killed, any number of things could happen."

"The guy's big enough to go anywhere."

"Just the reverse. Piantini is trapped, that's why he started talking to the Justice Department."

"If you were Piantini—"

The barmaid interrupts, "Detective Olearczyk, there's a phone call for you."

He looks at her then back at me. "It must be the precinct."

The barmaid smiles as she places the drinks on the table.

Olearczyk rushes back, downs the whiskey, and takes a large swallow of beer. His face is grave. "Two cops were involved in a shooting on Prince and Ivy."

I gulp the drinks. "I'll follow you."

He holds his arm out to me. "Not too close. I don't need the attention."

THURSDAY
4:20 P.M.

TEN DAYS AGO, a crowd like this needed to be kept in a line across from St. Vincent's Hospital when Nickie Piantini lay in the street. As I approach, I hear all the usual taunting remarks, the forged misinterpretations on both sides. Yesterday, I walked this street. Now the same hate-filled faces feel another scar etched on their souls.

Up ahead, there's an ambulance. A body lies in the street. The hot, putrid air carries the smell of blood and the sense of helplessness. A small group of cops is to one side. Sirens abruptly stop and car doors slam.

"He's a dark-skinned man that's dead."

Off to the side, I hear the muffled laughter of two old timers with sunglasses, guns, and beer guts. To those of the neighborhood, we are the enemy without opened eyes or compassion.

I hear the story secondhand in the wind from a young cop who doesn't know quite how to act. His voice is full of excitement. "The nigger was running down the street, he just got done burglarizing one of the apartments. He tried to fire at the cop who was chasing him."

From the apartment building, two cops lead a hysterical young woman in a cheap dress to a patrol car.

The dead man's brains leak from a shattered skull, and his face is partially gone. Blood oozes from holes through his back and heart.

The cop who did the shooting wasn't very far away when he killed Dickie Green. A medic stops me from touching the body.

I can't comprehend it all, but I notice the vet sitting on the curb with a rag in his face. Over my head, I hear a conversation, explanations. I slowly turn away from the wasted vet. Sergeant Peter Wrobel is taking statements. Quick, neat statements from the two cops I met at Marlowe's. I stare at them. I remember biceps telling me to keep the bottle of Remy and his slippery partner, who just killed Dickie Green.

Slippery has his arm on Wrobel's shoulder. He has a smirk painted on his miserable face. We're all members of the same club. We all know the real rules beneath the politics of the game. Death is routine, part of the job when you're given a gun. And then there are the fringe benefits like drinking for free in night spots and wasting little men like Dickie Green.

The vet's eyes are empty beacons. Authority never loses. Something repulsive begins to turn inside me. It's guilt with claws somersaulting in every fiber of my being. It rips through my heart and bursts into my brain. Hatred and helplessness swallow me for the second time today. Dickie Green is dead. Probably, somewhere in the Bronx, a punk named Filippo is being wrapped in mortuary white. Green was killed because he was a frayed lose end. He spoke with me, he fucked over Nickie, and he was at the scene of the shooting. Authority, power, and money never lose.

I look at my hands, visualizing the second scenario—the underlying message in the puzzle I put together. If I get in the way, I'm expendable too. That's what McConnell meant this morning. He wanted to protect me from the high-speed train; he wanted me off the tracks, but it's too late.

I move into the crowd, slipping past the jeers. My stomach is queasy, and I try to puke by the side of my car, but nothing comes up. I slam the car door. Once inside, I race into the filthy, trash-ridden streets.

On Prince past Joyce Avenue, I slam on my brakes and run to a telephone booth. I rip out a page from the phone book Jean Moderna's address.

Prickly heat has become a layer of grime coating me. I try to make my way through traffic to Lincoln Street—gas, brake, gas, brake. It takes too long to get there. Maybe I'm just paranoid. They probably left her alone. Maybe something will work out today.

I'll get there, and we'll laugh. We'll have a drink and make plans to go dancing. She's probably on her way home from work right now. Two more blocks then Lincoln. I race, making the right turn on two wheels. Midway down the block, my car screeches to a halt. I run up the entrance steps and bound up the wooden stairs to the fourth-floor landing. I turn the knob, and the door opens.

The smell of sweat and blood.

"Jean!" Each room is a blur. I push open the last door as my heart catches up with me. She cowers on the bed semi-conscious, sobbing hysterically, staring forward. She's been brutally beaten and probably raped. Thin lines of dried blood running down her breasts. As I move toward her, she screams.

I yell at the voice on the other end of the phone that I need help.

The screams continue. It's the same chilling scream over and over. I rest my head against a wall and shut my eyes. I straighten up and pound the thin plaster with my fists. Noises echo around me, objects crash to the floor. I hit harder and faster, harder and faster until most of the wall is missing.

I hear the calling card of the police and the medics. The sound of importance, of urgency. The high-pitched noises become one loud clamor. Brakes and metal, voices and footsteps. Blue and white uniforms enter the apartment. Everybody wants answers. I hear orders and directions given. I hear my own voice. A lieutenant has taken control. The painful, pitchfork screams continue.

I tell a sergeant the little I know. The medics must be trying to comfort her because the rhythmic screaming has changed to a more frightening one—it's higher pitched and more frantic. It tears at my brain, and it will always be there.

Before I leave, I tighten my jaw and walk into her bedroom. Jean is sedated and restrained. I lift a sheet spotted with blood. A medic looks at me. "They cut her vagina and sodomized her."

THURSDAY
5:30 P.M.

I FIND myself in front of the Sixth Precinct. The only name Gage didn't mention who distrusted me was Rocca's. I have nowhere else to turn. That thought makes me smile. Was it only a week ago I was a respected cop doing his job? I could ask questions, request help, make lives more comfortable, solve crimes. Now I'm precisely what Gage pointed out I was, a nuisance, no, worse, a pariah. Yet, I feel so sure, I need to continue. A sign of a psychopath is his total belief he is correct. I understand logic doesn't exist if there are no rules.

Unannounced, I walk into Rocca's office. His expression tells me how horrible I must look. There's blood on my pants and on my shirt sleeves.

Rocca stands.

"Captain." It doesn't sound like my voice—it's mechanical, controlled. "An Italian-Latin woman has just been beaten, cut, and sodomized. Your men are attending to her right now. They're gonna find nothing. Nobody will be caught. It means something to you for Calabrese to be proven innocent. I will do that and more. I'm going to keep him from being murdered. I need a favor. Andre Gabriel, for sure, and maybe Manuel Vasquez had something to do with what happened to the girl. If Emilio Reyes and Sergio Diez made bail, they are also involved. There's a dead kid on his way to the morgue. He was killed by a cop—he and his partner, a guy with huge biceps are both on Cellini's payroll. He was sacrificed I think because he was a witness to Calabrese's innocence. Or maybe just retribution for talking with me." I swallow hard. "Have anything to drink?"

Rocca walks to a bookcase at the back of his office. "Grand Marnier or Sambuca?"

"No bourbon? Grand Marnier then."

I take a large gulp and ask for more. "Two Coney Island pieces of shit, Martin Floriano, and Richard Stone are set to murder Calabrese, probably tomorrow in Asbury Park. I don't know exactly how it is all tied, it's so convoluted, but I know it's connected. The feds, cops, gangsters—I know it's not my paranoia."

Rocca sits uneasily in his chair but says nothing.

I continue, "I can't prove anything I've just told you. No one can. Take what you want from it. I'll save Calabrese; you find a way to even up the score for what has been done to this girl and the dead kid."

Rocca has measured me since I walked into his office. "Who is the girl and the kid to you?"

"Innocent friends."

"What could happen to these four Hispanics?"

"The system has been corrupted. Justice lies in the hands of the connected and that justice seems to be arbitrary."

"Are you asking me to kill these men?"

"I'm asking for you to examine your conscience. What you can't accomplish, if I am not killed, I will."

"What else do you want?"

"Do you have any connections in Monmouth County, New Jersey?"

"My nephew's a state trooper."

"Give me his name."

"I'll call him for you," he says. "You're pretty sure of yourself, D'laska."

"I know, that's what really frightening me."

"What if you're walking into a trap?"

"A moth to the flames."

He pours himself another drink. "I don't know if you're incredibly bold or incredibly dumb."

"Does it make a difference?"

He downs the liquid. We shake. The pact is sealed. I've joined the hypocrisy. I believe Reyes, Diez, Vasquez, and Gabriel will all have unfortunate accidents or wind up in jail. Biceps and his partner, they might be on my to do later list. I'm involved in something parallel to what I am trying to prevent. It's all so absurd, yet it's happening.

Rocca hands me his business card with a name and a number on the back. We exchange knowing glances as he begins dialing.

THURSDAY
7:15 P.M.

I CALL the Innfield from a phone booth on the other side of the Holland Tunnel. New Jersey smells of corrupt America selling bad dreams. Britt asks me to hold.

Suzanne tells me that once I left, the phone calls never stopped. The office became a nightmare with McConnell and John Gage arguing fiercely. I'm to be brought up on charges, and if Paul isn't back soon, he'll be suspended. McConnell tried to defend my actions, but he's being overpowered. Suzanne continues her frantic explaining, and it takes me several tries before I can interrupt, "Did you get an address for Calabrese?"

She takes in a deep breath. "Did you know we were being filmed?"

"There was a chance."

"I don't have the address," she says.

"What about Paul?"

"He's at the amusement park in Asbury Park."

I hear the ice cubes clink against the glass as she takes a sip.

"Did you like that blues club we went too?"

"Yes, why?"

"That was a great night. We're going to visit that club again…soon, but…now I have to go."

THURSDAY
9:05 P.M.

THE CIRCLING LIGHTS of the Ferris wheel are always visible first at an amusement park. From a distance, everything else seems to radiate from the twirling lights that travel from the orange glow of the park into the blackness of the night.

I hear the mechanical noises, barkers, screams of frightened joy and the smell of fun—hot dogs, sweet confections, and salty air. Nothing is static, yet everything remains in place. I begin to divide what's in front of me into grids, squares hemmed by tumbling lights and popcorn vendors.

I move like a man in the dark. My eyes trace the perimeter. Faces blend into a creamy paste. People walk through the measured frames I create.

At nine-twenty-eight, I follow the blacktop to where several paths converge. The loud music bellowing from the merry-go-round seems inappropriate I stare at the painted faces of the animals as they pass. They all seem to be in pain.

A husky voice breaks my trance, "Detective D'laska?"

I turn. A broad-shouldered young state trooper with abundant dark wavy hair gives me a broad smile. He nods. "I'm Captain Rocca's nephew, Joey. I have the information you requested over the phone."

We shake hands. "Thank you."

I can feel him measure me, mentally confirming his superior strength. "My uncle told me to give you full cooperation." He hands me a folded sheet of paper. It contains the plate numbers for both Guzzetta and Calabrese's cars.

Joey Rocca remains smiling, like a dog who has performed a task and now wants a reward. I'm too distant to feel friendly. I tell him the skeletal story and ask him to go into Toms River and find the lodgings where these cars are registered. He doesn't question my request. He just tells me where to meet him at eleven-thirty.

I move out again, into the lights that roll and crash. Back to the grids, the imaginary squares with twisting machines and fanciful smells. My eyes cross proud winners parading their booty and losers scoffing at their luck. Calabrese would agree to meet here. He would feel comfortable and somewhat in control here.

I lean against a cotton candy booth and comb the complete area. Various intensities of music whirl with the acrobatic lights flashing in the air as rifles fire at targets and balls thud against backdrops. To my right are food concessions. In the center is a big island flanked by two good-sized entrance pathways. Squarely on the island is a large, clumsy, barn-shaped building with a tinseled, Arabian facade horseshoeing a grassy courtyard filled with cheap statues. Stoops circle the building where large carnival caricatures bellow out recorded messages. The building houses Sinbad's Carpet, the only walk-through amusement on the grounds. I study the amusement and the building that houses it.

I spot Paul standing below a grotesque laughing mannequin. His presence here assures me I'm right about this amusement park.

I approach Ainsworth.

"How are you holding up?" I ask.

"I've been here three times today. I don't have much sanity left."

"And?"

"They're all here, at the food concession, eating: Calabrese, Guzzetta, their families, and Floriano. Stone stayed back at the motel with the hookers."

We step farther back and closer to the building away from Calabrese's perspective.

I ask already knowing, "Floriano and Stone were here earlier?"

"Alone and with the women. This Sinbad's Carpet has been a popular attraction for everybody."

"What's on the other side of the building?"

We stroll, marginally outside the park around the bulky building. Behind Sinbad's Carpet, part of the structure is a harshly lit room where working machinery hides on the other side of a rickety screened door. Above the door is a faded emergency exit sign. The smells of grease and grinding gears waft from the room.

On our left, between us and that door, is a grassy hillock surrounded by waist-high shrubbery. On our right is the street.

I take a closer look at the room, asking over my shoulder, "What's on the final side of the building?"

Paul yawns before answering, "A small bus terminal with a couple of offices above."

I force my way through the shrubbery to examine the room. The misshapen door opens quickly. One dim wall light illuminates a room full of churning greasy metal wheels, cabling, and machinery. Aged well oiled machines continually grind, repeating the same monotonous pattern. Smaller devices hiss with movement. Thick wiring runs from substantial metal pulleys through groaning gearboxes. Jumbo chains tug at screeching gears. The smell of hot burning grease hangs in the air. Twisted steel riggings, frayed from age, belch sparks as they shorten and lengthen through worn steel lockets. Compressors add heat to the sour atmosphere. Metal scrapes along with worn, rusty iron. Metal is always grinding, grinding then halting, moving then screeching—old heavy iron against old heavy iron. There's a shaky, vibrating black metal stairwell suspended by wall rods. The steps are caked with years of grease, and the railing is slick with splattered oil. The staircase ends above the black, oily floor. It was once an emergency exit that still leads to a door opening into Sinbad's Carpet. The room's a grinding casket made for an accident.

Returning to the sidewalk, Ainsworth hands me a fistful of shelled peanuts. He takes more out of his pocket before asking, "What do you think?"

"That's the only amusement you walk through, isn't it?"

"Sure is. It's mostly interiors except at the end when you ride Sinbad's Carpet out. It takes ten, twenty minutes, depending on how many kids are in front of you."

"Did they check out this room?"

"Stone poked his nose in there."

"And?"

"And, nothing, they bullshitted here for a while then went on the ride. Why?"

"Let's take a walk through."

"What about Floriano?"

"Nothing's going to happen until tomorrow."

THURSDAY
11:35 P.M.

. . .

THROUGH THE GRIMY WINDOW, I see Joey Rocca's head bobbing as he walks from the parking lot into the brightly lit diner. He's wearing tight jeans and a snug tank top. The gold chain around his neck bounces with his snappy gait. He finds me in the back booth.

He talks while approaching, "Order the Italian waffles, they're unbelievable."

I give him a cautious smile. "I'm just having coffee."

He slides in the booth. "Calabrese and Guzzetta are staying at bungalows not far from the park. Nice clean place, back out of the way. Off the main drags. They're in adjacent cabins."

A pretty waitress lingers to take our order. She looks at Joey adoringly. He takes her hand. "Missy, this is my friend, Mike, from NYPD."

She gives him a warm smile, then says to Joey, "Italian waffles, sausage, and coffee?"

He nods.

I order another coffee.

Joey watches Missy walk away. "She's married to a bum. A real bum. I can't believe it. You see her, she's beautiful."

"Pay attention," I say. "I want you to arrange for a maintenance man to meet us at the amusement park tomorrow morning around nine-thirty before it opens. Can you do that?"

"I know the superintendent of the park, it shouldn't be a problem." He raises his eyebrows. "Why?"

I place my elbows on the table, making a steeple with my fingers. I look across at Joey. "If you and a partner felt confident you would get away with it, how would you plan a murder in the amusement park? Remember, one, you want the murder to look like an accident. Two, you will be in the company of a confidant of the man you plan to kill. The aim is to kill one man and have the other man believe, once the act is committed, that it was an accident—not a shooting, not a poisoning, or a mugging, but a legitimate accident. Finally, you and your partner have to look completely innocent."

Joey turns his head toward the window to think. He takes his time.

He looks at me. "Tough question. I'll take it in stages. An accident in a park usually happens around fast-moving rides, but all those are popular and in the open with witnesses everywhere. No good for murder." He thinks for a moment longer. "A ride that goes into a darkened area, but then, what about the friend of the person you're trying to kill? Where's he? Nobody dies by falling out of a car moving less than a mile an hour. And if you kill him in the car and dump his body in the darkness, you still have the same problem, the friend."

Joey's face tightens before he continues, "Behind the concessions along the back alleyways, that's a possibility."

"What about Sinbad's Carpet?"

He blows air between his lips. "It's dark in the passageways, but with all the traffic walking through, the body would be discovered within minutes."

"I know."

"So, where would you murder somebody?"

Missy returns with two coffees. She lingers. "Missy come on, join us."

She sashays off with Joey watching her every move.

"Joey," I say, breaking his reverie.

"Yeah, I know, where would you murder somebody?"

I stir my coffee. "I won't know until tomorrow morning."

He shrugs. "You didn't give me that option."

"Where's the closest lodging to the bungalows?"

"There is a motel across the road."

"Can you see the bungalows from there?"

"Yeah, from some cabins."

"Call there and arrange a room for me with a view of Calabrese's quarters."

I stand.

"Anything else?" Joey says.

"Directions."

He draws a few lines, writes some interstate numbers and fills in a few street names, then he hands me a napkin. "That it?"

"Meet me in my room at eight a.m."

He sighs. "That's awfully early."

I look at the counter. "Tell Missy I said good night."

CHAPTER 11

FRIDAY, JULY 11, 1975
7:56 A.M.

THE KNOCK STARTLES ME. I sit up in bed not entirely sure of my surroundings. I let out a groan from the sharp pains that shimmy up my back. More knocks. I wrap the sheet around me and open the door. Joey Rocca steps into the room. He gives me a cup of coffee and an Italian pastry.

He clears his throat. "Mike, I was thinking about what you asked last night. Why not just go across the street and talk with this Calabrese, we're all cops and tell him what's happening?"

I run my hands over my face and push my hair back. "Because he wouldn't believe me. He'd think I screwed up his chances of clearing himself with Reno Piantini. Remember, that's who he thinks he's meeting."

He struts to the back window and moves the shade to peek across at the cabins Calabrese and Guzzetta occupy.

"Looks like they ain't up yet."

He's edgy. I look at him. "I'll shower, and we'll be on our way."

Joey removes lint from his starched uniform before he speaks again, "Floriano and Stone checked out of their motel last night. They're now at the Villa in Long Branch."

"Ainsworth still with them?"

"Sure."

"So?"

"It's a real high-class place."

"That confirms my theory about today. Someone should be stationed there."

We stare at each other, and he hesitates before nodding.

"What's wrong, Joe?"

"The Villa has always been neutral territory."

"What goes on there?"

He sighs. "Regular shit. A gambling, prostitutes. It's a place to relax."

I nod. "Mob run?"

"That's what they say."

"I understand. I'll take care of it. Anything else?"

He hesitates, not knowing how to phrase what he's thinking,

"Come out with it."

"I've put my neck out. I just hope you're right."

———

FRIDAY
9:13 A.M.

WE MEET Ainsworth at the amusement park before it opens. A taciturn maintenance man in oily overalls walks us through the various indoor rides. He flicks on a light switch, leans against a wall, and leaves us alone to inspect the rooms. They're mostly large, open areas with tracks running across. The opium of the trip is the darkness. Anticipation in the rider's mind to be frightened, combined with the surprise of the freakish displays, unlocks all of our double-edged sensations. In the light, the only thing that's frightening is how filthy everything is. I have little doubt in the dark, creatures do run free.

The maintenance man methodically moves us along. After a slow walk around the grounds and three indoor rides, I ask him to take us through Sinbad's Carpet.

Sinbad's Carpet is a series of rooms, hallways, and landings connected by narrow corridors. It's laid out to weave the customer up three levels both inside and outside the housing without them realizing it. The passages are pitch black, and I need to follow the walls with my hands to creep forward.

The maintenance man allows us to roam freely while he smokes a cigarette on one of the outside landings. With the use of his flashlight, I walk through the passageway, back and forth. Ainsworth follows. Joey, with growing skepticism, joins the park worker.

At first glance, the exit seems a joke—a trick exit. An odd door in a black wall, leading nowhere. I open the door and lean my head into the greasy room housing the machinery. There are fresh footprints on the metal landing of the stairwell. The drop between the door and the landing is a good fifteen inches. That is a longer than a normal seven to eight inch rise we come to expect on steps. In the dark that could be a real hazard.

Ainsworth looks down over my shoulder into the ugly guts of the room. He says, "Scary, isn't it?"

I motion to the footprints. "What kind of shoes are Floriano and Stone wearing?"

Ainsworth bends lower to look at the prints on the stairwell. "That doesn't look like a worker's boot, does it?"

I nod in agreement.

"Stone is wearing a trendy shoe like that, with a blunted toe and wide heel."

I run my hand over the handle. There's a bolt lock that's been recently sprayed and the carriage removed to prevent the door from locking.

"It's going to happen here. Stone is going to get Calabrese to open this door. Then he's going to push him into those machines."

Ainsworth says, "How?"

"My hunch is Calabrese will be told Reno Piantini is waiting for him down the steps and on the other side of the screened door.

Supposedly, Piantini will be outside on the grass surrounded by the shrubbery."

Ainsworth takes the flashlight and shines it directly into the machinery. He steps back and looks down the corridors in both directions. He asks while I close the door, "What about Guzzetta?"

I turn on my heels, thinking as I walk in the dim light. "Floriano will be with him somewhere in the vicinity on one of the landings facing the courtyard or outside, ready for retaliation if things go wrong."

"Guzzetta is in a vice between his best friend and relying on his blood cousin. He's being set up royally."

I look at my partner. "Stone and Floriano are banking on Guzzetta trusting them and encouraging Calabrese to follow through with the plan. Without Guzzetta's unshaken belief in his cousin's ability to put this deal together, it would never happen. That's why he'll let Calabrese out of his sight."

Joey's voice echoes down the hallways, "You guys done or what?"

The maintenance man stares at us with indifference.

Joey approaches. "I've been thinking. This is all ridiculous and, if it gets out of hand and Calabrese gets hurt, I'm gonna get fucked cause I could have prevented it."

Ainsworth stares hard at the young trooper. Joey squares his shoulders before speaking again, "I'm confronting Calabrese."

Paul shakes his head coolly. "No, you're not."

I say, "Joey, I told you earlier—he's not going to believe you. He trusts the men he's coming here with."

Paul moves away to the maintenance man. "When's the lull time in the afternoon?"

"Between three-forty-five and five. One group of people getting tired, the other's just arriving."

"How often does someone go into the room with all the machinery?"

He takes an unfiltered cigarette from his inside shirt pocket. "Just before opening and at closing. If something works, no sense in fixing it." He lights the cigarette. "Are we done?"

The maintenance man leaves us in front of the structure. Joey asks, "What did we learn?"

"The old exit is perfect," I say. "It can't be viewed from the grounds, and it's in the center of a dark corridor."

Paul pulls a peanut from his pocket and plays with it. He's tense, and his voice has an edge. "Calabrese could have been killed anytime in the last eight-ten days and by more experienced men."

"Nothing was set up till now," I say. "And as long as it looks like an accident, everybody is happy. Reno Piantini gets revenge. Gage gets information. Floriano and Stone get recognition. Roberts and Ring gloat. Mulvaney will continue to poison the department, and Calabrese will have helped a lot of careers. Guzzetta is the fall guy because he will be blamed for setting it all up. Remember, it's documented his family has mob ties."

Ainsworth glances at his watch. "We know why and where. Any ideas on how exactly?"

"Once in the dark corridors with a growing sense of anxiety, Calabrese will be a ripe target. While walking through the maze, he'll believe his friend has his back. As planned, Stone will quickly open the door for an anxious Calabrese. He'll hit Calabrese over the head and toss him down into the black churning jaws. Later, Guzzetta will find his partner's body chewed into unrecognizable pieces."

"Calabrese and Guzzetta must have an alternative plan," Paul says. "We would if we were in his shoes."

"They do! They're gonna synchronize watches and base a strategy on time. When I was with them back at Calabrese's summer home, when they were making plans to leave Monticello and drive in the city they synchronized watches for their meet up. I'm sure that's a tactic they used in Street Crime. Guzzetta will go along with the plan because he has loyalty to both men."

Joey shrugs. "It's just too strange. This isn't an accident."

"It will be when it hits the papers," Paul says. "A lot can happen between New Jersey and New York." He looks at his watch again. "One more question before I leave. What about the other customers walking through?"

"Simple, before the corridor leading to the exit door is a large open space where you can loiter, and people can pass each other. Stone will have time to choose a good distance between himself and anybody else."

Joey scratches his head. "I have voiced my skepticism."

I look at Sinbad's Carpet, I trace the building in my mind. I've got the puzzle solved. I have every piece, but I don't know how to move the puzzle without it falling apart.

Ainsworth slips on a pair of sunglasses. "We have time. I'll expect to hear from you within an hour."

Paul leaves the parking lot and heads north for the Villa. Joey opens my car door and leans against it. "What's the plan?"

"Call me at two-thirty."

"That's the plan?"

"Do what I ask, please."

Joey takes off with stones and gravel flying. Once he's out of sight, I walk into the amusement park again.

The long-faced maintenance man isn't hard to find. He's in his shack, sitting on a hard chair and reading a magazine.

"Forget something?" he asks.

"I need a hammer, nails, and some thick wooden blanks. We have to secure the old emergency exit door in Sinbad's Carpet."

He blows smoke from his nose. "There's a bolt on that door."

"It's been removed."

His face comes to life. "You sure?"

"Positive."

He crushes his cigarette in a tin can. "Sounds like serious police business?"

Glancing at my watch, I nod. "Let's get started. The park will be opening shortly."

FRIDAY
1:00 P.M.

. . .

I WATCH Calabrese from the window. He's nervous; his neck seems to be on a swivel, moving from side to side as he paces by the cabins. Guzzetta puts his arm around his partner, and they disappear behind the cottages to where the women are sunning themselves.

I pick up the phone then set it down again. I want to talk with Suzanne, but I have no words to convey. I shake my head to dissolve her image.

I walk to the mirror. I see tired eyes begging for answers that no one can supply. What if I'm wrong?

The phone startles me.

After speaking with Paul, the phone rings again. I instruct Joey to be at the park in plain clothes. I want him inside Sinbad's Carpet. His job is not to interfere unless necessary. He's to watch Floriano and Guzzetta no matter what happens with Stone and not react when it looks like their plan has fallen through.

FRIDAY
3:00 P.M.

GRACE CALABRESE WALKS her husband to their car. He gives her a kiss. I take a deep breath and open the cabin door.

I'm hit squarely in the gut with a club. My knees hit the ground hard. There's a gun at my temple and a voice telling me to get up. Stone pushes me into my room.

"I'm smarter than you, cop." He quickly flattens my right hand on the wooden table and smashes a heavy sap against it repeatedly, breaking the bones in my hand. He pushes me to the floor, kicking me in the face, chest, and gut a few times.

"I am so much smarter than you! You hear? Try to fuck with me." Stone pounces on my already pulverized right hand. The pain hovers then radiates throughout my body and is followed by a reverberating ache that pulses through me.

I must have lost consciousness because as I gather my senses, my legs are duct taped to my chair and my swollen bloody right hand and wrist are taped to the table. My left wrist is taped to the table. Three fingers are taped so that only my thumb and first finger can move. Everything has a blurry double image to it.

Stone is delighted, smug, almost giddy. He can't seem to stop moving. He keeps looking at his watch. He comes over and grabs the index finger of my right hand and bends it back till it snaps. I didn't think my already broken knuckles could crack any further. I was wrong.

When I come around, the pain reaches a peak, goes numb, then awakens again and explodes through me. My mind is on full alert except full alert is dumbed down, slow-motion thoughts trying to figure out why fight or flight isn't working. My brain can't decide whether to remain in this world or make that step into complete abandoned madness.

Stone places the phone in front of me. "Call the front desk and ask to be connected to room nine. When someone answers, hang up." I hear myself, but nothing comes out of my mouth. Focus, D'laska, grab a piece of yourself, catch a tangle of thoughts and make them sensible. You are still you, and you need to try and think clearly at all costs.

Stone rips the bandage from my neck. "You fucker, I'm gonna open you up. Your blood is gonna be all over this room. Fucker." He dashes to a drawer next to the sink. He finds a fork.

I shake my thumb trying to point to my mouth, and the word "water" tumbles out.

Stone slowly walks to the bathroom and fills a small glass. "Open your mouth." He throws the water into my face. I feebly attempt to grab whatever moisture I can. My tongue is thick, and I can feel crusted blood on my lips. Stone uses the fork to rip the stitches from my neck. I can't halt the screams that follow.

Stone barks, "Call!"

I do what he says. I force myself to recall things, anything, and relay what I can. I need to separate the instinctive protective layer my mind is trying to create from what I must concentrate on to find a solution. There is always an out, isn't there? I tell myself to approach it like a puzzle, move the mental fragmentation into a comprehensive whole, start with the edges, and work toward the middle. Rely on reasoning—since I'm physically anchored, action is no longer an option—but is my thinking rational? Discerning what is and what is not possible is my only alternative. Survival 101: Do not go to that safe pace in your head—be mindful of other options. Keep trying to separate truth from delusion.

I hear myself speak into the phone and ask for the room, but the voice I hear is not familiar.

Stone asks with a giggle, "Wondering why I'm so bright, and you're an asshole? He stabs my hand with the fork before tossing it away. The dumb state trooper told that waitress everything while trying to get into her pants. She then told her husband, and my New Jersey friends made sure I got the info about your plan. And, bringing us to date, that shit head trooper is with her now but, not at the park as you planned. For a few bucks, she's keeping him occupied." Stone is ecstatic. "Oh, you were mostly right about the park, but now I've moved from a good plan to a great one."

He moves the curtain to look out the window. "Cop, you know how made I'm gonna be after today? My dreams are gonna be fulfilled! I'm gonna be working with a killing crew, I know it. No more penny-ante shit. Easy street is where I'm gonna be living while you and Calabrese are in the ground." Relishing his imagined future, Stone comes over and slaps my face multiple times. I feel the separation of flesh as his ring digs into my skin.

The door opens slowly. Through watery eyes, I see an average-looking, medium-sized man in a brown polyester suit enter. His right arm rests inside his jacket. He cautiously walks around the room, looking everywhere including the bathroom, under the bed and cupboards and dresser, never removing his right arm and using a white handkerchief to not touch anything. He then stops at the table between Stone and me. Stone is all smiles. He moves toward the man, in a gesture that looks like he wants to acknowledge him with an Italian embrace, but the man shakes a finger at Stone.

He says, "I am waiting."

Stone goes to move behind him, but the man steps back quickly, his arm tensing as Stone must cross him to get to me. I notice there's open unfriendliness here and Stone is definitely of lower rank.

Stone slams his gun butt against my right hand. He spreads my fingers and hits each one seperately. I'm prepared for the move, but that doesn't stop the pain. He pokes the gun barrel in my neck. "The shooting wasn't a hit, was it? Nickie and that cop were both at the wrong place at the wrong time. Right, that's what you proved?"

It's hard to open your mouth when your body is screaming, *Get me out of here*. I point to my mouth again, and the brown-suited man, who I recognize as Reno Piantini, fills a glass with water and places it in front of me. It's the first time I notice how much I'm shaking. Somehow this reality calms me a bit; it means I'm still alive. I close my thumb and finger and grasp the glass. I'm reminded what the mind can do to manage situations too painful to endure. I suddenly know the true meaning of the word sublime—this liquid that I am gulping, swallowing and spilling, is sublime. I bring my head down and wipe the drool from my chin.

"Calabrese did not commit premeditated murder," I say without knowing how long it took for me to formulate the words and spit them out.

Stone looks at Piantini and they exchange glances. Stone then orders me, "Pick up the phone and ask for an outside line."

I watch tiny beads of blood seeping from underneath the tape of my mangled right hand. They gather to form a thread that creeps the short distance to become a drop that then falls to the gray linoleum floor and bursts.

Piantini first looks at me, then Stone, and drags the phone over to himself. When the outside line is connected, he begins to dial, he waits, then says, "Off." At that instant, Stone moves slightly and lifts his gun toward Piantini, but it fumbles in his hand. Piantini swings the receiver across Stone's face knocking him backward. Quickly, he has Stone by the back of his hair. A knife appears, blood splatters and flies across the room, Piantini slit Stone's throat and pushes him to the floor.

Piantini walks to the bed, drops the pillow from the pillowcase, and uses it to wipe the blood from his knife. Slowly, methodically, he regards the room and uses the case to clean everything he may have touched. He seems like a man going about everyday business without a worry in the world. Job completed time for cleanup, then head home—except I'm still here. Tears run down my face as the futility of my situation fully hits me. I'm going to die. My mind is a photo album of partial pictures, running into one other, all surreal, Suzanne, my mother, mountains… "Stop it!" I hear myself say.

Water runs in the bathroom after a while Piantini appears from the room and pats his face. He stands behind me. "What's your name?" he asks without any trace of emotion.

I'm suddenly aware of the noise from a chainsaw. These are my last moments. I feel myself climbing all inside myself to a small, safe space where all is calm, and in moments, I will not be anymore.

It isn't a chainsaw—it's the air conditioning unit rattling. It has probably been making noise the whole time; I just wasn't aware of it. The human psyche rallies whenever a vestige of hope is available, and I grab an uncertain hold once again.

From behind me, a voice as ordinary as a summer's day, asks, "What is your name?"

My name? I know my name, but can I say it? I dig down as far as I ever reached inside myself before.

"D'laska." I hear it, clear and direct. But what is he doing behind me? There is movement.

"Delasker, ah?"

Is that knife coming around any instant now?

I hear footsteps pace behind me. Then, they stop. I take the silence as a warning and anticipate my demise. Suddenly, a hand appears on my shoulder, I scream. It lingers there for a second, large and menacing. Then it disappears.

I am a million pounds of dynamite about to explode, but I don't. I gather myself and try to concentrate. I swallow hard, I am going to speak what may be my last words. "John Gage…part of this?"

There is a loud snort. "Without us, the Justice Department would have nobody to blame their crimes on."

Moments pass. Long moments.

From behind, I hear: "My son's killing was an accident?"

I get it, make me comfortable and as I begin to speak, then slit my throat. "Ya...yes."

The toilet flushes in the bathroom, water runs in the sink then all goes quiet.

Silence has never been so loud. It clangs in my head.

I feel him directly behind me. I am going to die. Please do it quickly.

Piantini walks past, stops, he taps the blade of the knife against his palm, "Delasker, ah! Not Italian."

I am frozen. I cannot move my mouth. I want to beg for my life, but I know it won't matter. His eyes never leave mine. I know he is deciding my fate. How best to kill me.

Reno Piantini, nods, then tosses the knife on the table. He doesn't look back, he just walks out of the cabin into the sunlight. The door closes behind him.

The moment is incomprehensible. My heart becomes all of me, that is all there is, just my heart beating so fast each beat catches the last and surpasses it. Is that door going to open again? Is there more helplessness and horror to come? Nothing else exists except fear.

The unknown is terrifying. I think that I'm moving to grab that knife, but I'm fastened to this chair. Best to reset my thoughts, push aside the flooding and choose a singular path of thinking with an objective. Then like a huge wave, one extraordinary thought explodes on me: I am alive.

I twist, push, and pull my left wrist, trying to loosen my arm to get to that knife. On the millionth try, I succeed enough to tap it toward me.

My right arm is all dead weight and falls to my side. I cut the tape around my legs. I am free, but the door remains. I am free of one situation, but only so far as the moment. My legs don't lengthen quickly—it seems I straighten in segments. Battered, bruised, in tatters, breathing in gulps, but I am standing.

My desperation to get out of the room is all-consuming yet tempered with the cautionary thought that someone may be waiting outside. Maybe my status is beneath Piantini and killing me will be left to someone else. The overwhelming feelings come in waves—how long will I be alive? Is somebody waiting out there?

I become aware of the metallic stench of blood that has been filling the room. I find my gun under Stone's dead body. I feel little remorse for this death, but the sight of a man's nearly decapitated head bathed in blood will never leave my memory.

I cannot take the time to adequately assess my injuries. I know I'm running on adrenaline, which will soon deplete. What happened in this room was a complete surprise to Stone. This means something has gone wrong and Calabrese is still in danger from Floriano, maybe Guzzetta, too. Ainsworth might be walking into a trap. I need to act.

In the bathroom, bending into the sink, I turn on the tap with my barely useable left hand. Cold water rushes over my head making me feel somewhat tuned into my surroundings, my situation. My thoughts begin to become mine again and stop finding ways to either hide or escape. All the bloody fingers of my right hand are thick and cramped together and connected to a red, swollen, black and blue fleshy mass. Moving back into the room, I cut the threadbare bed sheet with the knife and make a sling for my arm. I cut another piece and wrap it around my neck. I check the rounds in my gun.

I stand to the side with every neuron on full alert, breath held in my lungs, and push the door open. First, there is stillness, and then I hear movement, birds, flies, bees, cars passing, even voices. The voices of sane people.

FRIDAY
  4:30 P.M.

I QUICKLY PASS THE MERRY-GO-ROUND, the Twister, and the Scrambler. Funny how sheer determination overcomes agony. Two little boys run into me as I round the cotton candy stand. Their eyes widen and mouths open when they look up. I'm something from the House of Horrors.

Calabrese, Floriano, and Guzzetta are at the opening on the second landing of Sinbad's Carpet. Calabrese grasps the guard railing, weaving back and forth. Guzzetta plays with the chains around his neck. Floriano between them seems to be searching the immediate area. A warm breeze blows against them. Voices crackle over loudspeakers. Joey isn't visible on the landing. Neither is Ainsworth.

I shout, "Floriano, Stone is dead!" Screaming anything else would mean questions, but Floriano knows if Stone is dead, whatever plan they had is over.

"Hey Floriano, Stone is dead." This time I catch his attention. Calabrese moves his head, looking for the source. Guzzetta is lighting a cigarette.

Floriano locks on to me. I smile as I aim my gun. I anticipate his movements. In a flash, I rush past the hedges to the back of the building and rip open the door to the engine room. Machines grind, and the smell of grease hangs in the air. The thick cabling runs from small holes in the ceiling to large pulling wheels and pinches through gearboxes. Metal grinds and halts, moves, and screeches.

The wooden planks are missing from the emergency door. Creaking thuds come from the footfalls on the wooden floor above. I begin making my way up the slick metal steps.

Sparks fly when a chain rigging swings into the climbing steel cables. Compressors rattle. Sweat rolls from my face in this grating hell. The old metal steps begin to wobble. I cling to the oily railing. I slip; stumbling down, my chin bounces on a step. The faster I try to move up the steps, the more they swing. Muffled voices come from inside the Sinbad.

The door swings open and both Floriano and Calabrese spill out. They lose their footing and tumble down the oil covered stairs into me. Once on the floor, Floriano is up, but Calabrese quickly spins him around by the shoulder. Calabrese wastes no time like a flurried boxer, jabbing him in the mid-section then landing a punch to the jaw. Floriano comes back and pounds Calabrese in the stomach with both his fists. Calabrese falls to his knees. Floriano attempts to kick Calabrese, but Calabrese catches his foot and pushes him back. Calabrese picks up a small metal cylinder. When Floriano attacks,

Calabrese strikes him just above the groin. Floriano flails. Calabrese makes it to his feet and hits Floriano square in the face. Floriano flounders again, moving backward, then slips. A chain wraps around him, lifting him into the grinding guts of the machinery. Within seconds he's hauled into the vortex of the machine and ground beyond recognition by the innards of the hungry monster. I spot a fuse box, but it's too late for Floriano. Calabrese and I are frozen mannequins staring at each other while the cranking machinery hisses furiously before it halts.

Guzzetta appears above us at the top of the stairs. He looks down into the blood-stained machinery, the pieces of flesh, then at Calabrese and me. With his gun in hand, he comes toward me. "What the fuck is going on?"

Guzzetta stomps on the blood-soaked towel around my hand. I scream so loud it echoes in my head forever.

"What the fuck is going on?" he repeats.

"Put the gun away," shouts Ainsworth, his gun pointed at him.

"After I get some answers!"

Calabrese looks to me. "If you have answers, now is the time to tell us."

I want to ignore all that is around me, walk into the nearest liquor store, grab the first bottle I see, drink it down, pass out, and wake up days from now on a beach in Aruba. Instead, it takes all my strength to gather myself up, step past Paul, and stagger outside into the sunlight and heat. They follow.

I drop on the patchy grass. "Stone and Floriano planned a double cross that went terribly wrong for them."

My eyes find Calabrese. "I watched Piantini slit Stone's throat in self-defense. Floriano was going to kill you." All of a sudden, I really feel it. It had started in my gut, butterflying in my chest, and heads directly with growing speed to my brain. "One last thing, there's no longer a contract on your life."

CHAPTER 12

SATURDAY, JULY 12, 1975
10:00 P.M.

"D'LASKA, are you awake?"

I hear a voice, but it takes a long time for me to respond to it.

"D'laska."

My eyes, slowly open. I glance at my hand. It's a white knot of wires and plaster. I can barely make out pink fingertips. My body feels heavy like it's tied to anchors.

"Where am I?" My tongue is enormous, too big for my mouth.

"Hospital," Gage says. "Broken fingers, knuckles, wrist, and a number of your ribs are bruised, a couple busted. You have stitches under your eye and beneath your chin. Your neck had to be re-re-stitched. Aside from that, you look great!"

Blood has crusted in the corners of my mouth. I rub some water over my lips before speaking, "How long have I been here?"

"Over twenty-four hours."

I remove a rose from my chest. "Are you asking me to go steady?"

"Suzanne Baxter and Ainsworth were here earlier."

Gage sucks at his lips. "Here's the good news: from what my informants said, it was Piantini who murdered Stone. Seems Stone was a bit too ambitious. Once the contract was off Calabrese, Stone knew there would be peace among the Mafia families in New York. They hate the attention, especially heat from the cops, particularly from the ones they're paying off. But Piantini had begun talking with us. He's too bright and savvy to step on big toes around here, but he will give us valuable information about drugs coming into the States from Europe, especially Marseilles. But the fact he was talking to the feds became known to New York crime families. His talking would result in a distraction, which means interference in business and a loss of money. So, Mr. Stone and Floriano figured they'd become major players quick by killing Piantini making sure nothing relevant came out of his mouth."

"And Calabrese?" I ask.

"A dead Calabrese puts this whole incident to bed, no backlash, no loose ends, and there are many of Calabrese's fellow cops who still have doubts about his loyalties."

A pretty, petite nurse wrapped in a fruity perfume walks into the room, puts a thermometer under my tongue, takes my vitals, picks up a clipboard, jots a few things down, and shakes her head. "I hope you have no plans to play shortstop. There are twenty-seven bones in the hand, and all of yours are broken some in more than one spot."

"Will I be able to hold a cold beer?"

"Does that include a glass of Chardonnay for me?"

When the nurse leaves, Gage comes as close to the bed as possible. "Okay, D'laska, here's the bad news: informants lie, change their minds, or forget. There's no sign that Piantini was ever in your motel room, no witnesses, no fingerprints, nothing. You can easily be charged with Stone's murder. And who's going to take the word of a murderer—you—that Calabrese didn't kill Floriano in cold blood? So, both of you could be sharing a cell for a lifetime. Are you listening?"

"Gage, I'm not feeling powerful. Why not just pump up the morphine and put a pillow over my face?"

"I have thought about it. Pinning everything on you would be easy. Oh, it seems Suzanne Baxter rifled through classified documents in McConnell's office. Hate to see her dragged into this. One more thing, Ainsworth disobeyed a direct order from Chief Roberts, and a concerned citizen just happened to snap a photo of him at the exact moment he pulled a gun on a fellow officer out of New York jurisdiction. Your whole clan is in trouble, D'laska. Oh, and there is that little tantrum you pulled at our lunch, but as of now, neither the club nor I will be pressing charges. But, my suit was ruined."

"What do you want?"

"Your word on a few matters. One, you have no positive recollection of who might have been in your room when Stone was killed. Two, neither you nor Calabrese will ever attempt to contact Piantini again. If you or he tries, you will both be charged with murder—you for Stone, and he for Floriano—and you will be found guilty. I have all the documentation sealed away. I have been assured this morning that Mr. Piantini would like to have a dialogue with the Justice Department to help fight illegal drugs from entering the country."

"I can't speak for Calabrese."

"Oh no, you two are inextricably tied together. You get the message to Calabrese that he must never try to get ahold of Piantini again. If he does, we'll come down on you two, and it won't be pretty. We, meaning the department, could benefit from Piantini's information as opposed to needing anything from two shit heel cops suspected of murder. Both of you are very expendable. It may be just my good nature keeping the two of you alive right now. Oh, and I wouldn't make any life-changing plans to move to Seattle."

"So, Calabrese is safe?"

"As far as I know, but really, what does safe mean? It's a dangerous world out there."

CHAPTER 13

FRIDAY, JULY 18, 1975
1:00 P.M.

"That barmaid is wearing a Red Sox tee shirt. If you live in New York, there should be a law—you have to be a Yankee's fan or if you're a pansy, a Met's fan." Calabrese sits across from me in a back booth at the Innfield. He's wearing a light gray suit with the collar of his light blue shirt over the lapels.

"She's from Boston," I say.

"They run out of bartending jobs there?"

"Did you hear about Tito Garcia?" I ask.

He shakes his head.

"They found him dead Sunday morning in the trunk of a parked car in Long Branch. Three bullets in the head. He went into hiding in Florida after the shooting. Garcia was asked to come back because Reno Piantini wanted to have a meeting with him. He was apparently guaranteed safe passage." I pause for a long moment before continuing, "The coroner found the bullet hole in Garcia's leg where you must have hit him."

Calabrese swirls the liquid in his glass. "They're giving me a medal and sending me back to Street Crime. Fuckers won't give me a detective's shield. Gino is still in Harlem."

"I heard."

"I also heard your partner put in his resignation."

"He took a job as head of security for a hospital system in Maine close to the Canadian border."

Calabrese smirks. "You're hated more than I am. No captain is going to want you attached to his precinct. Everybody will refuse to work with you."

"They hate psychopaths out on the streets more than they dislike me."

"No, you're wrong. Start looking for a new career or a new city to live in. Maybe both."

"Thanks for caring."

"I don't."

"I read in the paper the two Hispanics that were waiting outside the morgue to kill you are up on multiple Federal charges."

Calabrese shrugs. "When does the cast come off?"

"I'm thinking of keeping it. Doctors might stop prescribing the painkillers if they remove it."

Calabrese is a very literal guy and, he doesn't see the sarcasm. I grin, and he just sits there, nursing his drink. "I have a question for you." I ask, "Floriano? Did you know?"

"In Street Crime, you survive by your gut. It made no sense to Gino or me that Piantini would meet us at an amusement park in New Jersey, but we had no choice. When it registered what you shouted, and Floriano took off, I knew something wasn't right. And even if Piantini was in that engine room, do you think he would have given a shit if I threw some punk down a flight of stairs?"

I glance outside and notice the sheer, wispy clouds adding whiteness to an otherwise liquid blue sky. Who knows if it's Gage or Piantini who's responsible for Garcia's death.

I grin. "All charges have been dropped against us in the Stone and Floriano cases. There is still some official bureaucracy, but we've been cleared." I wave to Britt for another round.

When she arrives, Calabrese asks, "Aren't you embarrassed to wear that shirt? This is New York, show some respect."

Britt's come back is immediate. "We have assholes in Boston too. We call them New Yorkers!"

He breaks into a smile, nodding. "She's quick."

I'm still chuckling. "One last question, why didn't you try to join the force after high school?"

"I tried, but I kept failing the height requirement," he says. "Why did you want to meet?"

"Has an FBI agent named Gage been in contact with you?"

"No."

"Since the contract has been terminated, there's no reason for you to contact Piantini, correct?"

"Why didn't Piantini kill you too?"

"He really liked my last name."

"Oh really! That's funny. Maybe you two made a deal."

"I was a witness. Piantini killed Stone in self-defense. Also, he is a professional, no reason to kill me, no motive and no money in it for him."

Calabrese takes the cuffs of his shirt and gently pushes them down to his wrists. He presses his collar down, tilting his head. "Something ain't right. I'll believe there's no contract on my life when I hear it from someone other than you and I ain't heard nothing absolutely confirming that yet. So, till then, I need to talk with him."

There is a grayness that closes around a distorted echo in my head, an illogic that stays suspended near reality but without acknowledging it.

"I heard Piantini cancel the contract, myself," I say. "You and your family are safe."

Calabrese stands, guzzles his drink, and before leaving, says, "What does safe mean? It's a dangerous world out there."

ABOUT THE AUTHOR

Philip M. Butera grew up in Buffalo, NY, earned a BS degree From Gannon College in Erie, PA, served in the US Navy then received an MA in Psychology from Simon Fraser University in Vancouver, Canada. He has published three books of poetry, "Mirror Images and Shards of Glass," "Dark Images at Sea," and "I Never Finished Loving You." He is completing his second novel, "Far from Here," a domestic thriller about love going awry. His poetry appears in Journals and Magazines. He was a contributing editor for EatSleepWrite.net 2016-17 and a column in the quarterly magazine, Per Niente, 2016-2018. Philip won full scholarships to the 2017 Palm Beach Poetry Festival, 2017 Creative Capital Workshops, and Creative Capital Advanced Weekend Workshop 2018. The Cultural Council of Palm Beach County premiered his play, "The Apparition," and exhibited his poetry from February to March 2019. The Artists Guild Gallery/Boca Raton Museum of Art presented, "The Apparition" in December 2019. He has participated in the Arts Mentoring program developed by the Florida Department of State, Division of Cultural Affairs. Philip is the publicity coordinator for Mystery Writers of America - Florida Chapter, Sleuthfest 2018-2020. He lives in Boynton Beach, Florida.